GUNSLINGER

GUNSLINGER

THE DRAGON OF YELLOWSTONE

EDWARD J. KNIGHT

WFP
WordFire Press

EBook ISBN: 978-1-68057-167-7
Trade Paperback ISBN: 978-1-68057-166-0
Hardcover ISBN: 978-1-68057-168-4
Library of Congress Control Number: 2020951378

Cover design by Janet McDonald
Cover artwork images by Adobe Stock
Kevin J. Anderson, Art Director

Published by
WordFire Press, LLC
PO Box 1840
Monument CO 80132
Kevin J. Anderson & Rebecca Moesta, Publishers

WordFire Press eBook Edition 2021
WordFire Press Trade Paperback Edition 2021
WordFire Press Hardcover Edition 2021
Printed in the USA

Join our WordFire Press Readers Group for
sneak previews, updates, new projects, and giveaways.
Sign up at wordfirepress.com

PROLOGUE

GOLDEN CITY, COLORADO, 1878

Beth nearly dropped the water pitcher. The long-haired man at the parlor's back table—*it had to be him!*

Fortunately, the pewter pitcher just slipped in her hand and she only sloshed water over her faded gingham dress. It'd dry fine, and if she held the pitcher just so, she could block anyone from seeing the wet splotch. But no one else in the Astor's crowded parlor had even noticed. The teamsters and traders and miners all ignored her and the other serving staff as if they were part of the decor. Which they were, she thought with a grimace.

So, since no one was watching, she took a longer look. *Yes! It was Wild Bill Hickok himself!*

It couldn't be anyone else. His long brown hair curled about his shoulders, just like in the pictures. His eyes twinkled as he spoke with his companion, a plain-looking man in brown—

—no, a *woman* in brown.

Beth sucked in her breath and trembled. The woman wore a man's white shirt with silver buttons under a brown buckskin coat. She'd tied her chestnut brown hair up into a small bun and she smiled at whatever Hickok had said. A Colt .45 rested on the wooden table near her elbow.

A woman! In man's clothes!

The flush of imagined impropriety began to fill her cheeks, but Beth forced it down by looking away. Not that a woman in man's clothes was really improper here in Golden City. There were too many war widows just struggling to make it on their own for there to be a good sense of what was proper. Beth steadied her nerves and looked back at Wild Bill and his companion and found them looking at her. The woman smiled, held up a glass, and gave Beth a meaningful look.

Beth took a deep breath and wound her way past the other tables of drinkers.

"More water, ma'am?" she asked once she'd arrived.

"Beer," the woman said. "I understand Mr. Lake received a shipment from Mr. Coors earlier this evening ...?"

"Yes, ma'am," Beth said, eagerly nodding her head. "I'll fetch it for you immediately."

"And ask Mr. Lake if he still has some of those raspberry muffins from this morning," Hickok added.

"Yes, sir." Beth's eyes lingered on the Colt. She took a deep breath.

"Uh, excuse me ma'am," she said. "Is that your gun?"

"Why yes," the woman said. "Why do you ask?"

"They let you—I mean, you can ..." Beth stopped herself and took a deep breath. "How'd you learn to shoot?"

"Practice," the woman said with a chuckle. "Like anything."

"But now you're good, right?"

Hickok leaned over. "You're what, young lady? Twelve?"

"Thirteen," Beth said. "But that's old enough!"

"That it is," said the woman. She looked at Hickok. "I was fourteen." She reached out and fingered the ivory handle of her pistol. Then she extended a hand to Beth.

"Calamity Jane," the woman said as they shook. "And you are ...?"

Beth started in surprise. *Her too!*

"Beth Armstrong," she said. "My ma's the baker for Mr. Lake."

"Ah," Hickok said. "No pa?"

Beth shook her head and the familiar pang of grief grabbed her heart for a moment.

"But you want to shoot," Hickok continued. "Let me guess, you want to be a gunfighter."

Beth couldn't hide her blush.

"Why don't you stop by my room upstairs later," Jane said. "We'll talk then."

Beth nodded as the giddy smile drove her blush to an even deeper shade of pink.

Beth tried not to bound up the narrow stairs to the Astor's second floor. Given the hour, it just wouldn't do to wake any of the other guests, though she suspected few were yet asleep. She knocked quietly on Calamity Jane's door.

"Why Miss Armstrong," Calamity Jane said. "Do come in." She stepped back to allow Beth to enter.

The room was well lit from an oil lamp on the short dresser. Beth's eyes were drawn to the frilly pale blue dress hanging from a hook on the wall. A gorgeous dress. With white lace and silver stitches all down the sleeves.

"You like it?" Jane asked. "I don't normally carry on with such impractical attire, but Bill says it will be good when we meet with the president."

"You're going to meet the president?" Beth asked, her eyes wide. "Oh, my."

"We are," Jane said with an exasperated sigh. "Can't be helped, I'm afraid. We have to show him something."

"You don't like him?"

"I don't like most politicians. But as I said, it can't be helped."

Jane sat on the bed and gestured toward the chair. "Now Miss Armstrong, what do you wish to know about gunfighting?"

"So much," Beth gushed. "So much I don't know where to begin."

"Then one beginning's as good as the next." Jane smiled indulgently and tilted her head, waiting.

"What's it like?" Beth asked eagerly. "Holding a gun? Shooting? Or fighting? How do you do it? It's not like I don't have *some* idea, but—"

"Now hold on," Jane said with a chuckle. "One question at a time." She rubbed her chin. "Have you ever even held a gun?"

"Only once," Beth said. "I didn't know what to do with it."

Jane chuckled again. "Well, then that's the first step." She pulled her Colt out, checked it, and passed it handle first over to Beth.

"Now unless you're planning to use it soon," Jane said, "you should leave one chamber empty and lower the hammer on that empty chamber. That way you can't accidentally shoot your foot off."

Beth carefully wrapped her hands around the revolver. She ran one finger down the cool barrel and hefted it slowly, feeling its unexpected weight.

"Flip the barrel out," Jane said. "Here." She took the gun briefly, demonstrated the flip, and passed it back to Beth. "See how that chamber is empty?"

Beth nodded and ran her thumb over the empty hole, and then over the backs of the other bullets. A small shiver ran up her spine. The room felt cool, despite the warm flickers from the lamp. She pushed the cylinder back into place and then wrapped her hand around the grip, with her index finger just to the side of the trigger.

"Now you want to sight down the barrel," Jane said. "Don't aim at me! Point it at the wall."

Beth nodded and raised the gun. Her wrist trembled under the weight, but it was a good weight—a weight that felt right.

"Now—"

The door burst open and a burly cowboy rushed in. He pointed a fat revolver at Jane. "Don't move!" he growled, surprisingly soft.

Jane and Beth both froze.

The cowboy stepped in and closed the door behind him. He glared at them. A jagged scar ran along his cheek and disappeared into his scruffy beard. He looked fierce and serious.

Beth's pulse raced. She fought to keep her breathing calm.

"Hand it over," he said. With the barrel of his gun, he gestured toward the Colt in Beth's hand.

Beth glanced at Jane, who calmly nodded. Reluctantly, she passed the gun to the cowboy, who jammed it in his belt.

Jane cleared her throat. "And what might we do for you, Mr. ...?"

"Smith," he said reflexively, and then scowled when he'd realized what he'd done. "Just give me the Governor's ledger."

"Hickok has it," Jane said calmly.

He grunted, and his eyes darted from Jane to Beth and back again. His gun wavered and sweat beaded on his forehead.

A quick knock sounded on the door before it opened an inch. Smith moved away and another cowboy with curly black hair poked his head in.

"Hickok's gone!" the new man said. "Jumped out the window and took off!"

"Let's go!" Smith said. He waved his gun at Jane. "You too. Move slow and keep your hands where I can see 'em."

"Leave the girl," Jane said as she stood. "She has nothing to do with this."

"She knows my name," Smith growled. "She comes too."

Jane carefully stood and gestured for Beth to do the same. Smith stepped to the side and indicated for them to lead the way.

Outside, the cold night air stung Beth's cheeks and bare arms. Only a few lights spilled from the Astor, and the nearby buildings were dark. It took a moment for her eyes to adjust to the bright moonlight as Smith pushed them along, up the road, into the mountains. The other man raced on ahead until he was out of sight.

They left the last building behind and the road meandered around a curve in the hill. The night wind picked up, and Beth shivered.

Don't give into fear, she thought. *Don't give in. You've survived worse.* She could survive this. She just needed to keep her head. But her heart still threatened to pound so hard as to leap out of her chest.

"Go on ahead," Jane said to Beth. She nodded up the road.

Beth took a deep breath. There was something in Jane's eyes, something she wanted to say. She couldn't, though, not with Smith pushing the gun in her back.

Beth ran. Her legs wobbled like rubber. They held, though. Behind her, Smith shouted and cursed. Jane yelled. Beth lowered her head and forced her legs to move faster.

And then the gunshot.

She skidded to a stop and turned.

Jane and Smith seemed to be in a clench, almost an obscene dance in the moonlight, distant town lights silhouetting them against the sky. But then Jane slid to her knees and toppled to the ground.

Smith jumped back, a gun still in each hand, a look of shock on his face. His own gun was held high. Jane's—pulled from his belt—still pointed at the fallen woman.

He recovered quickly. With a jerk, he leveled both guns at Beth. "Come back here, girlie."

Eyes wide, Beth just stood, until he growled and cocked the guns. Slowly, she trudged back toward the killer.

He glared at her, but then looked down at Jane's body. "Killed with her own gun," he said with a smirk. He shoved the Colt back into his waistband but kept his own revolver pointed at Beth. He gave her an evil, wolfish grin.

Beth froze. Her knees locked. She struggled to breathe.

"C'mon," he said. He waved his gun. "I won't hurt ya if you do as you're told."

He's lying, Beth thought. She glanced around—the few scraggly pine trees near the road stood too far back. He'd shoot her down if she ran.

She took a deep breath and took a step toward him. Then another. Then another. Slowly, as her legs failed to collapse, she made her way forward.

Near Jane's body, a small fog formed. Light grey, and almost transparent, it slowly stretched up and solidified.

Beth's eyes went wide.

The fog took the form of a person, with arms and legs and a head. Slowly the features filled in, becoming a face.

Beth gasped.

Calamity Jane.

Her ghost, actually.

The ghost stared down at her body. She put her hands on her hips and frowned.

"C'mon!" Smith called. He didn't seem to notice the ghost standing right next to him.

He can't see it, Beth realized. *He doesn't know.*

To her surprise, she felt calmer. She picked up her pace but paused about three feet from the body and the ghost.

Smith sneered at Beth. "Search the body," he said. "Make sure she doesn't have any pages of the ledger on her." He stepped back, out of reach, to give her room.

Beth knelt. Her heart still pounded. She gently put one hand on the corpse's back and checked on Smith. He was watching the road ahead more than her.

She looked questioningly at Calamity's ghost. It pointed urgently toward the body's right boot.

Beth nodded. Smith's eyes were on her again, so she made a

show of patting down the corpse's back and sides. She tried not to vomit—the body was still warm, but the smell of the released bowels stank up the air.

She inched her hand down, slowly, over the hip, down the thigh. She took deep breaths to suppress the trembles in her arms. When she glanced at the ghost, it still pointed at the boot.

They heard yells from up the road and Smith's head jerked that direction. Shots followed.

Beth jammed her hand into the boot. Her fingers wrapped around the handle of a small derringer.

She yanked it out and pointed it at Smith. She squeezed the trigger.

It clicked on an empty chamber.

Smith had been looking at the road, his revolver pointed in that direction, but he instantly snapped his eyes down and pointed his own gun at her.

"Well," he drawled. "It looks like the girl's got some spirit. Too bad."

Beth pulled the trigger again.

The bang surprised her. The kick of the gun, too. Her arm flew back and she fell.

Smith's eyes went wide. His gun slipped from his fingers and clattered to the dirt. Crimson red blood soaked his shirt.

He collapsed into a lifeless pile.

Beth sat up, panting. Her arm ached, and she'd bruised her hand somehow. As she watched, a dark cloud formed above Smith's body. Instead of solidifying, it shifted and wavered like smoke, before a small grey disk appeared next to it and sucked the dark smoke in.

Jane's ghost smiled at her. It put its hands on its hips and nodded happily.

Behind her, she heard pounding footsteps on the road. She scrambled around, bringing the gun to bear.

She let out a relieved breath. Hickok raced toward her.

He skidded to a stop a few feet away. "Are you hurt?" he asked before dropping to one knee by Jane's side. Shock and grief raged across his face.

"I'm fine," Beth said.

Hickok rolled Jane's body onto its back and felt for a pulse on her neck. He cursed softly. Then he sat back on his haunches. His voice cracked when he spoke.

"She's gone," he said. He bit his lip, as if fighting back tears.

"Mostly," Beth said. "Her ghost's here." She gestured to where the ghost stood, smiling sadly at Hickok.

"Where?" Hickok turned wildly, looking all around. His gaze went right through the ghost not more than five feet from him.

"She's right there," Beth said, pointing.

He sighed. "Sorry," he said. "You must be one of the special ones that can see them."

Beth blinked as that sunk in. She stared at the ghost, wondering.

Calamity Jane's ghost cupped her hands over her heart and pressed them in. Then she pointed at Hickok. She repeated the hands on her heart gesture.

Beth nodded. She turned to Hickok. "She says she loves you."

He snorted softly, but the edges of his mouth still softened at the news.

"Tell her I love her, too," he said at last.

The ghost nodded, and her face beamed with an almost heavenly glow.

"She knows," Beth said.

Then the ghost drifted over to Smith's body. She pointed at something. Insistently.

Beth scrambled to her knees and crawled over to it.

"What is it?" Hickok called.

"She wants me to get something," Beth said. "Maybe the ledger?"

"I have the ledger," he said. "Or at least the pages that prove the governor's been stealing the army's money."

The ghost knelt and pointed at Jane's Colt. Beth looked at the ghost to make sure, and it nodded. She gingerly picked up the gun.

The ghost pointed at the revolver, and then at Beth. She repeated the gestures several times.

"You ... want me to have this?"

The ghost nodded.

With a deep breath, she squeezed the revolver tight. "Thank you."

The ghost smiled. A dark grey fog appeared behind her. Then it enveloped the ghost and they both faded away.

"She still here?" Hickok asked. He scrambled to his feet and extended a hand to pull Beth up.

She shook her head. She didn't relax her grip on the gun as she got up.

"She want you to have that?" he asked.

"I think so."

He nodded. "Then I suppose you oughtta keep it."

"Can I?" she asked.

"C'mon," he said and gestured back toward town. "We need to make sure everyone else is all right and get some help with these bodies."

"Then what?"

"Then," he said, "I teach you how to shoot. It's what she would've wanted."

CHAPTER ONE

GOLDEN CITY, COLORADO, 1881

Beth growled in frustration. She jammed her Colt into its holster. When she'd drawn it, the loose fabric in the shoulder of her dress had twisted. It'd messed up her aim. No one else was in the hotel's parlor, thank God. No one could hear her curse under her breath.

Should be in my shooting blouse, she grumped to herself.

But Hickok had told her, again and *again*, to practice in every outfit. "The gun should feel like a part of you," he'd said, "not just something you wear. It should be like pulling your hand from your pocket."

Except my dress doesn't have pockets, she thought sourly.

She took a deep breath and untwisted the thin cotton fabric. The gingham had gotten thread-worn. It tended to bunch at the seams and her ma had re-stitched it more than once. Still, she forced herself to be patient. She plucked at it and smoothed it as best she could until it lay straight all the way to her cuff.

Then she shook her arms loose. Just as Hickok had taught. Her right hand hovered over the Colt's handle. She stared at her reflection in the parlor mirror. She narrowed her eyes and—

—yanked the gun out, fast and smooth. She snapped her other

hand to the grip as soon as it was level. Her aim was right between her reflection's eyes.

Perfect.

She slowly lowered and holstered her revolver, and did it again.

Her aim was high and to the right. Only a few inches, but still. Hickok had driven it home, again and again. A few inches could be death instead of life.

She took a deep breath, lowered her gun, and practiced her quickdraw once more. This time her aim was dead on.

Pots clanged in the hotel kitchen. Her heart skipped a beat, but the kitchen door didn't swing open. She let out a relieved breath.

She glanced at the parlor's main door that led into the heart of the hotel. Not a peep. The Astor House of Golden City was quiet this morning. Most of the boarders had escaped outdoors. She couldn't blame them. It was one of the first truly beautiful Colorado spring days.

Another bang of metal rang out from the kitchen. She glanced around the parlor, with its dozen wooden tables and chairs.

Good enough, she thought. Mr. Lake wouldn't notice where she hadn't dusted. He'd only docked her wages once. She'd since learned all the spots he would inspect.

It wasn't that she *liked* cutting corners. She just needed the time to practice.

She checked her reflection in the mirror one last time. She'd tied her brown curly hair too loosely. It'd come untucked and she looked disheveled. She scowled.

You don't look like a "proper young lady" at all, she thought, mimicking Ma's regular phrase.

Still, it couldn't be helped. She brushed her errant hair back and glanced one more time toward the kitchen. It had gone relatively quiet as the cook moved to chopping or stirring or whatever his next step was.

So Beth unbuckled her gun belt and rolled it up around the gun. She headed to the polished upright piano that stood in the corner, where she scooted one of the wooden parlor chairs over and stood on it. With a small grunt, she lifted the heavy piano lid and carefully placed her gun inside. She rested it where it would only affect the keys with the lowest notes, the ones Mr. Lake never played. It wasn't the best hiding place, but it'd do.

At least until mid-afternoon. Then she could go down to the old battlefield like her friend Billy the Kid always did when he was in town. He'd taught her how to sit still, even in the hot sun, even in light rain, and wait. You had to wait, and then be fast. The prairie dogs popped out of their holes barely long enough to draw and shoot.

She smiled at the memory of practicing with Billy. He drew a crowd in town, but on the old battlefield, it was just the two of them. Just like it'd been with Hickok.

Most people avoided the battlefield. The giants and trolls who'd come through the rift from Jotunheim had destroyed too much and killed too many people. The battlefield felt haunted to them. And of course, they were right.

Neither Hickok nor Billy were scared of the ghosts that remained. Of course, they couldn't see ghosts like she could, but they wouldn't've minded if they had. The few ghosts left were friendly.

Not that it comforted Hickok. He always thought of Jane when they talked of ghosts. Beth had done her best. She'd listened to his stories. She'd held his hand when he needed it. More than once, she'd taken away his whiskey. She suspected she was one of the very few who'd seen him cry. Not that she'd admit it to anyone else.

She shook off the memories and set about straightening up the parlor's chairs. She'd gotten to the fifth table when Mr. Lake bustled in. Beads of sweat glistened on his forehead. His eyes darted nervously around, but he smiled when he saw her.

"Ah, Miss Armstrong," he said. "Miss Armstrong, Miss Armstrong."

Beth tensed. She stood straighter and brushed her errant hair back.

"Important visitors have come down from Fort Collins," he continued. "Would you be so kind as to prepare Room Four for guests?" He rubbed his hands together and glanced around. "Yes, we're ready here." He gave Beth a more pointed look. "Room Four, Miss Armstrong."

"Yes, sir," she said with a nod of her head.

She quickly walked through the door and up the stairs to the hotel's second floor. She paused at the top landing and took a deep breath. Then she continued on to the room Calamity Jane had stayed in the night she died.

Mr. Lake's "important visitors" didn't arrive for the midday meal. He himself disappeared a little after the clock struck noon. Instead, a couple of rough-looking teamsters joined the distinguished cattle merchant who was staying in Room Two for fresh bread and rabbit stew. The teamsters were unshaven and unwashed with greasy black hair. They laughed loud, but paid close attention to the merchant like he was their boss.

Beth served them quietly. She caught enough of their talk to realize they were discussing the way south, toward Santa Fe. The younger one had a stringy mustache and he leered at her. She bristled, but tried not to let it show.

When she brought glasses of Mr. Coors's latest brew, the younger teamster made a show of looking her up and down. He grinned, wide but cold.

"What's your name, missy?"

She stopped and stared at him.

"Mighty fine girl to be working in a place like this," the teamster drawled.

The merchant scowled at the teamster. "Mind yourself."

"Now why should I do that?" the teamster said. He gestured toward the glasses in her hand. "Gimme my beer."

Beth quickly set the glasses on the table. When she did, the teamster reached for her, but the merchant swatted his hand.

"She's Hickok's," the merchant said.

No, she thought, *I belong to me.*

"Hickok ain't here." The teamster waggled his eyebrows at her. "You lay an unwanted hand on her, and he'll hunt you down. God have mercy on you then."

"Aww ... but she's so *pretty.*"

Beth pushed down the growing fury. She squared her shoulders and faced the merchant. "Will there be anything else, sir?" she asked.

He shook his head.

She turned on her heel and strode steadily toward the kitchen. She ignored the feeling of eyes on her back as best she could.

Pick your fights, Hickok had told her again and again.

This wasn't one to pick.

In the kitchen, the fat cook looked up in alarm as she stormed in. He ducked his head and focused on chopping the winter potatoes. She glared at his back, but he just shrunk his shoulders and kept chopping.

The back door to the yard banged open. Beth spun and was about to say something tart to Mr. Lake but stopped. It wasn't Mr. Lake, but Rose, the other, slightly older maid and server. Her dark hair was perfectly in place under her bonnet and her dress was pressed and sharp. She carried a large wicker basket of clean laundry and gave Beth a concerned smile.

"Oh, honey," Rose said. "Men again?"

"They think I'm a whore," Beth snarled. She put her hands on her hips. Her fingers itched and she wanted her gun.

Rose shrugged and set the basket down. "Some've been calling me that since I was your age. You pay 'em no mind. They're not the ones that matter."

"No," Beth said, "but this isn't the shantytown outside Fort Chicago."

"There's nothing wrong with Chicago, dearie," Rose said. "Help me with the towels." She picked a stack out of the basket and opened the little linen cabinet.

Beth frowned but joined Rose at the basket. "One of them said I was Hickok's girl. I'm not."

"We know that," Rose said, "but they don't."

"I need to make a name for myself," Beth grumbled.

"Mmmm hmmm." Rose gave Beth her indulgent smile. "But don't let them bother you." She nodded toward the dining room and her eyes twinkled. "They're just men. They see a pretty girl and their brains stop working." She spotted Beth's start of a frown and continued, "And yes, you're pretty. You'd be prettier still if you'd let me make you another dress."

"I need new trousers," Beth said, "not a new dress."

Rose clucked her disapproval but didn't restart their old argument. Rose was all girl—well, at twenty, all woman. She'd never wear the trousers Beth favored. Still, she didn't exactly disapprove like most of the people in town. Beth had learned to ignore the looks and muttered comments. Most of the time.

They quickly finished with the towels and Beth pointed at the blankets that remained in the basket. "Are those for me, for Room Four?"

"Why yes, they are. Want some help?"

Beth shook her head. "The blankets are all I need." She tilted her head toward the dining room. "You can take care of the guests."

Rose's laugh rang merrily as Beth left with the basket.

Beth spread one blanket out over the top of the bed and left the rest folded at the foot. She'd brought in some fresh wild roses, but the room still smelled musty. It also felt warm, but there was no window she could open. She gave the dresser top and little writing desk one last check for dust. Then she sagged onto the little wooden chair and stared at the room. She couldn't get the teamsters out of her mind.

She wasn't Hickok's girl. She was his protégé! Why couldn't people understand that?

She snorted softly and shook her head. Well-worn thoughts, she chided herself. They wouldn't get the room ready.

She decided to give it a good sweeping, even though it looked like Rose had done it the day before. When she was done, she fluffed the pillows, adjusted the hang of the blanket, and made sure the small mirror hung straight on the wall. Then she headed back downstairs.

She heard the teamsters at the bottom of the steps before she saw them. With a silent curse, she ducked back on the landing and waited for their voices to fade. The door banged as they left the parlor for the dusty street. Then it banged again and other voices came in.

One of them was Mr. Lake's. Beth hustled down to talk to her boss.

The stairs ended in the front parlor next to the dining room. Whoever had been talking to Mr. Lake had preceded him through the connecting door, but Mr. Lake looked up at her footsteps. Tall and lanky with thinning hair, he looked a bit like a surprised scarecrow when he spotted her.

"Ah, Miss Armstrong!" he said. "I was just about to look for you. Please join us." He held the dining room door open for her. "Please."

She gave him her serious "What's this about?" look. He only smiled and motioned for her to pick up the pace.

Inside the dining room, two men and a woman were pulling out chairs at the large round table near the piano. The older of the men wore a dark black suit of the same cut and style that Hickok did. His long blonde hair fell in curls around his shoulders. He held his broad-brimmed hat in one hand.

The other man, with thin brown mutton chop sideburns, was dressed in a blue army uniform. He looked quite young and his coat hung awkwardly at the shoulders. He held the chair for the woman, but his eyes latched onto Rose as she approached with a pitcher of water.

Beth's eyes went wide as they fell on the woman. An Indian! She wore a beaded leather vest over a dark blue dress. Her braided silver-streaked black hair fell down her spine. Crow's feet wrinkles lined her eyes. After she'd sat, she turned and looked at Beth with a smile.

"Come, child," the woman said.

Mr. Lake gently pushed Beth between her shoulder blades. She lurched forward off balance, but didn't trip. *Stupid if I fell*, she thought. She caught her breath and forced herself to calm a bit.

As she approached the table, the woman gestured to the chair next to her. When Beth paused, Mr. Lake stepped around her and pulled the chair out. Without thinking, she sat.

"You are Miss Armstrong?" the woman asked.

"Yes," Beth said. "And you are ...?"

"Raven Stormchaser." Her slow smile showed her age. "With Mr. Weatherby and Lieutenant Tompkins." Her hand swept to indicate her companions.

"How do you do?" Beth said. She nodded her head since she couldn't curtsey, as Ma had taught, while she was sitting.

"Better than we were, Miss Armstrong," Raven Stormchaser replied. She leaned forward, placed her elbows on the table, and looked deep at Beth. "Much better."

"Ah ... and what can I do for you, Miss—Mrs. ...?" The Indian's head shake was almost imperceptible. "Miss Stormchaser?"

"Raven will suffice." Her eyes twinkled. "As for what you can do, that depends," she said. "Mr. Lake says you can see ghosts." She nodded toward him as he stood beside Beth's chair.

Beth willed her nervousness aside. "Yes. Yes, I can."

"Well then," Raven said, "we have much to discuss."

CHAPTER TWO

Beth folded her hands in her lap and sat quietly. She carefully studied the old Indian. Raven's eyes were wide and earnest. The corner of her mouth quirked up. Her breathing was steady and her muscles relaxed.

Hickok said to always watch their muscles, particularly their shoulders. "Those give you their intentions," he'd said. "They have to tense up before they can draw a gun." Then he'd given her one of his wide smiles. "And if they're not about to draw, sometimes their face betrays their thoughts."

Raven's face didn't.

Off to the side, Lieutenant Tompkins shuffled his feet. Then he coughed. Without looking, Beth could sense Mr. Weatherby's tight coil. He was ready to spring into action, but not at her.

She put on a warm smile and nodded at Raven. "Go on."

"We seek the ghost of one who fought against the Jotun giants in the Battle of Golden City." Raven nodded her head east, toward the old battlefield. "Mr. Lake says you spend much time there."

"There are some ghosts still," Beth acknowledged. "Maria wasn't able to persuade all of them to move on."

Raven looked over Beth's shoulder at Mr. Lake. "Who is Maria?"

"The witch that travels with Billy the Kid," he replied, but then added, "I believe they're in Texas now."

"Maria taught me about ghosts," Beth interjected, "once I knew I could see them."

Raven made a small shrug of acknowledgement and returned her attention to Beth. "We seek the ghost of an Arapaho warrior. He would be tall, with a long braid of black hair. Have you seen him?"

Beth frowned as she thought. Then she shook her head.

"He was a scout for the Army of the West," Lieutenant Tompkins said. "He might've been in uniform."

"Most are," Beth said. "At least on the battlefield."

"Are there many?" Raven asked.

"Ghosts?" Beth said. "No. Maybe a half dozen."

Raven pursed her lips. "We must speak with them all."

Beth raised an eyebrow. *She can talk with them? She's a witch!*

"Can you take us to the ghosts?" Raven continued.

"Yes," Beth said. "But we should wait 'til dark. I've never seen any of them during the day."

"That is the way of ghosts," Raven said. She looked at Weatherby. "We will rest and then set out after the evening meal."

He stared at Raven for a moment, as if asking a silent question. She met his eyes, but her expression didn't change. Then he made a small nod.

Raven turned to Beth once again. "You will join us."

"Right after supper," Beth said with a firm nod.

"No," Raven said, "I wish to hear about the ghosts, but after I have rested. Join us for the meal."

Beth twisted to look back at Mr. Lake questioningly.

"Oh, go on," he said with a flick of his hand. "Miss Chamberlin can manage serving supper on her own." He grimaced. "Or perhaps Mrs. Archer can be persuaded to fill in."

Beth fought to suppress a smile. Mrs. Archer always insisted on being paid with wine and Mr. Lake hadn't received a new shipment in months. No doubt he was worried about his dwindling reserves.

"Rose—Miss Chamberlin—can manage," Beth said. When she saw Raven raise an eyebrow, she added, "Rose can manage anything."

"Ah," Raven said. "Someone good to know."

The old Indian made to stand and Mr. Lake quickly moved to help her with her chair. She smiled gratefully at him. "My room?"

"Yes, ma'am. I'll take you right to it."

As Raven stood, Mr. Lake looked at Beth. "Perhaps you could assist in the kitchen?"

Beth forced a smile. There was always work to do.

Beth found Rose in the kitchen vigorously scrubbing pots. She'd filled a large copper tub with hot water and soap and set it on the little preparation table. Spots of grease splashed her apron but, as usual, not a hair was out of place. She looked up and smiled as Beth reached for her own apron on the nearby hook.

"What'd they want?" Rose asked.

"They're looking for a ghost." Beth finished tying her apron on. "A special one, apparently."

"Aren't they all special?" Rose said.

"To someone, I suppose."

Rose shrugged. She gave the pot she was working on a quick inspection and passed it to Beth. "Rinse tub is down there." She pointed toward the large basin on the floor.

Beth grabbed a towel and knelt next to the basin.

"Any idea why they want that ghost?" Rose asked. "I mean, it's not the ghost of a Jotun or a magic wizard or something, is it?"

"There are no wizards and no magic," Beth said, "and no one's ever seen a Jotun ghost."

"Doesn't mean there isn't one." Rose dunked a baking tin into her tub. "Maybe there's a Jotun wizard ghost! Who's haunting the battlefield!"

Beth couldn't help laughing a little, even as she rolled her eyes. She tried to glare at her friend, but the twinkle in the older girl's eyes just made her smile even more.

"Better take your gun," Rose said in mock seriousness, "in case you need to shoot the Jotun wizard warrior magic ghost."

"Actually," Beth said, "that's a good idea. I don't know these people, and that could mean trouble."

"Or you could get to know them."

"Or both," Beth said. She finished rinsing her pot and began to dry it. "I'm joining them for supper."

Rose's smile faded. "Huh. So I'm serving by myself." She passed Beth the baking tin.

"It's either that or have Mrs. Archer help," Beth said.

"By myself," Rose said emphatically. "Mrs. Archer always spills the soup."

At supper, Beth found herself sitting uncomfortably between Mr. Lake and Raven at the round parlor table in the back corner. He kept looking at Beth like she was some sort of cat. He'd smile and then nervously twist his spoon in his hand. It was like he expected her to jump on the table and lick the saucer.

She mentally sighed to herself. It was probably the trousers and gun belt. He knew she had them. He just hated that she wore them. The others had given her looks, but been too polite to say a word. Mr. Lake didn't, because he knew it was pointless. As long as she wasn't working, she'd wear whatever she liked. He wouldn't fire her, and she knew it. She wouldn't quit, and he knew it. Besides, other than her "unladylike behavior," they got along fine.

Of the others, Raven was the one more amused than scandalized by Beth's clothes. Except she annoyingly seemed to ask a question every time Beth's mouth was full. The older woman waited patiently while Beth chewed and swallowed, even if her eyes did dart around the table. Beth noted that Raven kept her shoulders relaxed. That helped Beth relax too.

It also helped that the creamy chicken soup was delicious. The baked winter potatoes had just the right amount of salt too. And the smell of the cracked wheat bread—heavenly!

But to Beth's disappointment, their visitors didn't say much about themselves. Mr. Weatherby was something of a government representative to the Arapaho and a longtime friend of Raven's. Lieutenant Tompkins had been attached as an army liaison. Raven revealed that she was an Arapaho and the three of them had come down from Fort Caspar. Beyond that, she politely deflected all of Beth's questions.

And to Beth's surprise, Raven also didn't quiz her about her own life. She only asked after Beth's ma, and was polite in asking Beth's opinion of her ma's new beau after Mr. Lake mentioned him.

"It's been six years since Pa died," Beth said. "She deserves to be happy."

Raven raised an eyebrow, but didn't comment on Beth's non-answer.

Otherwise, the conversation was almost all about the battlefield and the ghosts. Beth described the four she'd clearly seen and where they haunted. Raven was disappointed that Beth didn't know what they'd told Maria, if anything. None of their descriptions seemed to match the ghost Raven was looking for, either. But the older woman was heartened when Beth told her about a fifth ghost that she'd only kind-of-sort-of glimpsed a few times halfway up the North Table Mesa.

Near the end, Mr. Lake sent Rose to bring back a bottle of California whiskey. Mr. Weatherby lamented the loss of "the good stuff" now that the Jotun giants controlled Kentucky. Mr. Lake commiserated but they both drank more than one glass.

None was offered to the ladies, Beth thought sourly. Not that she liked the taste anyway. But shouldn't they have offered a drink of some kind?

When Raven gave her an appraising look, Beth pulled the frown off her face. She tried to keep her own shoulders relaxed despite how anxious she was to be headed out.

Finally, finally, the meal was over. Mr. Lake said a few polite words to Rose and then their whole party made their way to the street.

Beth took a deep breath of the crisp night air. It held the hint of winter past. She shook her arms to keep them loose. Once everyone had left the Astor, Mr. Lake said his farewells. He said he'd have hot cider ready for their return.

She stepped close to him and a bit away from the others. She pitched her voice low so they couldn't hear. "Raven and Mr. Weatherby enjoyed the bread. Perhaps you could serve some with the cider? With butter and the apple jam?"

"Thoughtful," he murmured.

She smiled and returned to the others. Raven gestured to Beth to lead the way.

They strode down the dusty street into the heart of Golden City. Two of the saloons popular with the miners and ranchers were lit and boisterous with music and loud voices. Beth's own party didn't talk as they passed them by. They walked beyond the darkened shops and stables and soon were among the shacks along the east side of town.

All too soon, the old earthen barricade rose up before them. It stretched from the North Table Mesa to the South Table Mesa, except where Clear Creek cut through it. At ten feet high, it had been enough to slow the Jotun giants, but not enough to save the men. None of the ghosts haunted it, even though most of the men had died there. They'd been the easy ones to find and lay to rest.

Beth led their small party to the winding footpath over the barricade that Billy had shown her. She paused and looked back. They were single file now, with Mr. Weatherby behind her, followed by Raven and with Lieutenant Tompkins bringing up the rear. Mr. Weatherby and Raven carried small lamps.

Mr. Weatherby paused at the bottom of the climb. "What's on the other side?"

"Uh ... the battlefield?" Beth said.

He scowled. "Is there any cover on it?"

"No, not really," she said. "There's some small cottonwoods down by the creek. There's some scrubby bushes too, but it's mostly dirt and rock."

"Nowhere someone could hide?"

"Not unless he's a prairie dog. They've pretty much taken over."

He let out a dark chuckle. "They're small, but not that small." He started climbing again.

"What are small?" she asked.

"We don't know," he said. "We saw what looked like fat children watching our camp two nights ago. It was too dark to see them clearly, though."

That made her heart skip. Her hand drifted to her revolver as they crested the barricade and started down the other side.

The path wasn't steep, but it was tricky in the dark. Sharp rocks and the ends of decaying wooden stakes stuck up at odd angles everywhere. In a half-dozen places, the dirt had eroded and made the footing tricky. Beth focused on her steps to avoid slipping.

About halfway down the path into the old battlefield, Beth caught movement from further north along the barricade out of the corner of her eye. She froze, and then slowly turned her head to look more closely at it.

The squat figure was silhouetted against the lighter sky behind it. She couldn't make out any features, but it seemed to be holding something. It turned slightly and ...

... it held a bow.

"Down!" she yelled, but an arrow was already in flight.

She threw herself to the ground, where a rock stabbed her ribs.

Behind her, Weatherby cried out. Beth fumbled to draw her revolver and banged her thumb on the ground. She cursed and leveled the gun at the figure just as another arrow flew overhead.

She fired twice in rapid succession.

The figure jerked and then dropped behind the far side of the barricade.

Beth quickly scanned the area. She couldn't see anything else moving. Keeping her gun pointed where she'd last seen the figure, she scrambled to her feet. She glanced back over her shoulder.

Weatherby was down. She couldn't see Raven or Lieutenant Tompkins. Keeping her eyes mostly on where the figure—the enemy—had disappeared, she worked her way back to where she'd last seen Weatherby. She found him sprawled on the ground, an arrow through his chest. Dead.

She gasped, and her chest clenched.

No time to panic, she thought. *No time to panic.*

"Help!" Lieutenant Tompkins called. He knelt at the top of the barricade next to something. "Help!"

Beth scrambled back up to him as quickly as she could. She still didn't see any signs of the enemy.

Lieutenant Tompkins was on his knees next to Raven. He was trying to pull the arrow out of her gut, but it was already too late. When he tugged, Raven's head rolled against her chest.

"She can't die!" Lieutenant Tompkins cried. "She can't!"

Blood covered his hands as he tugged and twisted the arrow. The shaft broke in his hands. He cursed, his voice panicked.

Raven's body went completely limp.

Beth sucked in her breath. Behind Lieutenant Tompkins, the air shimmered and then fogged. Slowly, it took shape.

Raven's ghost looked down at her body. It frowned. And then it looked imploringly at Beth.

CHAPTER THREE

Beth swallowed hard as she stared at the ghost. Her pulse raced and, for a moment, she felt pinned to the spot. *It's just a ghost*, she reminded herself. *It's just a ghost.*

"Noooo!" Lieutenant Tompkins cried. He had his hands pressed against Raven's stomach over the wound. The blood still seeped between his fingers.

That shook Beth out of her trance. "She's gone." When Lieutenant Tompkins looked up, she gestured at the ghost. "She's here."

The lieutenant's head whipped around. "Where?" He looked left and right.

"Her ghost's right there." Beth pointed more directly at the spot.

Raven's ghost still looked at her with wide desperate eyes. It urgently gestured north down the barricade toward where—

"Down!" Beth cried. She threw herself into the lieutenant and bowled them both to the dirt.

An arrow hissed through the air nearby.

The lieutenant snapped out of his shock. Still pale, he scrambled to the side away from Beth and rolled onto his stomach. She shifted her weight and winced. Somewhere along the way she'd banged her knee hard.

They crouched near some foot-tall scrub bushes and a few large jagged rocks. Beth couldn't see anything ahead other than the scraggled barricade. The lieutenant crawled forward behind one of the boulders and peeked over it. The night, at least nearby, was still.

Beth started to crawl forward on her stomach. The air in front of her fogged. Raven's ghost had moved.

It pointed repeatedly over the barricade, toward the path they'd just climbed.

Beth bit back a curse. They were being encircled.

Lieutenant Tompkins shifted to his knees and drew his Colt. His focus remained on where the archer had been. Not the new threat.

Beth grunted in frustration. She twisted and crawled back up the path as best she could while keeping her gun pointed ahead. Small rocks stabbed her knees and hand. Dust stirred up and tickled her nose.

Raven's ghost appeared in front of Beth and slightly to the right. It pointed steadily at something ahead of her, and low.

Beth shifted onto her elbows and aimed her gun at that spot.

Something moved. She couldn't quite make it out other than it was dark and getting taller. Like someone coming up over the crest of the barricade.

She fired.

Something squealed and the shape dropped below the rise.

Beth scrambled to her feet. She advanced as quickly as she could safely walk. Sweat poured down her brow. Her pulse raced and she tried to calm her breathing. Her eyes darted everywhere— where is it? Where's the next archer?

She looked to Raven's ghost, but it now stared northward.

Beth let out a sigh of relief. *It must've fled*, she thought.

She reached the top of the barricade. She crouched at first, not wanting to make herself a target against the lighter sky like the archer had done, but she didn't see anything. Raven's ghost continued to look north.

Down below, something moved. She squinted. A dark figure ran north just below the lip of the barricade. She couldn't make it out well, but it seemed to be fleeing. It was too hard to get a good shot, though.

Lieutenant Tompkins climbed up the barricade to her side. "You see them?"

She shook her head. "You?"

"No," he said, "not anymore." He looked down where Raven and Weatherby's bodies lay and let out a ragged sigh. "It seems they did what they came to do."

Beth peered around for Raven's ghost, but it was gone as well.

"So now what?" Lieutenant Tompkins said. From his tone, it wasn't a question.

But Beth answered anyway. "We go back to town and get Mr. Lake and the others to help us bring them back," she tilted her head toward Raven and Weatherby.

Lieutenant Tompkins nodded in agreement.

Despite being nighttime, Mr. Lake had the bodies taken to the mortician's shop down on Washington Street. He sent a messenger to the militia commander and quickly organized a sweep of the battlefield.

While they searched, Beth sat wearily at one of the back tables in the parlor at the Astor. Every muscle seemed drained of strength, now that the terror had passed. She fought back yawns and forced herself to take sips of her tea. Rose had made her "special healing blend" and gave Beth a disappointed glare every time she came in from the kitchen and saw Beth wasn't drinking.

The parlor bustled with people coming and going. Mr. Lake had the cook making sausage sandwiches for anyone who wanted one, but Beth's stomach was too turbulent to even try. Mr. Lake himself sat at the table closest to the main door. He took reports and sent messengers with news. He repeatedly told them there was a reward for anyone who found the killers.

Rose came in from the kitchen with a basket of hot brown bread. She set it in front of Beth, and then sank into the chair next to her.

"My, what a night," Rose said as she fanned herself with one hand. "Are you sure you're okay, dearie?"

Beth nodded. Her thumb ached, but she could move it. The bruise on her knee hurt bad when she walked. Otherwise, she was mostly just exhausted.

"It's hard seeing people die like that, in front of you. It can be a real shock, a real shock."

Beth made a sour smile. "I've seen it before."

"So have we all," Rose said. "So have we all. It doesn't make it less of a shock."

Beth nodded. She took a sip of tea and thought for a moment. "It's not a shock when it happens. Not to me. I'm too busy thinking about how, or *who*. It's only after that when the shock sets in."

Rose nodded sympathetically. "Like now."

"Yeah," Beth said. "I barely knew Raven and Weatherby. I'm upset that they're dead. But I'm not sure how I feel after that."

"Why should you?" Rose placed a reassuring hand on Beth's arm. "Death's a hard thing to face."

"True." Beth smiled at Rose. She sipped some more tea. "I wish I knew what Raven wanted. She never told me."

"You could ask that handsome lieutenant. I'm sure he knows. And I'm sure it was important."

Beth nodded. *If it was worth killing her*, she thought, *it had to be important.*

"I'll ask him," she said, "when he gets back from the search."

The militia hadn't returned by the time Beth's yawns had become contagious. Mr. Lake told her to go lie down in Room One, so she wouldn't have to make the long walk back to her ma's in the dark. He'd send a messenger so Ma didn't worry. He didn't exactly say he was concerned about her safety, but she knew.

She woke up late, with sunlight seeping in through the cracks around the door. She sat up and saw fresh clothes arrayed over the wooden chair in the room. Besides her unmentionables and old trousers, a new pretty red and brown wool dress was prominently spread out. It had ruffles on the long sleeves and flared below the waist.

A small white plate sat on the little nightstand with two brown sugar cookies on it, Rose's specialty.

Beth shook her head in amusement. If Rose wanted her to have a new dress, she'd have a new dress.

As she pulled her clothes on, Beth realized that the dress could actually be worn over the trousers. She'd have to wear her gun belt on the outside. There was no helping that. She hesitated for just a moment. Everyone had seen her with the gun last night. There was no point in trying to hide it now. She buckled the gun belt over her dress and headed to the parlor.

She found Lieutenant Tompkins slumped at one of the tables with an open bottle of whiskey before him. It sat mostly empty. Half-nibbled bread lay tucked under a casually thrown napkin. His jacket hung over the back of the chair and his shirt was unbuttoned at the top and cuffs. He stared toward the windows to the street, but without focus. When Beth approached, he barely glanced her way until she stood tableside.

"May I join you, Lieutenant?" she asked.

"Dear Lord, yes," he said. He tried to stagger to his feet, but nearly fell out of his chair.

Beth sat before he had a chance to do himself harm for the sake of courtesy.

"You saw her ghost," he said. "You saw her. Did you talk to her?"

"I can't talk to ghosts," Beth said. "Like some others, I can only see them."

"I ... I dunno." He shook his head and then shook it again. It looked like he was about to cry. "We need ... we need her. We need to talk to her."

"Why?"

"She knew how to ... how to ... find it." He grimaced. Then he stared out into nothing again.

Beth fought back her frustration. "Find what?"

"The monster. It ... it killed a bunch of our men. A bunch of her tribe, too. But it flies. Too high to shoot. We ..." He turned back to stare at her with wide eyes. "We have to find its lair. Kill it there."

His face fell and his shoulders slumped. "You wouldn't understand. You're just a girl." His eyes went out of focus again.

Beth stared at him. She took a deep breath to calm her fury. Then she stood and walked out.

Beth found Mr. Lake in front of the mortician's office. He wore yesterday's suit, though brownish dust covered it. His face was hangdog worn with dark circles under his eyes. His hat's brim fluttered in the wind, making him look even more weathered.

When he saw Beth, his eyes darted to her gun and trousers. He let out an exasperated sigh. He'd just come out of the office and the door finished banging shut. He waited as Beth marched up to him.

"Did you find the killers?" she demanded.

He shook his head. "Some blood, but that was it. The army scouts weren't able to track them." His eyes narrowed. "How'd you know there was more than one?"

"I shot two," she scoffed.

He nodded without arguing.

"Lieutenant Tompkins is drunk."

"Why am I not surprised?" Mr. Lake turned to look at the mountains. "Hopefully he'll sober up by the funeral."

Beth blinked. *A funeral already?* she thought. "When is it?"

"When the militia commander gets back. We want it done before the storm rolls in."

She glanced up at the dark clouds that gathered behind the mountains. It might just be a spring rain, or it might be more. Either way, it wouldn't be long.

Still, the gathering gloom made her shiver. Ghost weather, at least on the battlefield.

"I should pay my respects," she said. She nodded toward the mortician's shop.

He nodded. "I'll see you back at the Astor."

The viewing room in the mortician's shop felt tight and cold. A scattering of candles in wall sconces provided the only light, as the black curtains over the sole window had been pulled tight. It smelled heavily of linen oil and lilies. Beth couldn't help wrinkling her nose.

The mortician, a kindly old man with stringy grey hair named Mr. Dooley, had let her into the room with the bodies. He hadn't blinked at her trousers and she decided on the spot to bring him some muffins from the Astor after the service. Then he'd stepped back out to the main shop, but left the door ajar three inches or so. At first she just heard him whistling to himself, until someone else came in and they began to talk in low voices.

She stood there, hands clasped, and stared at the bodies. They looked so cold and rigid in their pine coffins. Weatherby's hands lay by his side. His cheeks were collapsed in, which made him look like he was kissing the air. The wary man had been reduced to a clammy fish in a suit.

Raven looked more like she was asleep. Her chin tilted down

as if she were taking a nap. Her hands relaxed on her chest. She seemed to be praying.

Beth took a deep breath, studying the woman's face. Was there wisdom still within?

The voices from the other room rose. Only one seemed angry —the mortician. He told someone to leave. Beth turned and pulled the door nearly closed to block out the distraction.

When she looked back at the bodies, her breath caught. Raven's ghost now stood opposite her.

Beth willed herself to be calm. She couldn't hear ghosts. Could the ghost hear her?

"Thank you for your help," Beth said to the ghost.

Its expression didn't change. It just looked calmly at her.

"You saved us," Beth said. "I ... owe you my life."

This time, the ghost slowly nodded. Its mouth moved, like it was speaking, but no sound came out.

"I'm ... I'm sorry," Beth said. "I can't hear you."

Raven's ghost tried to say something again, but then stopped. Its eyes narrowed. Then it pointed at Raven's corpse.

"You ... you want something."

It nodded and pointed again.

Beth slowly stepped to the edge of the coffin. "You want me to do something."

It nodded, stronger this time. Then it pointed directly at a tiny pouch on the body's chest, right over the breastbone.

Beth frowned. She hadn't seen this pouch before. It was about the size of a thimble and made of soft deerskin. Thin leather cords looped from it around the corpse's neck. Light tan, it had some symbols branded into it that Beth didn't recognize.

The ghost jabbed its finger at the pouch once more.

"You want me to do something with this."

It nodded its head up and down.

Beth reached out and put her hand on the pouch. When the ghost nodded again, she lifted it from the cold corpse. The ghost nodded once more.

"You want me to take this," Beth said. "You want me to have it?"

The ghost smiled. It nodded its head yes. Then it faded away, leaving only cold air.

Beth hesitated. *What was this thing?*

Loud shouts came from the main room. More than one voice. Yelling.

Beth quickly grabbed the pouch and yanked hard. The cord cut into her hand but didn't break. *I need a knife*, she thought. The back end was under Raven's hair—it'd be hard to pull over her head. Beth tugged at the cord, spinning it around. A knot! The cord tied in a knot that was normally behind Raven's neck.

Beth picked at it. It took some work to loosen it. Meanwhile, the yelling outside got louder.

The cord finally worked free! She lifted her dress and shoved the pouch in the right pocket of her trousers.

A gunshot thundered in the adjoining room.

Beth jumped in surprise. Then she drew her Colt and edged to the door.

CHAPTER FOUR

Beth waited next to the nearly closed door and listened. Blood rushed in her ears and made it hard to hear anything in the next room. Her mouth tasted like milky cotton. Sweat beaded on her brow.

She grasped the cold door handle but then paused.

The door would open into her room. By the time she got it open far enough to see anything, they'd have seen her. And if they were armed ...

She didn't want to be easy to see. She quickly moved around the room and put out all the candles but one. Let it draw their eyes instead of her.

Then she crouched down as close to the hinges as she could. And pulled the door open.

No bullets came flying.

As the door slowly swung in, a gap between the door and its frame opened up, where the hinges were. When it was wide enough, she peeked through.

Nothing. At least not in the small sliver of room she could see. She couldn't hear anything either.

She took a deep breath. Then she scooted to look around the door itself.

The room was empty—no, not quite. Mr. Dooley, the mortician, stood in the doorway to the street, looking out. He panted hard and leaned against the doorjamb, with a drawn revolver held ready.

She scrambled to her feet and stepped into the main room. She lowered her gun to her side as she did.

Mr. Dooley glanced back and saw her, but returned his gaze to the street. He shifted his weight and stood up straighter.

"Did you hear that?" he asked when she approached. He didn't look back.

"Just some arguing and the gunshot."

"That was me. Thought they could push me around, did they?"

"Who were they?" She'd reached his side, but couldn't see who he meant. The street outside was nearly deserted. Only one of the ragged hoping-for-a-gold-strike miners from the shantytown was stumbling along. He held a brown bottle in one hand that he drank from every third or fourth step.

"Two cowboys," Mr. Dooley said. "Never seen 'em before. Said they were friends of the deceased. They needed to claim the woman's things." He snorted. "Like I'm that stupid." He glanced at her. "Mr. Lake said you were with the poor souls when they died, so I knew you was all right. Them?" His lip curled in a frown.

"Did you see where they went?"

He shook his head. "Must've ducked around the side."

She glanced left and right down the street. Only the miner was out. The clouds had continued to gather above, casting a grey pall everywhere. The wind had also picked up, stirring dirt from the road into mini dust devils. It'd be pure mud once the storm broke.

The miner slipped and fell. He twisted to avoid dropping the bottle and landed hard on his hip. Then he fell on his side.

"I'm going to help him," Beth said to the mortician.

"Why?" His lip curled as he considered the obvious drunk.

"Because he needs it," she said. "Besides, he might've seen where the cowboys went."

She holstered her gun and pushed past the mortician into the street. He waved her on her way and stepped back into his shop. She hustled over to the miner, but looked up and down the street as she did.

No cowboys.

She reached the miner just as he managed to sit himself up. He gave her a broad gap-toothed smile.

"Do you need help, mister?" she asked. She extended a hand.

"Why ... thank you, missy," he said. He let her pull him up to his unsteady feet.

"Where are you trying to get to?"

"Oh ... uh ... my shack's down that-a-way." He gestured toward the ramshackle shantytown that had grown up between the battlefield and the original town. "Got some beans. Some nice pork fat." He raised his bottle. "It'll cook real good in this."

"Perhaps I could help you to your shack?"

His eyes went wide and he stared at her. "Oh ... missy, that'd be mighty kind of you. Mighty kind. But it wouldn't be right, a sweet young thing going off with me alone. Wouldn't be right, mind you."

She pasted a practiced smile on.

"Perhaps I could help you to the Astor House?" she asked. "I'm sure someone there could get you home." She gestured toward the deepening clouds. "Or you could wait out the rain there." It looked like it'd hit soon, well before the militia returned.

"Why, that'd be mighty nice. Mighty nice of you." He coughed, and she stepped back to avoid his whiskey breath. "Mighty nice." Then he held out his hand. "I'm Jeb Miller."

"Beth Armstrong. Pleased to meet you." She took his hand and made a small curtsey.

"Oh, I'm charmed. Truly charmed." His grin was as wide as his face.

He started walking toward the Astor, slowly. One foot carefully planted before moving the other. But he didn't stumble. Beth's own steps were reduced to a stroll to stay by his side.

"So," she asked after they'd walked a bit, "did you hear that gunshot a little while ago?"

"Oh, yes. Oh, yes. Then those men! Such a hurry, such a hurry."

"Did you see which way they went?"

"Went? Which way they went?" He stopped walking and scratched his chin. "They were in such a hurry...."

She forced a smile. "A hurry to run toward the saloons?"

"No ... no ... no." His hand slid up and scratched his head.

"South of town?"

"No ..."

"Toward the stables?"

"No ..." He frowned. "The battlefield. I remember wondering if maybe they'd help me to my shack."

She let out an exasperated sigh. Maybe he'd remember something more. Maybe not. The cowboys were surely long gone either way.

She glanced back at the mortician's shop, but the man had gone back inside and closed the door.

She took Jeb's elbow and guided him up the street. "Let's get you to the Astor."

The first drops of rain splattered down just as the sandstone walls of the Astor came into view. With the rain, a light breeze blew down the mountain and brought the smell of grass and pine trees. One big fat raindrop plopped on Beth's nose. Then another hit her ear. Then they started smattering around and turning the dirt road to mud.

She needed a hat. A real one—not the bonnet Ma had bought for her when they'd first come to Golden City six years ago. Besides, she'd grown and it barely fit now. She needed a broad brimmed hat.

But a hat like that took money she didn't have.

Jeb still shuffled and stumbled along. He clutched his bottle tight and kept a hungry eye ahead. He seemed immune to her silent urgings to hurry up, but at least he didn't fall.

The Astor had the only balcony in town—a small one that stuck out over the main entrance a dozen feet. Some mornings she'd sat silently there with coffee and watched the sunrise.

Those were peaceful times.

Now the balcony was deserted, but several soldiers stood underneath it, out of the rain. They milled about talking quietly. One sipped from a canteen. Beth's chest tightened. The militia quartered on the far side of town. If they were here ... that meant trouble. As Beth and Jeb got closer, the soldiers turned to watch.

Jeb paused almost mid-step. His mouth fell open and he started to tremble.

"They're on our side," Beth said quietly. "Let's keep going."

"They're staring at me."

No, Beth realized, *they're staring at me.* In her dress and gun belt, she had to be quite a sight.

She lifted her chin and pushed her shoulders back. With a firm grip on Jeb's elbow, she walked them both forward. As she did, she met the stares she could eye to eye. Many of the men looked away. One of the soldiers sneered, but another looked amused.

The rain picked up, and then the wind. Beth fought off a shiver and kept her eyes on the soldiers. They made room for her and the miner under the shelter when they finally arrived.

"May we go in, please?" she said to a burly black-haired private blocking the Astor's front door.

His gaze skipped down her body and then his eyes went wide at the sight of her gun.

"My, my," Jeb said. His head swiveled this way and that as he took in all the soldiers. "What is all this?"

"Muster," the private said. "The militia's headed out."

"What?" Beth barked in surprise. "When? Why?"

He shrugged. "Word is, a huge army of trolls have invaded

Cherokee Territory by crossing the river south of Memphis. We're supposed to help."

Beth blinked. "That's a long way from here."

"I just follow orders," he answered. He gave her a dismissive wave and stepped aside.

Beth found Mr. Lake and the militia commander, Colonel Mosby, in deep conversation in the parlor. They sat surrounded by the colonel's aides and some of the other prominent town business leaders. The ones standing nearly blocked her view. Mr. Lake bent forward and leaned on his elbows. He only gave her the briefest of glances as she walked in. He somberly focused on the colonel's words instead.

Beth spotted Rose bringing stew and beer to a rumpled and clearly exhausted soldier huddled at the back table. She guided Jeb through the crowd. They reached the table just as Rose finished setting everything down. She turned with an inquisitive smile.

"Could we get some stew for my friend Jeb here?" Beth asked. "On me."

Rose's eyebrows went up. "On me" meant out of Beth's wages.

"Oh, you don't need to do that," Jeb said. "Not at all, not at all."

"I insist," Beth said. "Just sit right down. Please?"

"Better do like she says," Rose added sweetly. "I have yet to meet a man who could say no to her."

Beth harrumphed quietly and shot Rose a warning glare, but her friend just dismissed it with a friendly chuckle.

"Will you join me, missy?" Jeb asked.

"I'm sorry," she said with a shake of her head. She turned to Rose. "Will you take care of him, please? He saw some funny things earlier."

"Oh? Are you going to tell me about them?"

"After I get back from the mortician's." Beth turned to go but paused. "Um ... Rose?"

"Yes, dearie?"

"May I borrow your hat?"

Beth felt silly tromping through the rain and the mud in a red and brown dress and a pink hat. The dark trousers underneath didn't help her appearance either. They were warm, though. The initial torrent of the cloudburst had faded after about thirty minutes, like most Colorado storms. A slower drizzle still continued. So she wasn't *too* soaked. Still, the town only had wooden sidewalks here and there so she had to pick her way carefully through the sodden mud.

She inhaled deeply, breathing in the cleansing scent of the rain. She kept glancing around, just in case she saw some cowboys, but she was still alone on the streets. She didn't see another soul before she reached the mortician's.

As she approached the building, she froze. Something was off. She stood still, letting raindrops roll off the brim of Rose's hat and onto her shoulders. She let out a long breath and studied the building.

The curtains to the viewing room were open. They'd been closed when she'd viewed the bodies, not less than an hour ago.

The shop's door remained shut just like before, but the curtains were wrong. Completely wrong. Her hand started to twitch, so she rested it on her gun. She stole towards the window with glances left, right, and behind to check for danger.

Nothing.

She let out a deep breath to steady her nerves, just like Hickok had taught. Then she did it again.

She sidled up next to the window and drew her Colt. She tried to quickly peek in, but didn't see anything other than blackness. Which wasn't really surprising since she'd put out the candles in the viewing room herself.

Of course. She cursed under her breath. Then her gut knotted in realization.

Someone had needed light to see, so they'd opened the

curtains. It wasn't Mr. Dooley the mortician—he'd have just relit the candles. Which meant—

She strode over to the door, threw it open, and immediately dropped to one knee with her Colt pointed into the room.

No shots.

No one to shoot.

Just Mr. Dooley's body, sprawled on the floor.

They'd ransacked the corpses. Raven's now lay face down in its coffin. Mr. Weatherby wasn't so lucky—they'd tipped his body onto the floor. Raven's bracelets were gone and the pockets of Mr. Weatherby's pants had been slit open. Clothes had been tugged and untucked and pulled, leaving broken buttons behind.

They'd also torn apart Mr. Dooley's personal quarters, the ones behind his shop, but much more sloppily. Too much of a hurry, she suspected. It turned out his rooms had a back door, which remained thrown open. Tracked mud showed it'd been their way in.

Mr. Dooley's body they'd left alone except to turn out his pockets.

She clutched Raven's little pouch in her own trousers pocket. Her nails bit into her palm as she held it tighter than she'd ever held her gun. Her heart raced and her breath started to come in gasps.

She stared at Mr. Dooley's body—all splayed out like a broken doll on its face. One hand was twisted underneath his body. Blood pooled underneath. Already the stench was starting to turn her stomach.

If she'd still been there ...

Her imagination raced.

CHAPTER FIVE

The rain finally fizzled out as Beth trudged back to the Astor yet again. Birds cawed in the distance, out for their post-rain worm and bug hunt. The sun wasn't out, though. It looked like it might not appear before dusk. Already the western mountains were fading into the gloom.

Fortunately, the mud wasn't deep enough to be slippery. It clung to her shoes, which just made her wish for good boots. But she stepped carefully. No point in slipping and getting mud everywhere else.

She grimaced. Three people were dead and she was worried about mud. She couldn't help rolling her eyes at herself.

To her surprise, the soldiers were gone when she came in sight of the Astor. Long shadows filled the space under the balcony and nothing else.

Her gut tightened. She scanned the area—nothing.

No one.

Her breath quickened and she picked up her pace.

She let out a sigh of relief when she reached the door and heard multiple voices inside. She composed herself and strode in. The parlor bustled with people. Only the soldiers were gone.

A dozen of the town's merchants, stable owners, and even

Boggs the blacksmith sat at scattered tables. He looked up from his deep conversation and gave her a grim smile. Short and squat with bulging muscles, he once again reminded her of a troll. Not that she'd say so. He might not hit a girl, but the last man to call him a troll hadn't walked for a week.

Meanwhile Rose bustled from table to table with a frazzled look in her eye. She dropped off plates and picked up empty ones. She gave Beth a quick pleading glance before one of the merchants asked her for something.

"Ah, Miss Armstrong." Beth turned to see Mr. Lake beckoning from a nearby table. "Miss Chamberlin could use your assistance. We have a number of customers tonight."

"Mr. Dooley's been murdered," she blurted.

He paled.

"The killers were looking for something." She briefly recounted what she'd found, and then backed up and told him about what had happened when she'd been viewing the bodies. When she got to the part with Jeb, she glanced over at his table. The old miner was chewing some bread at the table where she'd left him.

"This is bad," Mr. Lake said. "Very bad." He gestured at the room. "Colonel Mosby wants provisions and supplies so he can ride out the day after tomorrow. Every able-bodied man who can is to go with them."

"So?"

"We can't rely on the army." He picked up a fork and tinked it against his glass. The conversation in the room died as he stood.

"Gentlemen," he said loudly, "there's been another killing. We need to find the culprits *now*. Let's gather outside."

She started to head toward the door when Mr. Lake put his hand on her arm.

"Thank you, Miss Armstrong," he said. "We'll take it from here. Why don't you see what help Miss Chamberlin might need?"

He gave her a pointed look and her objections died on her lips.

Beth waited for Rose in the kitchen. Her stomach rumbled at the savory smell of the stew on the iron stove. The cook only gave her a brief smile before he returned to chopping potatoes. She took a moment to pour herself a drink of water from one of the pitchers sitting on the side table. She sipped slowly to help calm herself down.

Rose bustled in breathlessly with an armful of dirty plates. "What's going on, dearie? You said there was a murder?"

Beth reached for the dishes. "The mortician, Mr. Dooley, was murdered. I found the body."

Rose stopped in her tracks and nearly dropped everything. Beth caught the plates just in time and only a wayward fork bounced off the floor.

"Murdered?" Rose said wide-eyed.

"Mmmm hmmm." Beth's expression soured. "I found the body, but Mr. Lake doesn't want me involved."

"Probably best you aren't," Rose said. She gestured toward the stove. "Help me fill the soup bowls while we talk? I also need more beer."

"But I *am* involved," Beth said as she pulled clean bowls out of the cupboard. "They killed him because they wanted something Raven had. And I was helping her."

"All the reason to let the men catch the murderer for you."

"If they can. They don't know who they're looking for."

"And you do?" Rose thrust a full bowl of stew into Beth's hands. "Here. Table Four. See if they need more beer while you're there, please."

Beth gave her an exasperated scowl, but Rose just smiled and shook it off. She nodded with her head toward the parlor. "Please?"

Beth glanced down. Her new dress had bunched around her hips underneath the gun belt, which revealed the lower half of her trousers. "I'm not appropriately attired for serving."

"Mr. Lake's left, and hungry men won't mind." Rose picked up two bowls. "And the sooner they're fed, the sooner we can talk in private."

Beth glanced at the cook, who remained hunched over, studiously ignoring them. She took the bowl and headed for the parlor.

She found the old miner Jeb hunched over his stew. He ate greedily and stuffed a heel of bread into his mouth between each spoonful of broth. He gave her a wide-eyed grin and watched her as she served the other tables. His eyes didn't leave her. He even spilled a little stew down his chin and unconsciously wiped his face with his hand.

She bristled and her right arm tensed. Since she was holding the stew, she couldn't rest her hand on her gun.

He's harmless, she told herself. *He's just looking.*

But why me? I'm not Rose.

At least he was polite, compared to the teamsters from the day before.

None of the other men in the parlor gave her more than a quick glance. They remained buried in their conversations and their plans with only the briefest attention to their food.

Since many had already left, the remaining service went quickly. Beth managed to steal a few minutes to wolf down some bread and stew of her own. Then she cleared and wiped down tables while Rose politely inquired if those left wanted more stew, or perhaps a little beer to wash down their meal?

Fortunately, other than Jeb, few seemed prone to linger. Within an hour, only the old miner remained.

"I should talk to him," she told Rose quietly as they wiped down a table two merchants had lingered at, discussing the price of feed.

"He does seem smitten with you."

Beth grimaced. "He's old enough to be my grandpa."

"Oh, honey, it's not like he's courting you. I'm sure he's just enjoying the attention of a pretty young woman."

"Well, I hope he can remember more about those cowboys. He's the only one that's seen them."

"I'll bring some tea." She held out her hand for Beth's cleaning rag and gave her a friendly smile. "Go on."

Beth let out a resigned breath. Then she went to Jeb's table. He dabbed some loose crumbs from his chin as she came over. His eyes danced.

"May I join you?" she asked once she'd reached his side.

"Oh, yes. Oh, yes." He started to stand, but she pulled out her own chair before he could. He slid back down into his seat, but almost bounced with energy.

"How was the stew?" she asked. "Filling?"

"Oh, mighty filling. Mighty filling." He grinned at her. "And I do thank you. I do."

"Happy to help," she said as sweetly as she could muster. "But ... I was hoping you'd be able to help me in return."

"Why anything, missy. Anything. Whatever do you need?"

She took a deep breath. "I need to know more about the cowboys," she said. "The ones you saw running."

"Oh, yes," he said, "oh, yes. They was in a mighty hurry, a might—"

"Toward the battlefield," she interrupted. "Yes, but what did they look like?"

"Cowboys," he said with a shrug. "Big coats. Hats. They was running. Hard to see much."

"Were they carrying anything? Did they have guns out?"

He sucked on his lip for a minute as he thought. Then he shook his head. "Nah. The big one yelled at the other one about it."

She snapped up and looked at him, but Jeb remained deep in thought.

"What'd he say?" she asked quietly. "Exactly? What were his

exact words?"

Jeb scrunched up his face. He wiggled his nose. Then he scratched it before nodding.

"He said, 'You fool! How could you not bring the gun?'"

Hmmm, Beth thought. *Mr. Dooley was shot less than an hour later. Where'd they get the gun? Or was it someone else?*

"Did the other cowboy reply?" she asked.

"No," Jeb shook his head. "He just ran along. Ran along after the big one." He shook his head once more. "That's all, I'm afraid. That's all."

"Well then," Beth said, "are you about ready for that walk back to your shack? I'm sure the cook would be happy to help you on your way."

"That'd be mighty nice," he said with a grin broad enough to swallow the sun. "Mighty nice."

The cook refused to escort Jeb to shantytown. He'd worked all day. It was already getting dark. He was tired. He was done. He was going home. He was even immune to Rose's charm and said they'd just have to find someone else. He walked out the kitchen's back door without even a glance back at the two women.

Beth sighed and leaned back against the prep table. She first ran her hands along the edge to make sure it was clean and she wouldn't dirty her dress. But when the handle of her gun bumped the table, she stood back up straight.

Rose's eyes followed her moves and danced with amusement. She stood in the center of the kitchen, and despite the frenzied dinner service, only her apron showed obvious stains.

"It'd be easier if he'd let me take him," Beth groused. "But he says, 'It wouldn't be right.'"

"He could go by himself," Rose said.

"I don't want him to end up like Mr. Dooley."

"Then have him stay here. Lieutenant Tompkins is passed out

in Room Three. If Jeb slept on the floor of his room, he should be safe."

"Hmmm," Beth said. "Wouldn't the lieutenant mind?"

"We won't know until we ask." Rose grinned. "And if we can't ask, because he's asleep, then he won't mind."

Beth rolled her eyes. "I'm not sure about that."

"Only one way to find out." Rose gestured toward the door.

They waved at Jeb as they passed through the parlor. He gave them a little wave in return and then sipped on his bottle. Rose shot Beth an amused look, but Beth just shook her head with a wry smile. Jeb would be happy whatever they did, she was sure.

Beth followed Rose up the narrow stairs and down the short hallway to Room Three. They paused outside and Rose leaned her ear against the door. Then she knocked lightly.

"Lieutenant Tompkins?" When no answer came, she knocked a little harder. "Lieutenant?"

A muffled voice called out, but they couldn't make out the words. Rose knocked again. The resulting yell was also unintelligible. Rose knocked once more, with even more force.

The door snapped open. A bleary, disheveled Lieutenant Tompkins glared at them. His mussed hair stood straight in places. His untucked shirt hung half-buttoned. He pressed one hand to the side of his temple. He leaned his other on the doorjamb, as if bracing himself against a fall. He looked hungover beyond hungover.

"What is it?" he snapped.

"We need your help," Beth said without preamble. "The mortician's been murdered. Raven and Mr. Weatherby's bodies were searched. The army's about to move out to fight the trolls—"

"Wait. What?" He shook his head and blinked hard.

"Oh, do sit down, Lieutenant," Rose said. "I'll fetch you some water and dry bread."

He grimaced. "I'd rather have some 'hair of the dog.'"

She tsked and shook her head with a smile. "Go on. Sit down, please."

The lieutenant opened the door wider. He staggered back to the unkempt bed and sat down on the edge. Beth entered and stood a few feet away, rocking on the balls of her feet, while Rose headed back to the kitchen.

Lieutenant Tompkins rubbed his eyes and then gave her a bleary stare.

"Murdered?" he said.

"Yes." She gave him an abbreviated version of what she'd seen and heard, only omitting Raven's ghost and the little pouch.

"They were looking for something," he said. "Something important."

"Yes. But what?"

He clasped his hands to his temples and rested his elbows on his knees. A strand of hair flopped across his forehead.

"Maybe ..." he started to say. Then he shook his head, but winced. He groaned and held his head tighter.

Rose returned. She held a ceramic mug, which she promptly thrust at the lieutenant. "It's nothing but water, but it'll help."

He took it with a skeptical look, but drank. After a couple of deep swallows, he lowered the cup and studied its rim.

"Oh. I can't believe I forgot this," he said. He looked up at them. "Raven once said that if anything happened to her, I was supposed to take this little pouch she wore and give it to another shaman. She never said why, though."

"Little pouch?" Rose asked. "What's it look like?"

"This." Beth pulled the pouch out of her pocket and held it up.

"Oh, my," Rose said.

"That's it," Lieutenant Tompkins said. He lowered his hands to his lap and sat up straighter. "Yeah, that's it."

"What's in it?" Rose asked.

Beth shrugged. She stepped closer to Lieutenant Tompkins so he could see and started to undo the ties. Rose looked over her shoulder.

The pouch held a small nub of polished bone.

Beth dumped it out into her palm and studied it. It was cool and smooth and no bigger than the last bone of her pinky, or maybe her little toe. She turned it over but found nothing different on the backside.

"A bone?" Rose asked. "Why was she carrying that?"

Beth's skin prickled as the room suddenly cooled.

"I think I know," she said.

She looked up into the smiling face of Raven's ghost.

CHAPTER SIX

Raven's ghost floated a few feet away, just at the foot of Tompkins's bed. In the light from the oil lamp on the nightstand, Beth could see partway through it. Like gauze or loosely knitted wool. It shifted slightly, fuzzing up the view. Apparently, the ghost could not stand perfectly still.

"Know what?" Rose prompted.

Lieutenant Tompkins's head snapped around, but he didn't see the ghost.

"She's here, isn't she?" he asked.

"Who?" Rose asked.

"Raven's ghost," Beth answered. "She's at the foot of the bed."

Both of the others stared that way. Rose grew very still. "Where?"

"Right there." Beth gestured toward the spot where the ghost still stood. Its hands were clasped and it continued to smile warmly.

"I ..." Rose began. She trembled slightly, her eyes wide.

"You can't see her," Beth finished. "Most people can't. See ghosts that is. But she can't harm you."

"What does she want?" Rose asked.

"I don't know," Beth admitted. "I can't talk to her. I'm not a witch or a shaman. But I know why she's here."

"To finish the mission?" Lieutenant Tompkins asked. He looked a lot more sober than he'd been a few minutes ago. Somber too.

"Probably," Beth said. "But that's not what I meant. I meant *here*, in this room. She didn't die here, so she shouldn't be here."

"I don't understand," Rose said. Her voice still had an edge as her eyes darted back and forth through the space where Beth had pointed.

"Maria—" She spotted Lieutenant Tompkins's furrowed brow and added, "she's the witch that travels with Billy the Kid. Anyway, Maria told me that ghosts either stay where they died or with the body."

"Which means ..." Rose began.

"Right," Beth said. "It's *her* bone. Probably her little toe."

Lieutenant Tompkins chuckled, long and dark and full. When he'd finished his eyes filled with amusement.

"Clever, clever woman," he said. "She *knew* she might die. She *knew* she might become a ghost."

"Mmmm hmmm," Beth said. Her blood raced with excitement. "And this way she can travel with us."

Raven's ghost clasped her hands together and nodded several times. She smiled happily and looked from the small bone to Beth's face and back again several times.

Just like Calamity Jane when she gave me the gun, Beth thought. Her chest tightened. She forced a smile, and then looked the ghost in the face.

"Yes," Beth said solemnly. "I will take you with me."

Raven's ghost nodded, and then faded away.

Beth slipped the bone back into the pouch, pulled it tight, knotted the cord, and hung it around her neck. Then she tucked it inside her dress. It hung cold outside her chemise.

"But where are we taking her to?" Rose asked.

"The battlefield," Beth replied. "The men don't want us

looking for the killers, so we're going to find that ghost she was looking for."

Lieutenant Tompkins asked for a few minutes to freshen up. Despite having slept most of the day, he was still badly hungover and didn't want to go out in his uniform until he was at least passably presentable. Rose promised to have more tea when he came down to the parlor.

Rose and Beth found Jeb snoring in his chair. He'd pushed it against the wall and his head lolled to the side. His shirt was damp with dribbled alcohol. His half-empty bottle lay on its side in front of him.

Beth stopped short, put her hands on her hips, and stared at him. "Really?"

"Oh, dearie," Rose said. "Let him sleep. He'll be safer here anyway."

"What is it with men and drink?"

"Not all men," Rose admonished. "And not all the time, either."

"True," Beth admitted guiltily. She took a deep breath. "I'm sure Jeb's had a hard life."

"So best let him sleep."

"What about when Mr. Lake returns? He won't like Jeb sleeping there."

"I'll handle Mr. Lake. You and the lieutenant go find that ghost."

A handful of torches lit up the street in front of the mortician's shop. They gave just enough for Beth to make out faces. The lieutenant had brought a small oil lamp, but not yet lit it. He wanted to save the oil, he'd said.

At first, she didn't recognize any of the men in the small

crowd. They dressed well—long coats, bowlers and the occasional top hat. Merchants, not cowboys or miners. Then she spotted Boggs, the blacksmith, next to the door. His face looked grim.

She and Lieutenant Tompkins halted their quick walk. She gestured toward the crowd. "Let's see what's going on."

The lieutenant nodded. She let him get a two step lead and fell in behind him. *I can tell Mr. Lake I'm only here because of Lieutenant Tompkins.*

The crowd parted as the lieutenant pushed forward. When he and Beth reached Boggs, the man looked up.

"The army's east of town," Boggs said when he saw the lieutenant's uniform.

"I'm assigned to Fort Caspar," Lieutenant Tompkins crisply replied. "I have work here." He gestured toward the shop. "And those were my friends."

Boggs barely blinked.

"So what's going on?" Lieutenant Tompkins asked.

Beth silently marveled. Despite being still clearly worn, with a touch of hangover, the lieutenant came across as cool and calm. A true officer instead of the drunk she'd seen earlier.

Boggs seemed to think so too. His tone became less surly. "Mr. Lake and the others are looking for clues. Then we'll clean up the place. The funeral will be first thing in the morning."

"We can help," Lieutenant Tompkins said. He included Beth with a gesture.

"There's plenty of men inside already. Besides, it's ..." He frowned at Beth. "... an ugly sight for the girl."

Beth clamped her jaw hard to avoid saying a thing.

Lieutenant Tompkins furrowed his brow. He glanced sideways at Beth. "Well ..."

"I'm sure they don't need our help," she said as sweetly as she could manage. "We should be on our way." She nodded in the direction of the battlefield.

Lieutenant Tompkins's eyebrows rose. "Yes. Yes, indeed." He

turned back to Boggs. "We'll see you at the service. May God speed your search for the villains."

"God speed indeed," Boggs said.

Lieutenant Tompkins turned and Beth followed him back through the crowd. They walked silently until they turned a corner, out of sight of the crowd. He slowed, until they were side by side. His stride was measured, his face firm.

"I apologize, Miss Armstrong," he said then, "for my behavior earlier today. It was unbecoming and irresponsible for me to have become intoxicated. I can assure you it will not happen again."

"Uh ... okay."

"I thought all hope was lost," he continued, "once Madame Stormchaser died. I should have known things were never as simple as they seem."

"Did you know her well?"

"No. But her mission ..." He broke off, grim-faced. They walked a dozen strides before he spoke again.

"We almost went to war with the Arapaho," he said. "They blamed us for the deaths of the buffalo herds, and for the wildfires that swept the plains. And when all the men in one of our patrols were killed, we blamed them. We were ready to fight."

They slowed their pace as they entered the shantytown. Beth breathed hard. She wasn't much shorter than the lieutenant, but he set a quick pace. She kept up, though.

"Our commander ordered us to prepare for battle," Lieutenant Tompkins continued. "But then Madame Stormchaser showed up with one of the Arapaho chiefs. She said our troubles were not as we thought. She said a 'monster from the sky' was responsible for the deaths."

"They saw it," Beth surmised.

"No, actually, they did not. She'd talked to a ghost. But our commander didn't believe her." At that, he did slow so that he could watch her reaction.

"It is hard to believe," she said. "The only dragon that came through the rift from Jotunheim was killed a long time ago."

"The only dragon we *know* of. Who's to say there weren't more?"

"But if no one's seen it?"

"Oh, but we did, much later. Or at least Private Johnson did, God rest his soul. He died ... slowly."

"I'm sorry to hear that," she said.

They walked in silence the rest of the way to the barrier.

Lieutenant Tompkins halted before they started the climb. While the rain had pushed on, a chill had descended with the evening. He shivered, which, like a contagious yawn, caused Beth to shake as well. The lights from town in the distance teased at warmth beyond reach. The moon and stars remained hidden behind the clouds. Over the barrier, it'd be black beyond black. They'd have only the lieutenant's small oil lamp for light.

"What if they're waiting for us?" he asked. "Like last night?"

She looked at the lamp. Without it, they'd risk treacherous falls. With it, they'd be easy targets.

"They won't be," she said with more confidence than she felt. "The army searched the battlefield this morning, so they had to have left. Why come back? They know they killed Raven."

He bit his lip, but then nodded. "Good point. But perhaps we should cross the barrier at a different location."

"Of course," she said. "There's a path further south, where the barrier meets the South Table Mesa. It's a bit of a walk...."

"I'd feel much better."

She shrugged. "We'll want to search that area anyway. We might as well start there."

"Lead on."

The night grew cold. Even the lightest breeze pricked at Beth's face and exposed wrists. She clenched her jaw and focused on picking her way up the slope past the boulders and broken timber. It was quiet, though. Only her own labored breathing and that of the lieutenant's broke the stillness.

They climbed further up the mountain's slope than she'd first planned. The South Table Mesa wasn't the largest mountain around and in most places it was a gentle climb.

But not where it met the barrier.

She'd never spent much time on its slope. She'd also never seen an Arapaho Indian ghost, so maybe the two went hand in hand.

Lieutenant Tompkins let her lead. He held the lamp low, almost at his knees. It lit their path, but not much more. He also shifted it from hand to hand, irregularly but deliberately. He always kept his body between it and the battlefield.

To make it harder for anyone else to see, she realized.

They stopped several times. He'd watch the battlefield while she slowly scanned the local area. She didn't see any greyish glow of a ghost at any of their stops. Once they were halfway to the top, she led them sideways, east along the edge of the mountain, away from Golden City. A few pinpricks of light shone from the Denver City ruins. In the distance they looked like stars scattered on the ground.

Still no ghosts.

After about an hour, they stopped for water from Lieutenant Tompkins's canteen. He stared out over the battlefield while she drank.

"Hard to believe so many died here," he said. "It must have been a heckuva battle."

"It was," she said. "At least according to Hickok."

"I can only imagine." He put his hands on his hips as he looked out over the valley. "It must've been glorious."

"Not to Hickok. At least not in private."

"Oh?"

"He's ..." She bit her lip as she picked her words. "He knows how important it is to have heroes. They ... don't tell most of us how they really feel."

"He was scared, huh?" Lieutenant Tompkins said. "That'd be embarrassing to admit."

He didn't look her way, so he didn't see her sour shake of the head. Hickok hadn't been scared.

Fear is not the enemy, Hickok had told her all the time. *Fear is just doubt with fangs. Fix the doubt, fix the fear.*

That's why they'd practiced shooting under so many circumstances—in the rain, at night, sitting, even lying down. *You never— never!—want to doubt you can hit your target*, he'd said. *That should be the one sure thing in a fight. You shoot at it, you hit it.*

She placed a comfortable hand on her gun. Then she stepped up to Lieutenant Tompkins's side.

"He wasn't afraid," she said. "He was sad. He ordered men to the barricades, knowing they were going to die. But he knew he had to. This," she swept her hand across the battlefield, "was our last chance."

"Oh."

It was all he said.

They took in the dark battlefield together. The lieutenant kept his thoughts to himself. Beth's mind drifted back to Hickok. Just scattered memories of their conversations.

The breeze pricked at her face.

She glanced down to the right and froze. About a hundred yards away the night shimmered grey.

"C'mon," she said to the lieutenant. "We've found a ghost."

CHAPTER SEVEN

Beth fought the urge to scramble down the mountain slope. Instead, they carefully picked their way around the rocks and scrub bushes. Once, the lieutenant slipped on the loose dirt, but caught himself before he fell. His swinging lantern flashed rays of light pell-mell but he covered it quickly.

As they drew close, Beth could make out more of the ghost. It seemed to sit on a small rock ledge that jutted out of the hillside. Its ghostly army cap sat askew and the sleeve of its jacket was torn. Its back was to them, and it didn't turn.

She slowed, and Lieutenant Tompkins halted behind her. He gave her a worried, questioning look.

"On the rock," she said quietly. She pointed at the ghost.

Lieutenant Tompkins squinted and frowned.

Beth made it down the rest of the slope. She slowly walked in front of the ghost. Her heart raced, but she forced herself to breathe calm, to breathe normal. It was only the ghost of a soldier with a long nose and scruffy beard. He didn't look Arapaho at all.

The ghost didn't look at her. It didn't even seem to notice her. It just stared, forlornly, straight ahead.

"Hello," she said.

The ghost didn't react.

Lieutenant Tompkins stepped up to her side. He suppressed a shiver.

"Hello," she said again.

Nothing.

"What's going on?" Lieutenant Tompkins asked.

"I can't get his attention." She waved her hand in front of the ghost's face. "Hello!"

Nothing.

"Is this ... normal?" the lieutenant asked.

"I don't know. Raven's ghost responded to me. So did Jane's."

"Oh."

She waved her hand again. Several times. Then she stepped close enough to feel its chill. She put her hand an inch in front of its vacant eyes.

It didn't move.

Beth stepped back and sighed with frustration. "It must be one of the broken ones."

"The what?" Lieutenant Tompkins asked.

"Broken ones. At least that's what Maria called them." She gestured for him to follow as she backed away.

The ghost still didn't move.

When they were about ten feet from the ghost, Beth carefully looked around. Nothing. No other ghosts. Or anything worse. Lieutenant Tompkins's eyes followed hers and he tucked the lantern loosely under his coat.

"I don't understand," he said.

"I'm not sure I entirely do either," she said. "But Maria and I talked after I discovered I could see ghosts."

Her gut tightened at the memories of Jane.

"Maria," she continued, "said that most souls became ghosts for one of two reasons. Either they had unfinished business, or they refused to accept they were dead. They had to be persuaded to ... 'move on' was what she said."

"Ah."

"The ones that refused to accept it—she called them the

broken ones. Or lost souls. I thought they'd do more than sit there, but ..." She gestured toward the still unmoving specter.

Lieutenant Tompkins squinted in the direction of the ghost. "So what now?"

She shrugged. "It's late. We go get some sleep. Maybe the men will have found Mr. Dooley's killers by the morning."

Beth found Mr. Lake in the Astor's parlor at breakfast the next morning. The smell of flapjacks on the griddle and fried bacon filled the air. Bright daylight streamed in the window and added to the freshness of the room. Beth quickened her pace as she approached.

He paused in wolfing down his scrambled eggs and looked at her. His eyebrows rose and he smiled happily at her. She'd changed into her gingham dress and tied her hair back. She'd also scrubbed her face and arms and left her gun behind. His appraising look told her he approved.

"Good morning, Mr. Lake," she said. She made a small curtsey. "Would you like some more coffee? Or tea?" She gave him a bright-eyed smile.

He arched an eyebrow. "What do you want, Miss Armstrong?"

"What makes you think I want anything?"

"Really?" He set his fork down and leaned back in his chair. His eyes danced from her hair to her dress to her face. "What indeed?"

She took a deep breath. "Did you find Mr. Dooley's killers? Did you catch them?"

"No," he said. "We haven't found the killers. We checked all the boarding houses and everyone's accounted for. Besides, we figure they've left town. Two horses went missing from Mr. Boggs's stable last night."

"Oh."

"It's a bit of a shame," he continued. "It means Mr. Boggs will have to remain behind when we all leave tomorrow morning."

She blinked in surprise. "Leave?"

"With the army. Every man that can fight and can be spared is to be ready to ride tomorrow. We leave at dawn."

"But ..." she looked wildly around the parlor. It was nearly deserted. Only one merchant quietly ate at another table while he read the Bible.

"I'll close the Astor House," Mr. Lake continued. "I'm sure you and your ma will be fine while we're gone. You're welcome to help yourself to the pantry here if need be."

"But ... but what about Raven? And finding the ghost she was looking for? And all those folks up near Fort Caspar?"

He let out a heavy sigh. "They'll have to do the best they can. *We* have duties elsewhere." He glanced pointedly toward the kitchen. "The joint funeral is in an hour. I'm sure you have work to do until then."

They held the service in the airy sanctuary of the Calvary Church. The sun streamed through the stained glass windows and gave the room a hallowed feel. The minister had ordered the side doors opened to allow the breeze in. It smelled of grass and the town's cooking stoves.

Beth wrinkled her nose and tried not to think about how the bodies smelled.

The three simple pine caskets rested side by side in front of the altar. They'd moved the lectern all the way to the right and the portly minister stood behind it. He tapped the top, idly but loudly, as he watched the stragglers file into the back. There weren't many —mostly merchant's wives in their fancy dresses and a few men with shops near Mr. Dooley's. Mr. Lake sat front and center, along with Colonel Mosby and his aide, but otherwise the only army officer in attendance was Lieutenant Tompkins.

Beth sat in the last pew. As the minister droned through the liturgy, she studied the mourners. No one acted unusual. She didn't see any of the tells Hickok had showed her to watch for. No one fidgeted, or stared at the caskets, or avoided looking at them completely. And no one looked like a cowboy.

When the service ended, Boggs and five teamsters came in. They carried Mr. Dooley's coffin outside to a waiting wagon with a high black awning covering it. Beth slipped out when they came in for Mr. Weatherby's. She stood near the horses and couldn't help smiling when one snorted and tried to nuzzle her face.

The men set Mr. Weatherby's coffin in the wagon with a loud thud. The wagon rocked and the tack jangled. The horse jerked its head and Beth put a calming hand on its cheek.

Boggs saw her and smiled. "She'll be all right, Miss Armstrong. She's a bit skittish, but she'll pull just fine when it's time."

"I'm sure she will, Mr. Boggs." She continued to gently stroke the horse as she spoke.

He nodded and went back inside for the third coffin.

She waited until he was in the church before she let the smile fade from her lips.

He knows this horse.

It's his horse.

Except he had two stolen.

It didn't add up. She knew Boggs regularly stabled horses, but if this was one of his, he'd still be able to ride off with the army.

Maybe he'd promised it to someone else.

That was possible, but it still didn't feel right.

The men brought Raven's coffin out and added it to the wagon. Boggs climbed up onto the driver's seat and took the reins. He gave her a friendly nod and then he and his helpers started down the street toward the edge of town and the cemetery.

Beth watched them go. Then she hurried back to the Astor.

Beth found Rose sweeping the upstairs hallway. She wore her plainer apron and had her dark hair pulled back and tied with a light blue ribbon. She'd propped the door to the balcony open, which let the sun and spring breeze in. The musty dust tickled Beth's nose. As she approached, Rose smiled and raised her eyebrows.

"You're loaded for bear," Rose said.

"It's Boggs. He said he had two horses stolen. I don't think he did. I think he's lying."

Rose gave her a questioning eye. "Now why would he do that?"

"I don't know. I don't think he's helping the killers."

"No." Rose propped her chin on the end of her broom and frowned. "He's been here too long. He wouldn't help strangers. Even if they paid him a lot of money."

"Well, everyone knows he does love money."

"Not that much." Rose laughed and shook her head. "Boggs drives a hard bargain, but he's fair."

"Yeah," Beth said with a deflated sigh. "Now that I think about it, I can't see Boggs lying. If he said those horses were stolen, they probably were."

"So why did you think he was lying?"

"He knew the horses pulling the wagon. Like they were his own."

"The wagon? With the black awning that they drive to the graveyard?"

Beth nodded.

"Oh, dearie," Rose said with a smile. "That's Mr. Dooley's. Or was. He kept it and his team behind his shop and Boggs drove it many a time for him."

Beth's breath caught. She narrowed her eyes.

"Mr. Dooley kept his *team* behind his shop?" she asked. "His horses?"

"He sure did. Though he may have moved them recently, I suppose. I don't know why he would've, though."

"So why would the killers steal *Boggs's* horses? Mr. Dooley's were right there!"

"That's ... that's a very good question."

Beth couldn't help her satisfied grin.

"They didn't!" she said. "The killers didn't steal Boggs's horses. Someone else did. The killers are still here!"

"Where?"

"Shantytown. They ran to Shantytown to get the gun they used to kill Mr. Dooley."

"Hmmm," Rose said. "I think you're right."

"Are you sure this is a good idea?" Lieutenant Tompkins asked quietly.

Beth nodded, but her hand still hovered over her holster as they walked. She'd strapped her gun belt over her dress after the midday meal. Mr. Lake and the other men had been too busy preparing to leave to notice. Rose had raised an eyebrow, but not said a word.

Instead, she'd decided to come with them as Beth and the lieutenant escorted Jeb back to his shack.

They walked through the main streets of town in a small cluster, with Beth and Lieutenant Tompkins slightly in the lead. She wore a broad brimmed hat this time, borrowed from the cook, which kept the warm afternoon sun off her neck. Other than the light breeze, yesterday's storm seemed like a memory.

Behind Beth, Jeb kept up a running stream of conversation with Rose. He nattered about the gold panning in Clear Creek. He hadn't found much yet, but he was sure it was there.

"It's just a matter of time," he said. "Just a matter of time."

"We could bring more men," Lieutenant Tompkins said.

"No," Beth said quickly. "They're all busy. Besides, this is mostly a hunch."

"And how often are your hunches wrong?"

She smirked in reply.

When they reached the stretch where the solid stores and homes gave way to ramshackle dwellings and then outright sheds and lean-to's, Beth slowed their walk to a stroll. She peered left and right and into every dwelling she could without being obvious. Many of the solid structures still hid their inhabitants, if any. After about fifty yards, she paused in frustration.

"Jeb," she said. "Most of these people have been here a while, right?"

"Oh, right you are." He pointed at a nearby shed with a tarp doorway. "Little Mike sleeps there. And the one to the right?" He pointed at what looked like half a teepee connected to an old outhouse. "That's Georgie's. He's got a busted nose, so he don't mind the smell."

"Oh, the poor man," Rose said as she placed her hand on her chest.

Jeb shrugged. "He says he don't mind. But we don't talk much. Mostly we keep to ourselves."

"Where would the new people stay?" Beth asked. "The ones that haven't been here a while?"

"Well, I don't right know." Jeb scratched his head. "Far from the creek, I suppose. Maybe that way?" He pointed south down a dusty footpath. It wound between some sturdier shacks and then turned downhill.

She looked at Lieutenant Tompkins.

He shrugged. "Lead the way."

"But my place is that way," Jeb said. He pointed north.

"My, it's such a nice day," Rose interjected. She hooked her arm inside of Jeb's, to his shocked surprise. "Perhaps we could stroll south for a bit first? I don't believe I've ever been that way."

He stared wide-eyed at her and swallowed several times.

"Oh my, yes," he said. "Oh my, yes. It *is* such a nice day. A nice day indeed."

Rose gave him a warm smile and then nodded toward the southern footpath. "Shall we?"

Beth and Lieutenant Tompkins stepped aside and let Jeb and Rose lead. He started talking a mile a minute describing everything they passed. He even started wildly pointing at the scattered pines and the distant peaks, as he explained how he'd once seen an eagle.

They followed the footpath down and around and then up a small ridge. The gaps between the scattered lean-to's grew and more scrub bushes and scraggly trees intervened. They swayed slightly in the breeze.

At the top of the ridge, Jeb froze. He clutched Rose's arm and stared down the path at something. Beth rushed around to his side.

A tall man in a full coat and Stetson hat strode up the trail toward them. His ragged beard didn't hide his shock.

"That's him!" Jeb said. He pointed straight at the man. "The cowboy I saw before!"

With a snarl, the cowboy reached for his gun.

CHAPTER EIGHT

Beth's Colt snapped to her hands.

Her arms out. Her aim straight.

The cowboy started to raise his gun.

She fired.

Twice.

He spun and dropped.

The sounds of the gunshots echoed off the hills. Only the rush of blood in her ears threatened to drown it out. Her breath came hard.

"My God!" Rose exclaimed.

Lieutenant Tompkins was already running toward the fallen man with his own gun drawn. Beth looked around—she didn't see anyone else. She hurried to catch up with him.

He quickly knelt by the man and touched his cheek. Then he rolled him onto his back. His head flopped lifelessly. His shirt was already soaked with blood and the stain was spreading fast.

"Right through the heart," Lieutenant Tompkins muttered.

Beth stared at the cowboy. His mouth had fallen open, his tongue partly out. His glassy eyes saw nothing. The blood on his chest continued to spread.

Her stomach twisted and heaved. She turned aside, dropped to her knees, and started vomiting.

"Whoa," Lieutenant Tompkins said. "Are you all right?"

She nodded as best she could as she continued to empty her stomach.

"Oh, dearie," Rose said from somewhere behind her. "Let's move back a bit."

Beth felt her friend take her hand and gently pull. She let herself be led at a half crouch to a small rock where they sat down together. Beth's stomach continued to heave, but nothing more came out.

"Want something to drink, missy?" Jeb asked from somewhere nearby. His dirty bottle appeared in front of her face. He'd taken the stopper out.

"Rinse your mouth out," Rose urged. "It'll help."

Beth nodded. Between heaves, she grasped the bottle and took a swig. The moonshine burned her gums, but it made the bile go away. She swished and spit.

Very unladylike, she couldn't help thinking.

She finally looked up. Lieutenant Tompkins had finished with the body and was walking toward them.

"First kill?" he asked when he'd come close.

She tiredly shook her head. "Second. But I didn't get sick the first time. I think it was all the blood this time."

"It gets easier, I'm afraid. The killing."

She sensed his black humor but only managed half a chuckle. "That's what I've heard."

"He didn't have much on him," Lieutenant Tompkins continued. "A few coins and this." He held out a leather bag and then loosened its drawstring. Then he tilted it over and poured several gold nuggets of various sizes into his open palm.

"Oh, my!" Jeb yelped. "Oh, my! That's a lot of gold! A lot of gold!"

"Several thousand dollars' worth," Lieutenant Tompkins

agreed. "There's no way a cowboy living in shantytown came by this honestly."

"They were paid," Rose said.

"*They,*" Beth said. Her stomach had settled to a low burble and she could breathe normally. "We need to find his friend, and quick. There's no way he didn't hear the gunfire."

Lieutenant Tompkins nodded grimly. He slid the nuggets back into the bag and extended a hand to help Beth to her feet.

Jeb and Rose decided to stay on the small ridge near the body. It had a clear view all around, and Rose promised they'd run if they saw trouble. Beth and Lieutenant Tompkins headed down the trail, both with guns out.

Beth kicked a loose rock through the dirt. It skittered past a row of thistles and sent a small field mouse running. But that was it—nothing moved in the few remaining shanties ahead. About twenty feet from the closest, Lieutenant Tompkins pulled up short. He shaded his eyes and looked west, up the slope, at a cluster of pines. Nothing moved there. They studied the broken-down shack, which was little more than a pole, a wall, and a tarp. Nothing moved there either.

"Circle around," Lieutenant Tompkins said. He gestured for her to go right, up the slope. When she started that way, he went left.

Still nothing moved in the lean-to.

Where was the other cowboy?

She could see three other shelters, here at the edge of town. No one moved near any of them. One looked completely abandoned. The others might've been, but it was hard to tell.

She also couldn't hear anything. No yells. No one running.

Lieutenant Tompkins crept closer to the shanty. He peered in and frowned in disgust. Then he waved Beth toward the next one.

This one was sturdier than the others. Three log walls and a plank roof implied it had once been a small cabin or barn, though it wasn't wider than maybe ten feet. Weeds already covered the side facing Beth.

She carefully circled around until she could see inside. No people, but some lumps. She waved Lieutenant Tompkins forward. Still looking left and right for any surprises, she went to investigate.

Two bedrolls and a couple of worn haversacks sat near a cold fire pit. Food scraps and chicken bones filled a corner of the shack. It smelled stale and overripe.

Lieutenant Tompkins joined her. He pointed at the haversacks. "Those are old, from the War Between the States. I'm surprised they're not falling apart."

He glanced around and then knelt by them. It took him a minute to undo the knots and look inside the first one.

"Rock hammer," he said, "mining pan, small drill ..." He glanced sideways and pointed to a small wooden box by the back wall. "That's a rocker box. It looks like they were looking for gold."

"Not successfully," Beth said, "or they wouldn't live here."

"True," he said. "I think this is where those cowboys were living, but we should have Jeb look at this stuff. He'll know." He stood and dusted off his pants. "But we should check out that last shack first."

They approached it with the same care as the others. It didn't take long to tell it was abandoned, though. The tattered canvas "roof" flapped in the light breeze and the walls creaked as they swayed. Tall weeds filled the inside.

With nothing in it, they stood at the entrance and slowly looked around the rest of the area. The valley between the South Table Mesa and the mountains continued its slow sprawl south. The scrub bushes and occasional pine scattered the land, but there weren't any more dwellings. The rutted trail leading south was empty as well. More sparse trees and bushes dotted the slopes, but no people.

"Let's talk to Jeb," Beth said.

They found the old miner and Rose waiting nervously on the rise. Rose kept glancing at the nearby body with a horrified look of disgust. Lieutenant Tompkins briefly described the tools they'd found and then they led Jeb and Rose to the old shack.

Jeb took one look at the rocker box. "Oh, my. That was Old Joe's."

"Old Joe's?" Beth asked.

"Yup. He said he sold it to some yokels. That was ... last week, it was. Yup. Last week."

"Where's Old Joe now?" Lieutenant Tompkins asked.

"Used the money to buy a stagecoach ticket to Santa Fe. That's all he got for it though."

Beth frowned. She looked at Lieutenant Tompkins. "If the cowboys bought this from Old Joe last week, then they were here before you arrived. They couldn't've been following you."

"They were hired." He tapped the pouch of gold nuggets. "I doubt they could've mined this much in a week."

"Not that much around here," Jeb agreed. "No sirree."

"The horses were stolen by the people who hired them," Beth concluded. "*They're* probably gone, leaving their hired guns behind."

"So what now?" Rose asked.

Lieutenant Tompkins grimaced. "We go back to town and I find a few men to help me bury the one Miss Armstrong shot." He snorted softly and smiled at her. "Good shooting, by the way."

Her gut still churned over the memory of the man falling. And of his lifeless face. But Beth couldn't help thinking, *Yeah, Hickok would've been proud.*

Beth's group found Boggs and Mr. Lake on Washington Street in front of Mr. Dooley's place. The men who'd helped carry the coffins sat in the bed of the now-empty wagon and talked quietly among themselves. Boggs and Mr. Lake looked up from their own conversation as Beth's party approached. Boggs took off his hat and wiped the sweat off his brow.

"We've got another body for you," Lieutenant Tompkins said. "One of Mr. Dooley's killers was hiding down in Shantytown. Jeb here recognized him."

The men in the wagon fell silent. Mr. Lake and Boggs stared at the lieutenant.

"You said 'body,'" Boggs said. "What happened?"

"He tried to draw on us," Lieutenant Tompkins said. He tilted his head toward Beth. "But Miss Armstrong was faster. Got him straight through the heart."

"That girl?" scoffed one of the men in the wagon.

"No way!" added another.

"He must've been slow," Boggs muttered.

"He was not!" Rose interjected. "His gun was already out before she touched hers."

"Bull," one of the men said. He turned and spat.

"Was too!" Beth snapped. Without thinking, her hand dropped to her Colt.

"Now hold on, Miss Armstrong," Mr. Lake said. "There's no need for that."

She turned on him. "You've seen me! You know Hickok trained me!"

"Yeah, but that don't make you a gunfighter," Boggs said.

"Why not?" she asked.

"Because you're a girl."

Beth saw red. Her blood raced. Her muscles tensed. She narrowed her eyes, but then Rose put a hand on her arm.

"We do need some help with the body," Rose said sweetly to Boggs. "If you big, strong men could help us, we'd be much obliged." She smiled sunnily at him and then the men in the wagon.

Breathe, Beth thought. *Deep breaths.* Hickok said to never shoot angry—it messed up your aim.

She forced herself to concentrate on her breathing and on calming herself down.

While she was counting her breaths, Lieutenant Tompkins arranged for the men to go retrieve the body. The path was too narrow and rocky for the wagon, so they went looking for a gurney. Meanwhile, Rose sweet-talked Mr. Lake into letting Jeb stay at the Astor.

"For his own safety," she said. "Besides, there won't be any boarders with you closing it up, so he won't be in the way."

After Mr. Lake acquiesced, Rose turned to Beth. "Let's get him settled," she said quietly. "Then we can plan our next move."

"Our?" Beth's eyebrows went up.

"You're not foolish enough to think you don't need my help, are you?" Rose teased. "Let's go."

At the Astor, Rose set about getting the big wash tub set up in one of the now-vacated rooms. She started heating water in kettles down in the kitchen and told Jeb that if he was going to stay at the Astor, he needed a bath. He nodded, wide-eyed. For once he seemed at a loss for words.

Beth helped tote the kettles to the room. They took a dozen trips until the tub was filled deep enough to at least pass for a bathtub, though more of Jeb would be out of the water than in. Then they left him and retreated to the now deserted parlor. Rose brought out a teapot and two cups. The two of them settled comfortably at the table by the piano.

"So what's the plan?" Rose asked.

Beth blinked. "You're asking me?"

"Ghosts and killers are your job." Rose gestured toward Beth's gun. "I wouldn't even know how to begin to use that."

"I could teach you."

"No ... no. Well, not now."

Beth nodded. There'd be time later, if needed.

"So figuring out what we do next is your job," Rose continued.

"I thought you wanted me to stay out of it and let the men handle it."

"And how well did they do?" Rose arched her eyebrow and kept it there until Beth nodded in agreement.

"Besides," Rose continued, "the army and most of the men are leaving town tomorrow. They're no help. But we've still got killers out there, and stolen horses."

"Don't forget the ghost," Beth said. "We still need to find the right one."

"Right. And Raven's ghost. Do you think she could help?"

Beth paused. "I ... I don't know. I don't know how to talk to her."

"What do you mean?"

"I mean, well. She just appears. I can't summon her or anything. At least I don't think I can."

"Hmmm." Rose leaned back in her chair and took another sip of tea. She stared out into space and pursed her lips.

"I think we should start by finding the ghost," Beth said. "That's what Raven would want."

"Right," Rose said. "If the other killer hasn't left yet, he probably will once he hears about his friend. And whoever stole the horses should be long gone. So that ghost is the only one we know is still here."

"If he ever was."

Rose shrugged. "You'll just have to look for him tonight."

"That's tonight. I wanna do something now."

"Well ... there is something you should do. You haven't been home in, what, three, four days?"

Beth grimaced.

"You need to talk to her. You know your ma will be worried."

"I suppose you're right." She let out a ragged sigh. "Just how upset do you think she'll be?"

CHAPTER NINE

Beth's heart hammered as she walked north on Washington Street. That was the only real thing wrong, though. Afternoon clouds flitted across the face of the sun and made it a very pleasant spring day. Insects whirred in the grass and a few birds sang in the nearby trees. As she crossed the bridge over Clear Creek, she heard a fish jump. Boggs's blacksmith shop and general store squatted just beyond the river, but she barely noticed it.

She was headed home. To talk to Ma.

She walked past Boggs's place without a glance. Her mind kept running through what she wanted to say.

Ma, I want to move into the Astor while the army's gone. I don't want to live way out here.

Except that wasn't all of it.

Ma, Mister Dooley was murdered. I want to look for the men who did it. And, oh, I already killed one in a gunfight.

She knew how that'd be received.

Ma, this Indian shaman wanted me to help her, but then she got killed. But don't worry, I'm carrying her ghost with me.

She snorted. Not even Rose could pull off that line.

Ma just wanted normal. But the world hadn't been normal

since the giants had come. It certainly hadn't been normal since Pa had been killed and they'd been forced to move to Golden City.

In some ways, it was better.

But Ma didn't understand that.

And while Beth's mind raced, her feet slowly carried her down the road, onto the side trail, and across the grass, to the little log cabin and goat pasture that Ma considered "normal."

The homestead came into sight as she rounded a small ridge. Ma stood outside in the vegetable garden, stubbornly hoeing a patch of dirt. Her thin body and weathered skin made her look older than she was. Like Beth, strands of dark hair perpetually escaped her bonnet. She looked lonesome, and a quick glance around confirmed her beau Wayne was nowhere in sight.

The half dozen goats whinily bleated from their pen between the prim cabin and the squat barn. Ma ignored them. She didn't even notice Beth until she was twenty feet away. Then she straightened up and rested her hands on the end of the hoe.

"So," Ma said, "you decided to come home."

"Ma," Beth said warningly.

Ma's eyes dropped to Beth's gun belt. She made a sour frown. "We heard what happened."

"Wayne's going with the army?"

"Already with them. I'll be fine." Her eyes flicked down Beth's body. "You need a new dress."

"I have one. Rose made it for me. It's back at the Astor."

"She's a good woman, Rose. She's always with a smile. Always polite." Ma snorted softly. "So you're staying there now?"

"Mr. Lake said he'd send word to you."

"He did." Ma let out another sigh. She slowly turned and surveyed the homestead. Her frown turned sad. "It's not much, I know."

"It was enough."

"Was."

Beth's chest caught. She took a few, hesitant, steps forward.

"I know," Ma said. "Ever since ... well, it's never going to be right for you, is it?

Beth paused. No words came to mind.

"I ..." She looked at Beth. "I'll just miss you."

"Oh, Ma!"

Before she knew it, Beth was running. She threw her arms around Ma and hugged her tight. Ma squeezed her back.

"Oh, Ma," Beth said through watery eyes. "I'll miss you, too."

They held each other tight, until it was almost hard to breathe. Then Ma pulled back. "You're going to live there now, aren't you?"

"I ... I have to."

"Well, come on inside. I made corn biscuits yesterday, and we have a little honey left."

"I'd love to."

Beth sat at the small polished pine table that Ma had bought when they'd first arrived in Golden City. She fidgeted. She didn't have anything to do with her hands, since Ma had insisted she just sit.

Like a visitor.

Ma bustled around the little kitchen and chattered about the goats and Wayne's enlistment. He'd made hints about proposing when he got back, she said, but hadn't quite come out and done it. She pulled out her two good china plates and the crystal glasses from San Francisco and set them on the table. The thick corn biscuits and small tub of honey quickly followed, then a pitcher of goat's milk, fresh from the morning's milking, she said.

Finally, she sank into the chair opposite her daughter. She gestured towards Beth's untouched biscuit.

"Eat up," she said. "You know it's good."

"This ..." Beth gestured at the crystal. "... is for special company."

Ma's eyes narrowed. "And you're not?"

Beth's eyes fell. "It's not like I'm leaving forever."

"No. You're just ..." Ma thunked her elbows on the table. She stayed silent. When Beth looked up, she was staring into space.

"Well," Ma finally said, "you've survived quite a bit. I suppose you'll survive what comes."

"I'll be fine, Ma. I know what I'm doing."

Beth's hand unconsciously drifted down to her Colt's handle. Ma noticed and frowned.

"You could go with Hickok," Ma said. "He'd take care of you. I'm surprised he's not sweet on you."

"I'm too young for Hickok."

"You're sixteen! Why, when I was sixteen—"

"He sees me as a daughter," Beth said. *The daughter he'd never had with Jane, he'd even said.*

"Then he shouldn't be teaching you *that!*"

Ma's finger jabbed toward Beth's gun. Then she shook it. Then she pulled it back.

Beth forced her face to be calm. She closed her eyes and took a deep breath. Then she took another. She put her hands on the table and made to stand.

"I'm ..." Ma's voice cracked. "I'm ... it's okay, honey. I'm just ... well ... I don't want to go to your funeral."

Beth opened her eyes. Her mother looked at her, pleading. One hand clutched the table's edge like it was a life rope.

"I'll be fine, Ma," Beth reassured. "I'll be fine. After all, I've got to come back and eat your biscuits, don't I?"

She reached for the nearest one.

Ma's death grip on the table eased and she forced a smile.

"I'll have strawberry ones in June," she said. "I know you won't want to miss them. Then raspberry in July."

Beth smiled at Ma's lighter tone. She spread honey on her biscuit and asked, "So what should I look forward to in August? I mean, if I'm gonna be coming back every month ..."

Ma let out a relieved laugh. "Well, that depends on how the garden does. And those rabbits. Say, do you have time ...?"

"I have to be back by dark. Otherwise, I'm all yours."

Beth walked in the kitchen door of the Astor just about an hour before dusk. She set down the heavy, worn haversack that contained all of her remaining clothes and other possessions. She shook the ache out of her arms and glanced around. Everything was neatly in place—the knives, the cutlery, heavy pans. Even the pitchers for water sat ready to fill and use.

Except there wasn't a single sign of the cook.

She listened carefully and didn't hear any movement either. So she walked into the parlor and found it similarly deserted. She went into the main entrance hall and found the front door locked. A handwritten sign hung on it, facing out. She turned it around and read, "Closed until trolls defeated.—S. Lake."

Upstairs, she found all of the tenants had departed except two. Lieutenant Tompkins's room still contained all his stuff, as well as an unmade bed, but he wasn't there. However Jeb had taken over one of the other rooms and he was. He sat on a chair just inside the open doorway sharpening a large Bowie knife.

"Well hello, Miss Armstrong," he said when he saw her. His smile overwhelmed his face. "Hello."

"Hello to you, Mr. Miller."

"Just Jeb. Just Jeb."

"So, Jeb," she said, "where is everyone?"

"Oh, Miss Chamberlin's out a-gathering her things. Lieutenant Tompkins is uh, um, oh yes, Lieutenant Tompkins is 'investigating the missing horses,' is what he said."

"Ah."

"I'm sharpening my knife." He held it up, as if she hadn't noticed it before. "See?"

"I see." She couldn't help grinning.

"Miss Chamberlin said supper was in the ice box," he continued, "for when you got back." He gave his knife one last look up and down. Then he wiped it on his pants and sheathed it. "And now you're back."

He stood and looked at her expectantly.

"Then," she said, "I suppose it's suppertime."

They were halfway through a supper of hardboiled eggs, boiled potatoes, and cured venison when Lieutenant Tompkins and Rose arrived within minutes of each other. Rose hurried to put her things in the room she'd claimed for herself while the lieutenant fetched himself some beer from the kitchen. He brought back food for himself and Rose as well. Once they'd all settled in at the table, Lieutenant Tompkins cleared his throat to get their attention.

"We learned some interesting things this afternoon," he said. He glanced sideways at Rose, who nodded. Then he looked squarely at Beth.

"Boggs recognized that cowboy you shot," he said. "He said he'd sold him a gun a few days ago—the same gun he drew on you. He came in alone, though, so he doesn't know anything about his partner."

"He also said he paid with gold nuggets," Rose added. "We compared them to the ones in the bag and they're similar."

"And they're not from around here!" Jeb said. "I know. I looked at 'em. I know!"

"The nuggets?" Beth said with a look of surprise.

"Yep," Jeb said. "Them. The other minerals are all wrong."

"They're not pure gold," Lieutenant Tompkins explained.

"What about the stolen horses?" Beth asked. "Did you learn anything about them?"

"One was a mountain pony," Lieutenant Tompkins said. "The other was Boggs's personal mount."

"He was not at all happy about that," Rose said with a roll of her eyes. "Went on forever."

"I can imagine," Beth said. She couldn't hold back her grin. When Boggs got worked up ... it was truly a sight.

"So how'd things go with your ma?" Rose asked.

Beth's grin faded. "Fine. It was fine."

"Ah."

Lieutenant Tompkins's eyes darted between the women and he frowned. Then he shrugged.

"So," he said, "I suggest we get to the battlefield by dark so we have more time to look for the ghost we want."

Beth nodded, and then realized all three of the others were, too.

"So we're all going?" she asked.

"Oh, no," Jeb said. "Oh, no. Miss Chamberlin and I are gonna stay here where it's safe."

Rose confirmed it with a nod and Lieutenant Tompkins just smiled in relief.

They didn't quite make it to the battlefield before dark. Lieutenant Tompkins wanted to bring his rifle as well as his sidearm and Rose insisted they have water bottles and a second lantern, but Mr. Lake had taken all the good ones to the army camp. They finally found one in a storage closet, but it lacked oil. Rose rigged up a candle to work, but again, it took time.

It turned out they didn't actually need it. With the swell of townsmen, the army no longer fit in their barracks. So they'd camped in the obvious large empty space near town—the old battlefield itself. Their scattered campfires looked scarily sparse. If the troll invasion was even a tenth of the rumors, it wasn't clear they'd be enough.

But they're just part of the army, Beth reminded herself. *Other men will be coming from all over the West to help.*

Beth and Lieutenant Tompkins started on the southern slope of the North Table Mesa. The evening air was still, which kept the night chill at bay. Stars above sparkled in almost a mirror to the campfires dotting the valley below.

Lieutenant Tompkins didn't try to hide his lamp this time.

Instead, he urged them to cover as much ground as they could. Beth led and looked for ghosts, but it was still slow. They had to keep a careful eye on their footing, and more than once she nearly slipped.

Finally, after several hours, they reached the eastern edge of the valley, where the mountain rounded north. Beth called for a break, and they sat on a small rock outcropping and drank from their canteens.

Lieutenant Tompkins guzzled his water and then grimaced in frustration. "A lot of ground to cover."

Beth shrugged. "If the ghost was close to town I would've seen it before. It's got to be out here somewhere."

"But where?" he asked. He gestured toward the wide valley mouth and the ruins of Denver City in the distance. "This place is huge."

"Yeah," Beth said. "But what do you suggest?"

"Can you summon it? I've heard it's possible."

"Witches do that. I'm not a witch."

"Aren't you carrying one?" He pointed at Beth's chest, where Raven's pouch hung from its cord around her neck.

"Yeah." Beth wrapped her hand around the pouch. "But we don't know how to talk to her." She rubbed the pouch slightly between her fingers, feeling the small bone within.

The air cooled.

Beth blinked. "Or maybe we do."

Five feet away, Raven's ghost stood, smiling.

CHAPTER TEN

Raven's ghost stood still. In the dark, her grey form seemed solid. The beading on her blouse was tight and textured. The wrinkles on her face, almost lifelike with their lines. But the monotone color and misty depths made it clear she wasn't alive.

"What?" Lieutenant Tompkins said. He looked around wildly.

"She's here," Beth said calmly. "Raven. Right in front of me."

He sucked in his breath and nodded.

"Hello, Raven," Beth said. She kept her voice slow and measured. "We're having trouble finding the ghost of the Arapaho scout."

Raven nodded.

"Can you help us?" Beth asked.

Raven nodded again. Then she smiled and pointed past Beth's shoulder, down the slope.

Beth turned and squinted. Darkness, darker lumps, a few obvious bushes—no grey forms. She turned back to the ghost.

Raven pointed again. Then she held up one hand and mimicked walking with two fingers.

"She wants us to go this direction." Beth waved her arm for the lieutenant to follow and then started down the slope.

They went slowly and quietly over the rough terrain. Beth kept her eyes ahead when she didn't need to watch her footing. The nearest campfires were far to the west, and the lamplight all came from behind her. But slowly, very slowly, they made their way down. They stopped and drank from their canteens when the slope evened out.

"Are we close?" Lieutenant Tompkins asked. He looked at Beth expectantly.

She shook her head. Then she turned and looked east, where Clear Creek meandered toward the Denver City ruins.

No grey figures anywhere.

"We keep going."

They hiked all the way down to the banks of Clear Creek. Still no ghost. They paused once again, and Lieutenant Tompkins sank wearily onto a large rock. He looked questioningly at Beth once again.

"Let's see if Raven can help," she said.

She pulled Raven's pouch out once again and rubbed it between her fingers.

A chill filled the air.

Raven's ghost materialized a few feet in front of Beth, almost on top of Lieutenant Tompkins, but not quite. He suddenly shivered and jumped to the side.

Raven's ghost looked at Beth and clasped its hands.

"Which way?" Beth asked.

The ghost pointed east, along the creek.

Beth squinted.

About fifty yards downstream, a grey figure stood in the middle of the rushing water.

"Found him!" Beth called out.

With a surge of excitement, she hurried toward the new ghost. It stood, or floated, knee deep in the water and faced her—an Arapaho face with long braided hair, but an army shirt, coat, and cap. It had its hands clasped in front and seemed to be studying her.

She caught her breath as Lieutenant Tompkins caught up to her. "Hello!" she called.

The ghost didn't respond.

"Hello!" she called again. "Do you hear me?"

No reaction.

If it won't respond, we can't play charades, like with Raven, she thought.

Raven.

She hadn't tucked the pouch back under her blouse, so she grabbed it and rubbed the bone again.

Raven appeared at the edge of the creek. She smiled at Beth and then turned to the other ghost. Her mouth moved, though Beth couldn't hear a thing.

The Arapaho scout's eyes went wide. He bowed to Raven and said something, though once again, Beth heard nothing.

"What's happening?" Lieutenant Tompkins asked. His eyes darted over the creek.

"We found the scout's ghost," Beth said. She couldn't tear her eyes off of him. "It's talking to Raven's ghost."

"What's it saying?"

"No idea."

"You sure it's him?"

"Raven's sure." She motioned for him to be quiet. She concentrated on the ghosts and tried to figure out what they were saying. After a bit, she shook her head in frustration. They weren't gesturing enough and she couldn't read their lips.

The two ghosts spoke for several minutes. Then the scout bowed to Raven. She returned the bow.

The scout's ghost straightened up and held its hands wide above its head. A grey disk opened behind it. Then the ghost and the disk faded away.

Beth blinked twice, but the scout's ghost was nowhere to be seen.

Raven's ghost still stood on the shore, facing Beth. Once she had Beth's attention, she pointed north.

"You know where the dragon is?" Beth asked.

Raven nodded and pointed north again.

"Ask her how far," Lieutenant Tompkins said.

"How far?" Beth repeated.

Raven's ghost held up one finger, then two, then all of her fingers. She quickly closed and opened her hands several times, flashing all ten fingers again and again.

"I think ..." Beth tilted her head as she thought. "I think ... a long, long way."

Raven nodded and smiled.

And then she was gone.

Several weary hours later, Beth and Lieutenant Tompkins finally reached the edge of town. Her legs ached and her mouth tasted of cotton. Their canteens had run dry well before they'd reached the barrier.

Golden City felt like a ghost town in the early morning hours. The taverns that spilled noise and light at all hours were shuttered. No lamps shone from any of the homes or stores. The streets were similarly still, with not even the strong breeze stirring enough to drown out the sounds of their footsteps.

They turned off Washington Street and the Astor loomed up the hill, a few short blocks away. Unlike the other buildings, it lit up the street. Light flowed out of all its windows and the open door.

Beth halted in surprise.

"What is it?" Lieutenant Tompkins asked.

"The door shouldn't be open," she said. "Mr. Lake always made us close it. Rose would've closed it."

Lieutenant Tompkins frowned. He extinguished the lamp he'd

been carrying and set it on the ground. Then he drew his Colt. Beth immediately did the same.

They slid into the shadows and crept forward.

Beth's heart raced and her skin danced as if on fire. The night fatigue sloughed off and she shifted to the balls of her feet. Beside her, Lieutenant Tompkins sprang equally alert.

They reached the corner of the Astor and Beth placed one hand on the rough sandstone wall. She just happened to be ahead of Lieutenant Tompkins and put out a hand to stop him.

"Cover me?" she said.

"No. You're a faster shot. You cover me."

She nodded, even as her heart soared at the compliment. She stepped out far enough into the street to have a clear view of both the door and the main parlor window beyond.

Lieutenant Tompkins quickly scampered forward. He crouched low so his knees almost brushed the ground. He knelt by the door and tried to peer in.

Nothing. No reaction from anyone inside. If there was anyone inside.

Beth had a vision of finding Jeb and Rose's corpses sprawled on the floor. She started to gasp for panicked breath. *Not Jeb! Not Rose!*

Don't give into fear. Hickok's words nearly rang in her ears. *Walk into it. Make friends with it. Become its master.*

She took a deep breath to calm herself. Then another. Then a third.

Lieutenant Tompkins rushed past the open door to a spot between it and the window.

No shots. No shouts. Nothing.

He peeked in the window, then looked back at her and shook his head.

Beth took another deep breath. Then she strode to the Astor's main door.

Lieutenant Tompkins crouched on its left. She paused on its right. She listened as best she could.

Nothing. Maybe a noise. Faint, far off.

Lieutenant Tompkins held up three fingers. When she nodded, he lowered one. Then the second. When he lowered the third, they both rushed into the entry hall, guns ready.

Beth's eyes darted everywhere. All she saw were familiar shadows.

Lieutenant Tompkins crossed to the door to the parlor. He peeked in, then turned back and shook his head.

Something thumped above them, on the second floor.

Beth motioned for Lieutenant Tompkins to come close enough for her to whisper.

"Some stairs squeak," she said into his ear. "Step where I step."

She crept up the stairs slowly. Her eyes remained peeled at the top, with only short glances down to make sure she was putting her feet in the right spots. The lieutenant only misstepped once, but the creak of the wood was soft, and nothing new stirred above.

Once on the second floor landing, Beth paused to listen. Muffled voices came down the hall, from Lieutenant Tompkins's room. The door sat ajar, with lamp light pouring out.

Beth quickly checked the other doors. All were closed and dark. She looked back at Lieutenant Tompkins. He gave her a reassuring nod. They crept toward the open door and the voices became distinct.

"There's nothing here either," Rose said. "Not under the bed or behind it."

"Check under the mattress," a man growled. Not Jeb, from the deep bass tone.

"It's a rope bed," Rose snapped. "I *just* looked under it."

"Look again!"

Beth sidled up to the doorway. The door opened the other direction, thankfully. Lieutenant Tompkins nestled in behind her. She held her gun up.

"Look," Rose said, "I told you. It's not here. If he has it, he has it with him."

Beth lunged into the room. Rose stood a few feet away facing a cowboy with a gun pointed at her.

Rose saw Beth and her eyes widened.

The cowboy turned his head and saw Beth. He brought his gun around—

Beth fired.

Lieutenant Tompkins fired too.

The cowboy collapsed to the floor. His chest pooled in red blood and he fell sideways, lifeless.

"Oh, thank God!" Rose cried. "Thank God!" she shuddered and sank to the bed.

Jeb sat on the floor against one wall. He held his arms around his knees, trembling, as blood flowed from a gash across his temple.

The rest of the room was a tossed mess with the lieutenant's possessions everywhere.

Lieutenant Tompkins rushed to Rose's side. "Are you all right?" he asked.

She shuddered and leaned into him. He wrapped one arm around her and held her tight as she fought back sobs. He looked at Beth meaningfully, as if he wanted her to say something.

"Any others?" Beth finally asked. Her stomach wasn't doing somersaults this time. For that, she was grateful.

Jeb shook his head. Then Rose did too. As strong as she'd looked a few minutes ago, she seemed frail, like all the iron had melted out of her.

Lieutenant Tompkins held her tight.

"I'll get Jeb's cut treated," Beth finally said. She turned to the old miner and extended a hand. "Come on. Let's get that cleaned up and bandaged."

"Please, missy. Please."

She got the full story out of Jeb while she tended his wound in the kitchen. They'd been waiting in the parlor when the cowboy had burst in with his gun. He'd demanded to know where the lieutenant was, and once they'd convinced him the lieutenant wasn't there, he'd insisted they help him search the lieutenant's things, without saying what exactly he was looking for. Jeb had tried to grab the gun, and gotten the cut for his effort.

"He's a bad man," Jeb said. "A bad man. I saw him before, you know."

"One of the ones running from the mortician's?" she asked.

"Yes, indeed. Yes, indeed."

"Well, you don't have to worry about him anymore." The memory of the dead cowboy up in the room churned her stomach.

"No, no indeed."

"Did he say what he was looking for?" Beth asked.

Jeb shook his head.

She'd just finished bandaging his cut when Lieutenant Tompkins and Rose joined them. The lieutenant asked Jeb to help him with the body. Jeb nodded and followed him out of the kitchen. Rose immediately poured herself a glass of water.

"Are you all right?" Beth asked.

"Oh, Beth!" Rose said. "I was so frightened! All I could think to do was to keep him busy and keep him from hurting Jeb, and I was wondering where you were, and the lieutenant—"

Beth placed a hand on her friend's arm. "You did fine. Just like you always do."

"I was scared."

"So was I," Beth admitted. "But we do what we have to, don't we?"

Rose nodded. She shuddered, holding back a sob, but then wiped her eyes. "We do, don't we?" she said. "And the men are going to need food when they get back. You, too." She gave Beth a grateful smile and then glanced around the kitchen. "Now where did that flour get to?"

CHAPTER ELEVEN

Dawn broke before the men returned. The four of them gathered in the Astor's parlor. It promised to be another beautiful spring day, so Rose had opened the curtains to let the sun in.

Beth sat with her back in the warm light. She'd changed clothes and abandoned her dresses entirely in favor of a man's shirt and her most comfortable trousers. The sun pleasantly soaked through the shirt and her chemise underneath. She slowly sipped hot berry tea, tart and a bit bitter, and let it warm her belly. The crumbs from Rose's biscuits still adorned the plate in front of her. She idly scooped a large one up with a finger and popped it in her mouth.

The smell of fried pork filled the room as Rose bustled back in with a steaming plate. She slid it in front of Lieutenant Tompkins, who was seated at Beth's right, gave him a quick curtsey, and headed right back into the kitchen.

A small smile creased the lieutenant's lips as he watched her go.

Jeb didn't notice. He was too busy wolfing down his eggs on Beth's left.

After Rose returned and took her own seat, Lieutenant Tompkins turned to Beth.

"Boggs will take care of the dead cowboy," he said. "The army's leaving. I think we should, too. You said we had to go a long way north?"

"We do," Beth said with a nod. "But we should be careful. The killers are still around and they were probably looking for this."

She pointed at her chest, where Raven's pouch now rested underneath her clothes, cool against her skin.

"Right," he said. "You think they'll try again?"

"Yes," she said, "just as soon as they can figure out how."

Rose furrowed her brow. "What do you mean? They tried last night."

"Their hired gun tried," Beth said, "but they don't have any more of those, or they'd have sent more than one."

"Why not come themselves then?"

"They can't. If they could, they wouldn't have needed to hire the cowboys."

"Of course," Lieutenant Tompkins said. "Why pay all that gold if you don't need to?"

"Uh ..." Jeb said. "I don't understand."

Beth smiled at him. "The people who ambushed us at the battlefield and killed Raven and Mr. Weatherby hired those broke cowboys to retrieve Raven's pouch, because they couldn't do it themselves. They couldn't just walk into town on their own."

Lieutenant Tompkins nodded. "They're not human."

"No," Beth said. "I think they're dwarves."

"Of course!" Lieutenant Tompkins said with a snap of his fingers.

"But ..." Rose said, "I thought the dwarves were all over in the Black Hills, minding their own business."

"Me too," Beth said, "but it's the only thing that makes sense." She looked at Lieutenant Tompkins. "They followed you down and struck when they realized what Raven was trying to do."

"That explains the small figures we saw watching camp," he said.

"Maybe we should go north, anyway," Rose said. She gave Jeb a side-eyed look. "Fewer bystanders are likely to get hurt that way."

Beth looked at her. "We?"

"You think I'm not going with you?" Rose's eyes darted from Beth to Lieutenant Tompkins and back. "I'll be safer with you than on my own. Besides Mr. Lake's closed the Astor and you need me."

"We do?" Lieutenant Tompkins said. He fought to hold back a grin.

"You do," Rose said firmly. "You need someone to cook and to make camp and to help you with the horses." She gave Beth a sly look. "*Some* people don't do well with them."

"I can ride!" Beth protested.

"Barely." Rose's eyes twinkled, daring Beth to disagree.

"It doesn't matter," Lieutenant Tompkins said. "We're walking. The army took all the horses, remember?"

Rose sagged in her seat with a frown.

"What about yours?" Beth asked. "You and Raven and Mr. Weatherby rode here, didn't you?"

"But that's only three horses. There are four of us." He gestured at Jeb.

"No siree. No." The old miner shook his head. "I'm not going. Not gonna go. I'm gonna take my share of the cowboys' gold nuggets and go to San Francisco. I'm going there. That's what *I'm* gonna do." He gave Lieutenant Tompkins a deep look. "I do get a share, don't I?"

"You do," Lieutenant Tompkins said, "and I think that's the right choice. You've already done plenty."

"Yes," Beth said. She reached over and took Jeb's hand. His eyes went wide at her touch. "We couldn't have done all this without you." Then she gave his hand a squeeze.

"Oh, my," he said. "Oh, my indeed."

They spent the rest of the day getting ready to journey north. When they weren't searching for provisions or packing, they napped. Lieutenant Tompkins insisted they sleep in shifts, just in case.

Nothing disturbed them, though. Boggs stopped by to tell them that they'd buried the second cowboy, but found nothing to tell them who he was or where he'd come from. He had his own bag of gold nuggets, which Lieutenant Tompkins took. He gave some back to Boggs and also gave him some to hold for Mr. Lake's return. A small handful went to Jeb and the rest went into Lieutenant Tompkins's pocket in case they needed them in Caspar.

The next morning started as one of those beautiful spring mornings with forever blue skies. A chorus of birdsongs filled the air as they left the Astor to take Jeb to the coach headed to Salt Lake City, where he could catch the train to San Francisco. The old miner had a spring in his step that threatened to become a skip as he led the way.

"He's happy," Lieutenant Tompkins said to Beth as they walked behind the exuberant man. His head darted this way and that and he actually whistled as he went.

"He has more gold than he ever expected to find," Beth said.

The wind tugged at the old bowler hat she'd found in Mr. Lake's lost and found. She'd chosen it instead of a bonnet because it didn't look nearly as ridiculous with her trousers and shirt, though it didn't stay on nearly as well. She slapped a hand on top to keep it down.

"He's also going to be safe," Rose said from Lieutenant Tompkins's other side. "That'd put a spring in *my* step."

"You could still go with him," Lieutenant Tompkins urged her. "I could still write that letter for you."

"We've already had this discussion," Rose said firmly. "I'm sure your sister's family are nice people, but I'd fret too much in California. No. I go with Beth."

Lieutenant Tompkins shook his head in resignation.

Jeb slowed up from time to time to let them catch up, but then he'd scamper ahead once again. By the time they reached the coach, he'd already stowed his one small bag and stood at the open door.

He smiled back at them and waited until they were close.

"Thank you, oh thank you," he said. "For all the help."

"Oh, sweetie," Rose said, "you helped too."

His face brightened.

"Can I give you a hug?" Rose asked.

Jeb's cheeks reddened, but he nodded. She stepped in, wrapped her arms around him, and gave him a quick kiss on the cheek.

His mouth fell open in surprise as she stepped back.

"Now you take care," Rose admonished. "And write us once you get to San Francisco."

"Oh, I will. I will."

Lieutenant Tompkins stepped forward and extended his hand. "It's been fine working with you."

Jeb shook the lieutenant's hand, but his stunned expression didn't fade.

Lieutenant Tompkins stepped back and looked expectantly at Beth.

She took a deep breath. *Hug or handshake?*

She stepped forward and extended her hand.

Jeb caught her hand, turned it, and kissed the back.

"Thank you, missy," he said. "You are the Queen of the West."

Then he gave her his familiar loopy grin.

She stepped back, blinking, while Rose tried to suppress her snickers. Then Jeb bowed to all three of them and boarded the coach.

They stepped back and waited patiently as the driver boarded and snapped the reins. Then they watched the coach and Jeb drive out of sight.

The three of them headed back to the Astor. The wind had picked up, forcing even Lieutenant Tompkins to hold onto his hat. Rose's skirts billowed with the gusts and swirled around her. Beth had to keep scrunching her eyes closed against the grit stirred up from the road. When they arrived at the hotel, Lieutenant Tompkins held the door firmly to keep it from banging as they went in.

"Should we leave a note for Hickok?" Rose asked as she brushed the blown dirt from her dress.

"Or wait for him?" Lieutenant Tompkins added.

"No," Beth firmly said. When she saw Lieutenant Tompkins's look of surprise at her tone, she added, "He's not supposed to be back for several weeks. Do you want to wait?"

Lieutenant Tompkins grimaced, but was clearly giving it some thought.

"If the dwarves thought it urgent enough to follow you," Beth continued, "I don't think we can wait."

"And you don't want to wait anyway, do you?" Rose gave Beth a critical, knowing look.

"No," Beth said quickly. "It's too urgent, and we can handle it."

Lieutenant Tompkins rubbed his chin. "I don't know...."

"We can leave a note," Beth conceded. "We're going to Fort Caspar first, right? We'll tell him that."

"Good," Lieutenant Tompkins said. "He might come back early, you never know."

Beth bit her tongue and forced a smile. *We don't need Hickok to do this*, she thought.

"I'll write a note," Rose said. "Then we should get going. If we can make it to Boulder before dark, we won't have to sleep outdoors."

Lieutenant Tompkins called a halt partway across the rocky flats south of Boulder. Dusk had fallen and the wind had finally died.

The stars had begun to twinkle but they weren't far enough along to see the lights of Boulder.

"There's water here." Lieutenant Tompkins pointed to a small creek that flowed nearby. "And we can see in every direction. It'd be hard for anyone to sneak up on us here."

"Boulder's not that far," Rose said. She leaned over the back of her horse and peered north.

"True," Lieutenant Tompkins said, "but the hills between here and there would be perfect for an ambush. I'd rather not go through them in the dark."

"Ah."

"Should we risk a fire?" Beth asked.

"I'd prefer not to." Lieutenant Tompkins patted his horse's head and dismounted. "They probably know we're out here, but why call attention to ourselves?"

"We have some jerky we could eat cold," Rose said, as she too climbed down from her horse, "and a few of yesterday's muffins."

"As long as I get first watch," Beth said. She was too keyed up to sleep anyhow.

"Fine," Lieutenant Tompkins said. He looked up at the stars and then pointed. "See the Big Dipper and the North Star?"

"Yeah." She stepped up close so she could see exactly where he was pointing.

"Wake me when the Big Dipper's rotated around the North Star to there."

"So an hour after midnight."

He snorted in surprise and turned to face her.

"I learned to tell time by the stars years ago. You go and get some rest."

Beth rocked back and forth to keep warm as she sat on the cold ground. She'd wrapped a blanket around her and had another under her, which helped. The breeze had faded, thankfully, but its occasional whispering touch still chilled her. It carried the smell of the horses when it did. The beasts also shuffled and snorted from time to time, but that was the only noise. Thankfully, neither Rose nor Lieutenant Tompkins snored. They curled up tightly, each under their own blankets. Rose used her hat and a saddlebag as a pillow.

Beth had tried walking around the small camp, but then thought better of it. The horses were largely still, even though they stood tall in the flats here. Her motion would be more likely to draw the eye of any watchers than anything else.

So instead, she'd picked a spot and just changed the way she faced every few minutes.

All she saw was blackness. Dark black low, where the ground was. A less inky black above, with a swath of stars.

Nothing to see. Nothing moving. Except ...

Something did move. South of them, back along the trail they'd ridden from Golden City.

From their height, it looked like two horses or ponies, silhouetted against the sky. Not more than shadows, really. But they were coming closer.

She squinted to get a better look. Her hand drifted to her Colt. It'd be awkward to draw while sitting.

Slowly, she climbed to her feet.

The shadows halted.

She drew her gun, but held it at her side. *They could be friendly*, she thought.

Her gut said otherwise.

But she couldn't see. Not that far. Not in the dark.

It's worse than looking for ghosts on the battlefield, she thought.

Ghosts. Raven's ghost could see just fine in the dark.

Beth pulled the amulet from under her shirt and rubbed it hard.

CHAPTER TWELVE

The air in front of Beth shimmered and fogged into grey. Everything cooled, and a shiver ran down her back. Slowly the grey coalesced and took form.

Raven's ghost smiled at her with questioning eyes.

"Someone's approaching," Beth said. She pointed toward the shapes. "Can you see them?"

The ghost turned to look, but the shapes were now quickly receding in the distance. They had to be riding hard the way they'd come.

Why?

Beth turned back to Raven. The ghost still stared after the retreating horsemen. Beth studied her.

Despite the grey, despite being more fog than flesh, the ghost's features stood sharp and clear. Each wrinkle in Raven's sleeve twisted just as if it was cloth. Each braid of hair hung exactly as it had in life. Except they didn't move. When the ghost turned back around, her head turned, and then her body, but the hair didn't swing or flow. It didn't move naturally at all.

Beth suppressed a shudder.

The ghost raised an eyebrow, but its knowing smile didn't fade.

Not in the mouth, Beth realized. The eyes, though ... she checked the shoulders, the arms, the chest.

Tense.

The ghost's smile was pasted on.

Beth took a deep breath. She looked the ghost in the eye as best she could. She tried not to flinch.

"Raven?" Beth asked.

The ghost cocked an eyebrow.

"Are you hap—I mean, are things okay?"

Raven gave a confused nod.

"I ..." Beth paused and tried to pick her words. "Well, we didn't get to know each other before you ..." She gestured at the ghost. "And I have no idea what it's like. But you're not a broken one, are you? When this is ... over, you'll ... move on?"

Raven's face shifted to a real smile and she nodded.

"I wish I could hear you," Beth said. "There's so much I want to ask ... so much to know. Even things I'm not sure I want to know."

The ghost seemed to chuckle at that. Then it motioned for her to go on.

"Oh ... okay," Beth said. "Does ... it hurt? Being dead?"

Raven shook her head.

"And what happens next? When you ... move on?"

The ghost held up her hands with a shrug.

"You don't know either," Beth said with a soft snort. She rocked back on the balls of her feet. A few old sermons Ma had made her attend flashed through her mind.

"I hope it's a good place," she said. "Though maybe it's different for everyone." She looked at Raven, whose expression was unreadable. "I've sometimes seen the grey cloudy disks when people die. Those are rifts to the afterlife, right?"

Raven nodded.

"But the rifts didn't look exactly alike. They don't all go to the same place, do they?"

Raven nodded again.

"So you didn't go through." Beth mused. "You stayed." When

Raven didn't respond, Beth continued. "When Jane died, she only stayed long enough to make sure I took her gun." Beth gestured with the Colt in question. "She'd been planning to teach me, so Hickok did. I like to think that's made her happy. But I don't know for sure."

Raven nodded in agreement.

"So if we stop this dragon, or whatever it is, that'll make you happy, right? That's why you're still here."

The ghost nodded once again.

"I wish I could hear you," Beth said once again with a sigh. A thought struck her. "Say—can you read English? I could write something and you could point to the words."

Raven shook her head.

"Well, I'm glad you've stayed," Beth continued. "I don't think we could do this without you."

The ghost smiled. Then it faded away.

They rode hard the next day and didn't stop in Boulder. Instead, Lieutenant Tompkins pushed the pace until they reached the Lyon farm many miles further north. Mr. Lyon was happy to let them spend the night, especially when Lieutenant Tompkins offered him some flakes of gold from the cowboys' nuggets. He stared at Beth's clothes and gun, but didn't say a word.

The next day, they continued to ride north along the foothills. They passed a small herd of cattle with a pair of cowboys tending them. These men looked nothing like the cowboys from Golden City. They waved and were clearly clean, healthy, and in good spirits.

And alive, Beth thought. She grimaced and tried not to think of the men she'd killed.

You just have to put it out of your mind, Hickok had said. Not that he'd always managed it himself.

But it was part of being a gunslinger. The man you faced wanted to kill you.

It was him. Or you.

The best survived.

That's what Hickok said was worse. Not the guilt of killing. Especially not when they were trying to kill you. But the guilt of being alive when maybe you shouldn't be.

Like after a battle where your friends died.

She couldn't stop the shudder as memories of her own dead flooded through. Pa. Jane. Mr. Weatherby and Raven. Mr. Dooley. So many.

At least none of them had died because of her. Hickok didn't have that luxury.

And at least one person was alive because of her. She couldn't help smiling as she thought of Jeb, safely on his way west.

She remained lost in her thoughts for most of the day.

They spent the night in Namaqua, inside an old fort that a rancher had built years ago. Only a couple of farmers manned it now, but the walls were solid, the food passable, and the floor dry and insect free. There was a bathhouse down by the river and Lieutenant Tompkins stood guard outside while Rose and Beth washed off the dirt from the road.

The bathhouse was small—really just four walls around an old pot-bellied stove with a fat kettle on it and a large iron tub. Smoke and steam had long blistered the wooden walls and ceiling and only the dry Colorado air kept the mold under control. It smelled of burnt wood and lye, but Beth still sighed in relaxation as she sank into the warm water.

Rose pulled up the sole chair and sat nearby. She stripped off her outer blouse and started washing her arms with a washrag. She, too, closed her eyes for a moment with a happy sigh.

"I'd forgotten how dirty one gets when traveling," Rose said when she opened her eyes. "I'm so glad I didn't bring my best dress."

"You left the blue one behind?" Beth asked.

"Mmmm hmmm. I decided three was enough, what with our limited saddlebags and all."

"I wouldn't have brought any, if you hadn't insisted."

"You never know when they'll come in handy." Rose finished with her arms and started washing her neck. She arched her back with almost a purr as she did.

"I brought as many bullets as I could."

"Oh, I noticed. Do you really think you'll need that many?"

"You never know when they'll come in handy," Beth parroted.

Rose laughed and swatted at her with the washrag, though not close enough to be anything more than symbolic.

Beth had sat in the water long enough, just relaxing, so she reached for the soap. She studied her friend as she did—very carefully scrubbing each bit of dirt away. Rose's skin almost glowed like fine porcelain when she was done. Even after a few days on the road, her hair was still shiny and smooth and tied neatly in place.

Of course, she brought three dresses, Beth mused. But then she thought some more.

"So ..." Beth asked, "why did you come along? You know this is going to be dangerous."

Rose sighed and lowered the washrag. She gave Beth a deep look.

"And it's not dangerous for you?" she asked.

"It has to be done," Beth replied. "The army may not care about a murdered Indian, but I do."

"Oh, they care."

Beth shrugged in acknowledgement. "But they have other priorities. And it can't wait."

"No," Rose said, "it can't."

"So why are you coming?"

Rose snorted softly. A thin smile crossed her lips. She stared off into space as she thought.

"Well," she said at last, "not everyone needs a gun to do what's right."

She sat still, the washrag in her lap. Then she pursed her lips and gently shook her head. Finally, she turned to Beth.

"Besides," she joked, "who's going to make sure you don't turn into a boy if I'm not along?"

"I don't think that's possible," Beth said with a laugh. She looked down at her naked body in the water. "I'm all girl."

"Mmm hmm. Now hurry up so I can get my bath before the water cools."

The ride to Fort Collins the next day seemed to take no time at all. The day was bright, with just enough clouds drifting through to keep it cool. Even Lieutenant Tompkins seemed relaxed and happy, as if all his cares had been washed away in his own bath the night before.

His happiness grew even further in Fort Collins when they discovered a small squadron on their way to Fort Sanders to relieve another squadron there. Most of the replacement soldiers had grey in their hair and a few clearly didn't know how to hold a revolver, to Beth's disgust. Still, it meant a much larger party on the road. Lieutenant Tompkins immediately arranged for them all to travel together. A few of the men stared at Rose and Beth, but after a few strong words from Lieutenant Tompkins, they largely kept to themselves.

The three-day ride to Fort Sanders thus became quite pleasant. Lieutenant Tompkins didn't see any point in trying to hide from the dwarves, or whoever was following them. The watchers either knew they were in the group or they didn't, and the group itself was impossible to hide. So they had fires and hot meals every night. Beth didn't have to take any watches. If she was quiet at the evening campfire, the men would forget she was there and tell stories of the Indians and army life.

They didn't always forget, though. The last night, the whiskey came out. After one grey-haired skinny private with buck teeth told a story about tracking some Cheyenne that had stolen some horses, he turned to Beth.

"You see," he said, "we call it Arapaho Territory, but there's lots of Injuns there. Cheyenne, Arapaho, Shoshone, Crow. They look all alike, though. You gotta look at their warpaint, if they're wearing any."

Beth gritted her teeth and pasted on a smile. *Does this fool think I'm ignorant?*

"Of course," Buck Teeth rambled, "they don't wear much paint these days."

She felt her blood starting to rise and bit her lip through the smile.

"I'd call 'em cowards, but they're not. Cut your throat in a heartbeat if they could. The Cheyenne are the worst."

"They're still mad about Sand Creek," one of the other old soldiers, one with stringy hair, said.

"Nah," Buck Teeth said, "they're just ornery." He grinned gleefully at Beth. "They love carrying off the womenfolk and making them their own, if you know what I mean."

"No," Lieutenant Tompkins said. His tone was sharp and he glared at Buck Teeth hard. "All of them have abided by the Medicine Lodge Treaty, except for a few rogue braves here and there. And those were dealt with by their tribes."

"We gave 'em too much land, sir," String Hair whined. "They don't need it all!"

"You want to fight the Jotun *and* the Indians?" Lieutenant Tompkins couldn't keep the look of disgust off his face.

"Don't mean we won't fight if we have to," Buck Teeth said. He leered at Beth again. "They'll ride down on you in small bands. Eight, ten, twelve warriors. And they'd love to scoop a pretty little thing like you up and take her away!"

"I'd like to see them try." She slowly pulled out her Colt and set it on her lap.

He laughed. "I forgot! This one's got spirit!" He turned to Lieutenant Tompkins. "I pity the poor man who takes her to wife!"

"And I pity the poor man who makes her mad," Lieutenant Tompkins said. "She's already killed two men in fair fights. I'd hate to be the third."

Buck Teeth laughed even harder and louder. "Oh, you are funny!" His eyes darted from the lieutenant to Beth and back again. "You're funny indeed." His voice faltered. "Funny."

"Two men? In fair fights? Is that true, sir?" String Hair asked. His voice caught and he looked wide-eyed at Lieutenant Tompkins, as if he dared not look at Beth.

The lieutenant stared back. "Two men. Now, tell me what the tribes have been doing up near Fort Sanders in the past few weeks while I've been gone."

Buck Teeth took another swig of whiskey and then turned away from Beth. The others studiously ignored her as they caught Lieutenant Tompkins up on the happenings and rumors they'd heard.

They arrived at Fort Sanders the next afternoon. None too soon, as far as Beth was concerned. The other soldiers had been quiet the whole ride and stayed away from her. Not that she minded. Instead, they flitted and hovered around Rose. She talked with them merrily, much as she did with customers at the Astor House. And like at the Astor, she rolled her eyes at Beth when the men weren't looking.

Once one of the fort's stableboys took their horses, the women were shown to a small spartan room just down from the commander's office. Two thin beds with bare mattresses nestled against the side walls, with barely enough space between for them both to stand at the same time. The blankets on top were threadbare and faded. The sole dresser leaned against the back wall, but rocked an inch when Beth set one of her saddlebags on it. It'd been swept, but the lack of windows made the room tight and stuffy.

"My," Rose said. She sat on one bed, frowned, and shifted her seat to a softer spot. "They must not get many visitors."

"Not much out this way," Beth said.

"True." Rose looked around. "Do you think Fort Caspar will be as bad?"

"This isn't bad," Beth said. "Just ... neglected."

"You know what I mean."

"Yeah. But why spend the effort? The war with the giants is nowhere near here."

Rose grimaced. "Still, you'd think they'd care."

Beth snorted softly. "They're here because the army doesn't want them on the front. They know that. And it's hard to care when you know no one cares about you."

Rose shook her head. "Just because they're not at the front doesn't mean they're not important."

"Tell them that."

She shrugged. "Maybe I will. Perhaps when we dine with the commander tonight. Though I'm a little nervous about that."

"Why?"

"Something Lieutenant Tompkins said. He told the stableboy we needed a room with a lock because the commander couldn't be trusted."

Beth's eyes went to the flimsy latch on the door and she grimaced.

CHAPTER THIRTEEN

They dined outside under an awning with the commander, Captain Whitaker, and his top aide. Captain Whitaker, a portly man with thin sideburns and black curly hair, had ordered two chickens butchered in their honor, and they were served in a wine sauce with a scattering of mushrooms. He offered the ladies some wine, but Beth's face soured when she took a sip. It'd been watered down to the point of being tasteless. The chicken was acceptable, but the cook at the Astor would've made it sing.

The conversation started light and general, with Lieutenant Tompkins and Captain Whitaker exchanging stories of army life and rumors about the troll offensive. Captain Whitaker also regaled them with stories about his time with one of the scientific expeditions that had explored the area "back in the day." Yet his stories were more about the scrapes he and the other young men had gotten into than the discoveries the expedition had made.

One story was particularly gruesome. A Private Sterling had apparently died by falling into a mud pit while running from some of his fellows who'd been threatening to shave off his unkempt beard. Captain Whitaker seemed to think the moral was better hygiene, but Beth was just appalled.

So she kept silent and watched the captain closely. His shoulders remained tense except when he discussed the scientific expeditions. Any casual comment about Fort Sanders caused his throat and arms to tighten. He still forced smiles, but the only genuine ones came when he talked about his time in the mountains when he was younger.

Lieutenant Tompkins looked nervous too. His shoulders weren't as tense, but his jaw was. He swallowed multiple times and took long pauses to gather his thoughts before asking questions. The sun had just started to set, with orange and red tints across the scattered clouds, when he turned to the subject of their own trip.

"So," he said, "what's the news from Fort Caspar, sir?"

Captain Whitaker blinked. "Why ... I don't believe we've heard from Fort Caspar in several weeks. Not since you came through, I believe." He looked at his aide, who nodded.

"That's ... strange, sir," Lieutenant Tompkins said. "Not a single rider?"

"No, not a one."

"Were any expected?" Beth asked.

She leaned forward, but ignored Captain Whitaker's surprised blink. He looked at her for a long few seconds before turning back to Lieutenant Tompkins.

He didn't expect me to talk, she silently grumbled.

Lieutenant Tompkins ignored the captain and turned to her. "There's usually a mail rider once a week. Not always, though." He looked back at the captain. "That didn't bother you, sir?"

"We've been busy," Captain Whitaker said. "The orders to send men south have taxed us. We did send a messenger to Fort Caspar when the mail rider didn't arrive ..." His face grew strained and he looked at his aide.

"An Arapaho, already headed that way, sir." The aide at least had the decency to look chastened.

"Ah, yes," Captain Whitaker said. "A local. Yes. We knew Fort Caspar would respond as best they could."

"But ... sir ..." Lieutenant Tompkins said, "They sent no men this way. No response of any kind ... didn't you at least—"

"Lieutenant!" Captain Whitaker put his palms on the table. The muscles in his arm and neck all tensed, though he held his face neutral. Only his eyes held his glare.

"Fort Caspar," he continued, "has a capable commander. I am sure he can handle any issues that might have arisen. Lieutenant."

"Yes, sir." Lieutenant Tompkins looked down at his plate, as if his chicken was suddenly fascinating.

"Would you like some more, Lieutenant?" the aide asked. He looked at the ladies. "Miss Armstrong? Miss Chamberlin?"

"I would love some," Rose said. "Your cook has quite outdone himself."

Beth nodded, though not quite in full agreement.

"Ah, yes," Captain Whitaker said. "His chicken is divine. You should see what he does with elk though. Which reminds me of this one evening on our expedition ..."

Beth settled back for the rest of what promised to be a dull mealtime conversation.

Beth latched the door after they returned to their room. Then she checked it again. It wouldn't hold if someone forced it, but it'd be noisy if they did. She put her Colt on the bed next to her pillow. After she'd taken off her outer clothes and laid down, she shifted the gun around so it was an easy reach.

"You really think you'll need that?" Rose asked from her own bed. The flickering light from the dirty oil lamp cast her face in shadow.

"No, but as Hickok says, better to have it just in case."

"I don't think the captain will do anything."

"It's not the captain I'm worried about," Beth said. "I just think he wouldn't want to be ... bothered if something did happen. He'd find a way to ignore it or make it our fault."

Rose suppressed a shudder. "Oh, yes. One of *those* men." Her eyes stared out at hidden memories that she didn't share.

"We'll be fine. Some things can't be ignored." *Like a gunshot in the night.*

Rose pulled herself out of her past and smiled sweetly. "We should get some sleep. I'm sure Lieutenant Tompkins will want to leave first thing in the morning." She reached out and put out the lamp.

Beth lay in the darkness, listening to the wind and the distant sounds of the fort. It took a while for her eyelids to finally flutter closed.

Beth snapped awake. Her hand was already on her Colt before the soft knock came on the door again. She sat up and aimed at the door when another knock sounded, but no one tried to open it.

After a few sweat-filled moments, all went quiet again. She waited another thirty heartbeats before she pushed the blanket aside and stepped out of bed. The cold floor was rough against her bare feet. She stole forward slowly, with no rhythm to her steps, as Hickok had once taught her. Pause. Step, step. Pause. Step. Pause, pause. Regular patterns were what people heard, he'd said. Not random noises. She reached the door without a single board squeaking.

She stood to the side of the door, listening, for another fifty or sixty heartbeats. She didn't hear a thing outside. Either whoever it was stood as silent as she, or they'd moved on.

Carefully she lifted the latch.

Gun leveled, she opened the door. Nothing. No one.

She quickly looked all around. On the ground, something flat and pale. Paper.

Keeping her eyes out for people, she quickly knelt and scooped it up. Then she shut the door and secured the latch once again.

"Huh ... whatizzit?" Rose mumbled.

"A note," Beth whispered. "Light the lamp."

As Rose fumbled for the light, Beth strode back to her bed. She sat on the side and began to read once the oil lamp flared into life. Rose looked over her shoulder.

Ask Captain Whitaker to assign Private Bannock to go with you, the note said. *He speaks Shoshone.*

It was unsigned.

"Who do you think it's from?" Rose asked.

"The aide," Beth said promptly. "Anyone else would've given this to Lieutenant Tompkins."

"But why give it to us instead?"

Beth paused for a moment of thought.

"Because," she said, "he either doesn't trust Lieutenant Tompkins to ask for someone to accompany us, or Captain Whitaker to listen to him. But he knows I'll speak up."

"That," Rose said, "is an understatement."

Beth just nodded.

"Well," Rose said, "we still have a few hours before morning. Are you going to try to get some more sleep?"

Beth smiled. By Rose's tone, it wasn't a question.

"Sure," Beth said, "but we'll talk to Lieutenant Tompkins first thing."

They found Lieutenant Tompkins in the stables early the next morning. Its doors had just been opened, so the smell of hay and animals still pervaded everything. The sounds of the fort coming alive filtered in, but otherwise they heard only the snort and shuffle of the horses mixed with the jangle of the harnesses and Lieutenant Tompkins packing the saddlebags.

He turned at their approach and then frowned at their grim expressions.

"What?" he asked.

Beth thrust the note out. "Someone left this outside our door last night."

He took it and quickly skimmed it. "Interesting."

"You said you didn't trust Captain Whitaker," Beth said. "Why?"

Lieutenant Tompkins sighed. "I don't have a good reason."

"But you have a reason."

"None of us in Fort Caspar trusted him. It wasn't anything he did, really. We just ..." He shrugged. "We'd send a messenger here asking for help or supplies and instead of getting them, he'd send back a bunch of questions. There were a lot of things like that, where he kept challenging us, like we were stupid. So if he didn't trust us, why should we trust him?"

"Obviously his own men don't trust him either." Rose pointed to the note.

"No," Lieutenant Tompkins said. "But should we trust this letter writer?"

"Maybe we should find Private Bannock and talk to him ourselves first," Beth suggested.

"Good idea," Lieutenant Tompkins said. He handed the note back to Beth. "He'll probably be in the mess hall soon. Let me finish up here," he gestured toward the saddlebags, "and I'll meet you there."

At the entrance to the mess hall, they stopped two soldiers on their way out and asked about Private Bannock.

The first soldier blinked in surprise. "Bannock? He's in the stockade."

"Do you know what for?" Beth asked.

"Drunk out on patrol. He claimed it was his partner's fault, but no one believes him."

"And insubordination," the second soldier added. "He's always questioning orders. And he never says 'sir' when he should."

Beth looked at Rose with a raised eyebrow, asking a silent question. Rose nodded, so Beth turned back to the soldier.

"Where's the stockade?" she asked.

He pointed, and after they'd said thank you, the women headed that way.

Beth carefully studied the disheveled man behind the bars. He lay on his side, facing away. His black hair hung in greasy bunches. Sweat stains and black smudges covered his worn army uniform shirt. His pants similarly had mud stains around the cuffs. He'd taken his boots off and his left heel stuck out through a gaping hole in his sock. His ragged snores cut off in wheezes from time to time.

But worst of all, he smelled. Like sweat, urine, and a few other things she wasn't sure she wanted to identify.

"Should we wake him up?" Rose asked.

"You woke *me* up," the jailer grumbled. He banged a bent metal pipe down the row of bars like he was playing a xylophone. "Wake up, Bannock! Wake up. You got visitors! Women."

Bannock snapped his head up, but held still. Mostly still, Beth realized. His right hand hovered near his hip, where his gun would be. His shoulders and arm were tense. Even his leg muscles were coiled to spring.

But he didn't move.

"Women?" Bannock said. He hadn't looked back.

"Two. A pretty one and ..."

The jailer's eyes flicked up and down Beth. When they met hers, she glared at him.

"And her friend," he finished.

"Her friend, huh?" Bannock slowly uncoiled and rolled over. He swung himself up to sit on the side of the bed in a single smooth motion and his feet hit the ground together. He looked to be in his late twenties, but with the world weariness of an even older man.

His piercing sky-blue eyes found Beth's at once. He didn't blink.

She stared back and forced her eyelids to stay up.

The corners of his eyes softened, and then his mouth. Then his gaze dropped to her shoulders, her arms, her hands, and then back up.

He smiled, almost a handsome, roguish smile. His scraggly unshaven cheeks and split lip took the handsome away, though.

Then his eyes finally darted to Rose. His eyebrows rose and he pursed his lips. He snorted softly and turned back to Beth.

"What do you want?" Bannock asked.

"We want you to come with us," Beth blurted. "To help us find the dragon."

The jailer guffawed.

Bannock cocked an eyebrow. "The dragon Whitaker says doesn't exist?"

Beth blinked. She hadn't picked up even a hint of that over dinner. When Lieutenant Tompkins had mentioned the dragon, the captain had changed the subject to the Indians or the fort or the weather.

He *didn't* believe in it.

Her gut tightened at the thought.

"That's the one, isn't it?" Bannock said. "Then I'm coming." He looked around for his boots. "As soon as you can get me out of here."

Captain Whitaker was happy to release Bannock. Or more precisely, he was happy to transfer Bannock to Lieutenant Tompkins and the Fort Caspar command, in exchange for a different private to be sent later. Any private, it seemed. As long as he was able-bodied and not prone to insubordination.

He also had a few quiet stern words with Lieutenant Tompkins, but did so out of earshot of the ladies. When Beth asked about it later, Lieutenant Tompkins said it was not worth repeating.

So by mid-morning, their saddlebags were loaded with new provisions and a horse had been found for Private Bannock. He'd gotten a bath and a change of clothes and so at least resembled a soldier. Lieutenant Tompkins also requisitioned a rifle for Bannock from the armory. He went to hand Beth one too and she shook her head.

"You sure?" he asked.

"I'm sure. I'm better with this." She tapped the handle of her Colt.

"Better take one just in case, though," Lieutenant Tompkins said. "You can always give it to me if I lose mine."

She snorted in amusement but accepted the gun.

The warm spring day made for pleasant riding. The sun wasn't too warm, nor the breeze too cool. The horses kept a good pace as the road wound through the grasslands north, with nothing but the rolling hills to change the scenery. They saw a small herd of buffalo in the distance once but didn't approach them.

At their handful of stops to rest and water the horses, Rose asked Bannock about himself, but any questions deeper than what he liked and didn't like about the army were neatly deflected.

After the fourth go around, Bannock just chuckled and shook his head.

"I joined the army to forget, Miss Chamberlin," he said. "Not even a pretty girl like yourself will make me want to remember."

Rose responded with a sour frown.

But otherwise, Bannock told jokes and silly stories about minor happenings at Fort Sanders. He spun a tale about the night the chickens escaped the coop and pooped all over the cook's laundry that had Rose and Beth laughing. Even Lieutenant Tompkins couldn't keep a grin off his face as he rolled his eyes.

They arrived at a suitable campsite just before dusk. The road ran close to a small river, maybe ten feet wide. It was the only feature of note—grass grew in all directions. They found an old fire pit in a cleared area not more than ten feet from the trail. After they'd finished dinner, Bannock turned to Lieutenant Tompkins.

"I'll take second watch," he said.

"I'd prefer you took third shift," the lieutenant said. "I'll take second and wake you about two-thirty."

"He told ya, didn't he?" Bannock replied.

"Of course."

"Told you what?" Beth asked.

Bannock turned to her, one eyebrow raised. "He didn't tell you?"

"I didn't see the need," Lieutenant Tompkins said.

"I wasn't talking about you," Bannock said to him. To Beth, "The captain loved to tell anyone who'd listen what a deadbeat I was. Never enough to court-martial, but enough to earn a night in the stockade."

He grimaced before continuing.

"Last patrol, my partner brought some whiskey. We drank some at dinner and I had first watch. When I didn't wake him, he said it was because I was drunk."

"Were you?" Beth asked.

"I know my liquor. Yeah, I drank some, but I wasn't drunk. Not then, at least."

"So what were you doing?"

He grinned, that toothsome grin that just highlighted his eyes.

"Watching the dragon, of course."

Bannock's eyes glinted in the low light, almost as much as his teeth. His smile turned into a smirk as the others stared at him.

Lieutenant Tompkins broke the silence. "You've seen it? You've actually seen it?"

"Heck, yeah," Bannock said. "'Course, my patrol partner didn't see it, even after I woke him. He claimed it was the whiskey, but I know what I saw."

"What'd you see?" Beth asked.

"Flame." Bannock's brow furrowed as he stared into space, remembering. "In the sky. It was far away and moving, but it was clearly fire. It danced and flared like a torch. Sometimes it disappeared entirely. But it couldn't have been anything else."

"So you didn't see the dragon itself," Lieutenant Tompkins said.

"Didn't need to, uh, sir," Bannock said. "What else makes fire in the heavens?"

Lieutenant Tompkins didn't seemed fazed by the fumbled formality. He just shrugged and looked at Beth and raised his eyebrows in a question. She shrugged, too.

Rose pointed toward the northern sky. "Did it look like that?"

CHAPTER FOURTEEN

Beth's hand dropped to her Colt as her head snapped up. Her heart raced as she spotted the flicker. Like a candle in the sky, a light danced high above the horizon. It disappeared into the inky blackness. Then it returned. A flicker that jetted out a quarter the size of the moon.

Lieutenant Tompkins gasped.

"Where's it headed?" Rose asked. "Do we need to pack up camp?"

"It's too far away," Bannock said.

The flame damped and then flared again. After a minute, it did it again, with a burst now half the size of the moon.

"It's coming this way," Beth said. "We need to get under cover!"

Lieutenant Tompkins swore.

Beth glanced around—there wasn't any cover! Nothing that could hide the horses. The scattered bushes by the river weren't much either.

Bannock quickly smothered the sparks of the fire he'd started. Rose threw the pots and provisions she'd unpacked back into their bags.

"Beside the bushes!" Beth called. "It's the best we can do."

"I'll lead the horses further away," Lieutenant Tompkins said.

"No!" Beth said. "No time!"

The flame was coming fast. Almost directly at them.

Beth dashed toward Rose and grabbed her arm. The two women crouched next to a small wiry woody bush with small leaves. The men scrambled in other directions.

The flames disappeared. Then they appeared again, closer, larger. Then they went out.

It's not constantly breathing fire, Beth realized. *We can't see it without the fire!*

She anxiously scanned the skies. Beside her, Rose knelt, but also peered into the dark.

Nothing.

More nothing. Still nothing.

Then a burst! A jet of fire across the sky almost on top of them! She could see the dragon!

Well, she could see something—in the dark, it was still hard to make out more than a big black shape, as it blocked the stars and skyglow behind it.

Her heart pounded. She held her gun up and cocked it.

Would it even help?

Then it was above them and another huge burst of fire roared through the sky. Beth winced and Rose cried out, but the flame went up, not down.

Beth steeled herself and brought her gun to bear, but she could barely track the dark shape, much less aim.

Then it circled. A quick fire blast to their east. Then north. Then west. Then south.

Then it soared on south.

Rose let out a deep sigh. "We're safe."

"No," Beth said. She lowered her gun as her gut filled with dread. "No, we're not safe at all."

"It flew on," Rose said.

"But it marked our location for its friends, whoever they are. We're going to be attacked."

The night seemed suddenly still, with the flame dwindling in the distance. Some of the bush's branches scratched against Beth's side. She took a couple of deep breaths to calm herself.

Lieutenant Tompkins ran toward them. He had his own gun out, held high. Behind him, Bannock raced toward the horses.

"Let's go!" he shouted. "We need to move!"

Rose scrambled for the last of their unpacked stuff.

"Where to?" Beth yelled back.

He pointed east. "Across the river! It's our only possible protection!"

"Can the horses make it?" Beth asked. The river wasn't too wide, but it might be deeper than it looked.

"I'll get your belongings!" Rose called to Beth. "You keep watch."

Beth swallowed hard and turned in a circle. *Keep watch for what?* They were in flatland—she couldn't see anything in any direction. Just grass and sky. Like when they'd been south of Boulder.

She blinked in realization and fumbled into her shirt. She drew out Raven's pouch and rubbed it between her fingers.

The air cooled. In front of her, it shimmered and then clouded up. Grey mist solidified. Raven's ghost looked at her with worried eyes.

"Where are they coming from?" Beth asked hurriedly. "The dragon's friends. Where are they?"

The ghost nodded and slowly turned in a circle. Then she paused and pointed north, up the road.

"What are they?"

The ghost pointed to Beth and then Bannock and Lieutenant Tompkins.

"Humans?"

Raven nodded.

"How many?"

The ghost held up every finger on both hands. Then she pulled them into a fist and repeated the gesture.

"On horseback?"

Raven's ghost nodded.

Beth sucked in her breath. Her heart hammered in her chest. "Thank you."

The ghost smiled, and then faded away.

She glanced at the others. Rose and Lieutenant Tompkins were shoving the last of their things into the saddlebags. Bannock had mounted his horse. He stared at Beth, his face white.

She shook her head. *No time to explain.*

"They're coming from the north!" she called out. "Twenty of them!"

"We cross the river!" Lieutenant Tompkins cried. He rushed to Rose to help her get on her horse.

Beth rushed to her own horse. By the time she'd mounted, Bannock was halfway across. The water only rose to the horse's thighs. It moved slowly, though, nearly balking at every step. Bannock urged it on gently but firmly.

Rose and Lieutenant Tompkins followed. Her horse struggled. She spurred it and it slipped, but didn't quite fall. Lieutenant Tompkins reached over and grabbed the reins. The two horses stopped in the middle of the current, not going forward at all.

Beth looked upstream and downstream. They'd picked the widest, slowest moving spot to cross and now the two horses blocked the best route.

She turned her head. She could see their foes now, in the distance. A mass of dark riders raced down the road.

Rose and Lieutenant Tompkins sorted out their horses and finished crossing the river. Beth spurred hers into the water, but then sat impatiently as it picked its way across. She kept glancing back at the approaching horsemen.

They became distinct as they closed. The pack separated into individual horses with tall figures on their backs. They galloped fast and the nearest raised a dark arm against the sky.

It held a rifle.

Beth spurred her horse, which didn't do much but make it whinny in protest. Still, it kept going until it stepped up the far bank. As it shook off the water, she slid from its back.

Bannock and Lieutenant Tompkins had already dismounted. They held their rifles level and pointed at the approaching riders. Rose, too, had dismounted and she led the horses further away from the river.

The riders closed, and then slowed. The lead one pointed their direction.

Beth sucked in her breath. They were *so* many.

Bannock swore.

"What?" Lieutenant Tompkins asked. He kept his gun leveled on the approaching horsemen.

"Shoshone," Bannock said. "See the feathers on that spear?"

Lieutenant Tompkins swore in turn.

Beth furrowed her brow, but looked closer. The riders were now close enough that, despite the dark, she could make out their individual shapes. A rider in the back did indeed carry a spear.

"What's wrong with Shoshone?" Beth asked.

But before either man answered, the Indians arrived at the spot on the road just opposite the river and halted. Then they slowly rode to the river's edge, not more than twenty feet away.

Beth started breathing hard. She pointed her Colt, which she didn't even remember drawing, at the biggest Indian in front. He was burly, with a long black braid, but all else was hidden in shadow. She did a quick count—there were indeed about twenty Indians, facing down the three of them. Four of them, if Rose hadn't gotten far enough away.

The Indians sat on their horses and stared at them. Several held rifles across their chests, but none leveled them. The burly one nudged his horse forward a few steps.

Bannock shouted out something she didn't understand.

The leader growled something.

Bannock swore and then yelled again in what had to be Shoshone.

The leader barked back and then said something to his men. They cried out—war cries, Beth realized—and then turned and rode off south.

Beth let out a long breath and lowered her gun. She turned to Bannock.

"What'd he say?"

Bannock lowered his rifle and spat on the ground. "He said they didn't have time to kill us now, but if they saw us in their lands again, they'd take our scalps."

"But this isn't their land!" Lieutenant Tompkins said. "By treaty, it's ours."

"I told him that," Bannock said.

"What'd he say?" Beth asked.

"Not anymore," Bannock said. "He said 'not anymore.'"

"But—but ..." Lieutenant Tompkins sputtered.

Beth gasped with the shock of realization.

"What?" Bannock asked.

"Fort Caspar," she said. "It's been destroyed."

"Yeah," Bannock said. "It must've been."

Lieutenant Tompkins stared, mouth open, at her and Bannock. He finally forced himself to turn away.

Rose appeared quietly at the edge of their little group. "I don't understand," she said. "Lieutenant?"

Tompkins shook himself, like a man putting on a wet coat, and looked at her grimly. "By treaty," he said, "Shoshone land is west of Fort Caspar, Arapaho land is north and east, and American land is south. Besides being a trading post, Fort Caspar was meant to keep the borders. If the dragon destroyed the fort, then the Shoshone can take over all the land."

"But the dragon and the Shoshone were coming from that direction," Beth added. She looked north along the road. "Which means ..."

Her eyes swung south, and then widened with realization.

"Oh, no," she said. "They're attacking Fort Sanders."

"Oh, God!" Lieutenant Tompkins face went white. "We have to help!" He dashed for his horse. "Mount up!"

"We can't get there in time," Bannock said.

"Then we do what we can," Lieutenant Tompkins shot back. "Mount up!"

"We'll be lucky to get there by morning, sir," Bannock objected. "It took us all day to ride this far, remember? We'll be riding in the dark when we can barely see the trail and our horses are exhausted."

"The Shoshone won't be there much before morning either," Beth pointed out. "Hours after the dragon. They're not going for the fight."

Lieutenant Tompkins turned on his horse and stared at her.

"They'll be too late," she continued. "They're not going for the battle. They're going for the looting after."

"We should ambush 'em on the way back," Bannock said.

"No," Lieutenant Tompkins said. "We can still help in the fight even if we're late. We should go on."

"Are you sure ... sir?" Bannock asked. "Is that an order?"

A pained look crossed Lieutenant Tompkins's face. He looked over at Beth.

She sucked in her breath. *What would Hickok do?* "We can't abandon the men in Fort Sanders," she said. "We ride south."

"We can't make it in time," Bannock said.

Beth shook her head. "You'd be surprised."

"Let's go," Lieutenant Tompkins urged. "That is an order."

Bannock shot Beth a look that said, "We'll talk later."

They forded the river again and headed south on the road. The cool night air caused Beth to shiver more than once. Lieutenant Tompkins started them at a gallop, but it didn't last long as the horses were already worn down. Finally they slowed to a walk.

Then Lieutenant Tompkins bowed to the inevitable and had them stop so the horses could drink from a stream running near the road. They refreshed their own canteens and sat on dry grass that smelled like clover. Rose broke out a small bag of jerky and passed it around. It was tough and too salted, but Beth still chewed hungrily.

Lieutenant Tompkins was the first back on his feet. "We need to get there," he said through gritted teeth.

"Doesn't matter," Bannock said. "Everyone will be dead soon."

"Maybe not," Rose said. "Beth survived two days."

"What?" Bannock said.

"Giants attacked my town when I was ten," Beth said with a shrug. "They destroyed my house. I was trapped in the rubble for two days."

"Huh." Bannock said. "And you think the Shoshone won't finish off any survivors?"

Beth shrugged.

"We should go," Lieutenant Tompkins said. "Even on fresh horses, the Shoshone can't be more than an hour or so ahead of us."

"If we keep pushing these horses," Bannock said, "they'll be worthless when we get there. *If* we get there."

Lieutenant Tompkins glared at him. "We'll take that chance." He looked over at the horses. "They're ready. Let's go."

Beth looked around as she waited for the others to mount. Then she let out a gasp.

Flames danced on the horizon to the south. They lit the night sky, right where Fort Sanders should be.

CHAPTER FIFTEEN

Beth clenched the reins as she stared at the distant flames. In the cool dark, it was hard to look away. Her horse snorted and pawed the ground. Beth sensed Rose mounting her own horse nearby and then the other woman gasped.

"What?" Lieutenant Tompkins called.

"Fort Sanders," Beth said. She pointed.

"Oh, God!" Lieutenant Tompkins scrambled onto his horse. "Let's go!" He snapped his reins and took off at a gallop.

Beth looked over at Rose and Bannock. The private just shook his head and sagged in his seat for a moment. Then he started off at a canter after the lieutenant.

Beth spurred her own horse and caught up with Bannock. Rose was right behind.

They rode hard for several hours. Beth's legs and arms ached and more than once she thought she might fall off the horse. Then a small light flashed in the southern sky.

The light—no, the flame—happened again. Closer, and a bit larger.

The dragon is flying home, Beth realized.

"Quick!" She yelled to the others. "Take cover!"

Except, just like last time, there was no cover. Just grass as far as they could see.

"Scatter!" Lieutenant Tompkins called out. He pulled up on his horse and then rode west, away from the trail. Bannock spurred his horse east. Beth turned and rode back north, instead of heading south.

It didn't matter. The dragon flew high, and a little to the west. It passed over them without stopping and then was gone into the northern sky.

Beth pulled up on the reins with a sigh of relief. The dragon was gone.

But what about the Shoshone?

They came within sight of Fort Sanders as the sun rose. The wind blew cold from the west and so strong that Beth gave up trying to hold her hat. She tucked it into her saddlebag straps and groaned from the aches in her arms and legs. The non-stop riding had taken its toll on her as well as her horse.

The others seemed equally worn. Rose's hair actually hung in tangles under her loosely tied bonnet and her dress had mud stains around the hem. Lieutenant Tompkins yawned a few times before they sped up to a trot. Bannock looked as grimy as he'd been in the jail cell. Was it only a day ago?

The flames were long gone from the horizon, replaced by curls of smoke that drifted east with the wind. They rode until they could see just the hints of the fort itself—the walls barely rose above the prairie. Then Lieutenant Tompkins led them around to the west. They circled until the wind was at their backs.

Then they slowly rode toward the fort.

They stopped when Bannock spotted horsemen just outside the smoking fort walls. At least three, and possibly more. Given the lack of cover, they didn't dare approach.

So Lieutenant Tompkins motioned for them to ride west again. He called a halt after another fifteen minutes. They'd gone far enough that Beth couldn't see the Indians anymore. Bannock stared that way as well. Lieutenant Tompkins gestured them to form a circle so they could talk without the wind drowning out their words.

"We're too late," he said. "The enemy controls the fort. We must presume that any survivors have been taken prisoner."

"But the Shoshone won't stay," Bannock said. "Once they've finished looting, they'll leave. Normally they'd burn the place down first, but ..." He shrugged.

"The dragon can't have destroyed it all," Beth said, "or there'd be nothing to loot."

"The armory's in the guardhouse," Lieutenant Tompkins said. "That's stone."

"So they'll be better armed," Bannock groused.

"What difference does that make?" Beth said. "They're allied with a dragon."

"More weapons is always good," Lieutenant Tompkins said, "but the Shoshone have started a war here. Why do that for a few guns?"

"It's a war they could win," Rose pointed out. "With our army off fighting the trolls ..."

Lieutenant Tompkins vehemently shook his head. "Our army will be back, and the Shoshone are not strong enough to hold the territory."

"Even with the dragon?" Beth asked.

He sucked in air through his teeth. "That ... I do not know."

"Maybe it's something besides the armory," Beth said. "We need to explore the fort after they leave."

"They'll burn anything the dragon didn't," Bannock said. "We won't be able to learn anything."

"Then we'll have to talk to a witness," she said.

"After the Shoshone are done," Bannock said, "there won't be any survivors."

Beth snorted softly. "Who said the witnesses had to be survivors?"

She lightly touched her chest over Raven's pouch, and watched his eyes widen in realization.

Bannock volunteered to creep through the grass back toward the fort. He said he figured that if the Shoshone were watching for horsemen, he could probably get close. The stalks weren't really long enough to hide him, but when Beth started to volunteer, he cut her off with a glare.

"Your ghost won't help," he said.

Her mouth dropped open in shock. Before she could say anything, he'd dismounted and passed his horse's reins to Lieutenant Tompkins.

Lieutenant Tompkins blinked and said, "Well, then. We'll move further west."

Bannock nodded and strode off toward the fort.

Lieutenant Tompkins had them ride further west to a creek that flowed north to the Laramie River. Once the horses were taken care of, he just flopped forlornly on the grass.

Beth sank to the ground next to him. She drank from her canteen. When she offered it to the lieutenant, he didn't seem to notice. He just stared into space until she shook it directly in his face. Then he accepted it without a smile.

Rose joined them with something wrapped in paper. She stood in front of him and held out her hand for the canteen, but Lieutenant Tompkins didn't notice. He passed the water back to Beth instead.

"Lieutenant," Rose said, "where are your manners?"

He started as if slapped and looked up at her. "I'm ... I'm sorry. I've been thinking about the men in Fort Sanders. We ..." His eyes lost their focus as he stared into space.

"Oh, dearie," Rose said. Her voice was filled with sympathy.

"We couldn't've outraced the Indians." She unfolded the paper. "Here. It's not whiskey, but it'll help."

"Honeycomb?" he said as he accepted the paper and its golden contents.

"With a touch of mint," she said. "The taste is so heavenly, it'll take your mind off your woes." She put her hands behind her back and forced a smile. "Please, Lieutenant. Have some. Please?"

He snorted, but the corners of his mouth turned up.

"Please, Lieutenant. Eat a bite. Just a bite."

"You're not going to stop until I do, are you?"

"Just a bite!"

"Fine." He pulled the paper back from a corner and nibbled on it. His eyebrows rose. Then he nibbled some more.

"Oh my," he said.

"Rose knows her sweets," Beth said.

"That she does." He looked up at Rose and gave her the smile she'd sought.

"She also knows how to get someone out of a bad mood," Beth said. "She's had too much practice, unfortunately."

Lieutenant Tompkins's face fell. "Well ... it's just ... I just keep trying to come up with ways we could've saved the fort."

"Against a dragon, a Shoshone war band, and probably dwarves?"

He shook her off. "Who knows? We were so late, our soldiers never had a chance." He rubbed his temples. "Always late. Always."

"What's that supposed to mean?" Beth asked.

"Nothing important," he muttered.

"Oh, dearie," Rose said, "if it's important to you, it's important to us."

He shook his head, but he smiled. "Well, what's important now is for us to get some rest before Bannock returns."

"You rest," Beth said. "I'll keep watch."

"Fine by me. Hopefully you won't see a thing."

The hot sun beat down before Bannock returned. Beth kept her bowler pulled tight as the wind continued to blow, though not as fierce. It'd gust for a minute, then die, then go back to a steady breeze. She sat with her back to it, which helped a bit. Meanwhile Lieutenant Tompkins snored softly on his side. Rose slept under a thin blanket a few feet away.

In the distance, new curls of smoke rose into the sky. They blew low, and were hard to make out at times. Beth couldn't see the fort itself, but the black streak in the sky marked its location as well as any sign.

Bannock strode across the prairie toward them. He had his rifle slung over his back and walked with a steady gait. Twice he looked back over his shoulder at the smoke. Then his pace picked up a tad. Beth gently shook the others awake, so that everyone was on their feet by the time Bannock arrived.

"They've left," he said. "The twenty Shoshone warriors on horseback, and a wagon."

"A wagon?" Lieutenant Tompkins said. "Why'd they take a wagon and not the army's horses?"

"They had those, too," Bannock explained. "Fully loaded, it appeared. But it looked like children on the wagon."

"Dwarves," Beth said. "Of course."

"You said you ran into them in Golden City," Bannock said, "but dwarves don't make sense. Why would they be here? There's no gold here."

"The dragon doesn't make sense either," Beth said. "Why would the Shoshone be working with it? You'd think its attacks on the buffalo herds would be as much a problem for them as for the Arapaho."

"I figure they've made some deal with it," Bannock said. "I just don't know what."

"We can figure it out later," Lieutenant Tompkins said. "Let's get to the fort."

CHAPTER SIXTEEN

Beth silently gave thanks that they were approaching the fort with the wind at their backs. Her gut tightened as not only the burnt walls but the burnt bodies came into view. Rose turned aside, pale. She took a few deep breaths before she was able to look back.

The stone armory still stood, as well as partial walls of much of the rest of the fort. What remained upright mostly smoldered. Charred bodies sprawled where they'd fallen from the walls. Other corpses, without burns, had clearly been looted and scalped.

Beth forced herself to take deep breaths. There wasn't a lot of blood, which helped.

Just a lot of death. No survivors but scores of bodies....

"How are we going to bury all these people?" Rose asked as they rode slowly into what had once been the fort's courtyard. She'd recovered some of her composure, but still had to pause and close her eyes from time to time.

"We're not," Bannock said. "It'd take days or weeks."

"We'll identify them as best we can," Lieutenant Tompkins said, "and give them a service, but we can't linger, unless we find some survivors."

"Let's see if Raven can help with that," Beth said. She pulled her pouch out and rubbed it.

Nothing happened.

She looked around in confusion. Then she rubbed the pouch again and made sure to pinch the bone between her thumb and finger.

Still nothing.

It felt like it *might* have gotten cooler, but the sun shone so bright she couldn't tell. Worse, she couldn't see the ghost anywhere.

"Uhh ..." she said. "I can't talk to Raven."

"What?" Lieutenant Tompkins said.

"I can't talk to her," Beth repeated. "She's not here."

"Who's Raven?" Bannock asked.

"A ghost," Beth said. "She was, or is, an Arapaho shaman."

"Ghosts aren't out in the day," Bannock said. "Thank God." His eyes narrowed. "Are you a witch?"

"No," Lieutenant Tompkins interjected, "she can see ghosts like some, but she's not a witch."

"Good," Bannock said firmly. His shoulders tensed. He gave Beth a narrow-eyed look and tightened his hands around his horse's reins.

"I'll check the stables," he said. Then he rode off without looking back.

"What's going on with him?" Rose asked.

Lieutenant Tompkins shook his head. "No idea. But let's get started."

After a few hours, Beth's stomach stopped churning from the smell of the smoke and the burnt bodies. She'd wet her lips a few times from her canteen, but the hint of ash had almost made her throw up. Instead, she'd wrapped a bandanna across her face. It didn't block out much of the smell, but it helped a little. The smoke still made her eyes water.

She walked carefully through the destroyed fort. Embers swirled around, stirred up by the wind. Only the greenness of the spring grass had kept the fire from leaping from the fort to the prairie. Fortunately, there wasn't much debris. The buildings had been burned instead of smashed. Only corpses lay scattered across the yard.

There weren't many of those out in the open. Most of the soldiers and other fort residents had died trapped in burning buildings, though Bannock reported that some near the stables had been shot. He said the scorch marks indicated that the fire there had started inside. He figured the Shoshone had set it after they'd taken the horses.

The same was true of the armory, though being stone, it hadn't really burned. The soldiers outside had been shot. Beth found Lieutenant Tompkins studying a patch of dark grass about fifty yards from the armory door.

"What is it?" Beth asked.

"Blood," he replied. "A lot of it."

"But no body."

"No. It must've been one of theirs. They took it with them."

"So the guards got one." She looked back at the two corpses on either side of the armory door. They'd been looted of guns and ammunition, but were close enough to have had a good shot at whatever caused the blood.

Lieutenant Tompkins followed her gaze. "Something interesting about those two. Their wounds are too big for bullets."

"They were shot with arrows," Beth said.

"That's my thinking. But why take the arrows?"

"Good question," she said, "But a better one is, why use a bow and arrow at all? We know the Shoshone had rifles."

"The dwarves." He swore. "Just like the battlefield at Golden City."

"Mmm hmm," she said. "I've been wondering, though. If the

138

dwarves had rifles, they'd have killed us all, instead of just Raven and Mr. Weatherby. They can use them, can't they?"

"I don't see why not," he said. "Trolls can, if they modify ones they've taken from us to fit their hands. Dwarves would have an easier time modifying them. They might even be able to make them by now."

"But we've never seen dwarven-made guns."

"Rifles aren't easy to make," Lieutenant Tompkins said. "You can't just bang them out on a forge and get a straight barrel. You need special tooling, which we've tried to keep from the dwarves."

"Did the fort have that tooling?"

"No." He looked at the armory and scratched his chin. "When I was in there yesterday, it was mostly empty. They only had a few rifles...." His eyebrows rose. "The broken cannon!"

"Cannon?"

"There was a broken cannon in the armory," he said. "Private Bannock may know why, but it was there. The wheels and whole carriage were missing, so it was mostly just the barrel, but it was there."

"Could the dwarves replace those?"

"Maybe," he said. "Probably."

"We need to go in," Beth said with a nod toward the armory. Wisps of smoke still drifted out the door. "Think it's safe?"

"It should be. It's mostly stone, except for some shelves."

"Let's go."

The ruins of a big wooden desk smoldered just inside the armory door. One leg hadn't caught, and Lieutenant Tompkins used it to tug and pull the desk out of the building. He got a lungful of smoke in the process, which led to a huge coughing fit. While he recovered, Beth ducked into the building.

The armory consisted of a single large room with empty wooden shelves all around the walls. A high window on the far wall let in just enough sunlight to create deep dust-filled shadows. None of the shelves had been burned. The fire had never spread from the desk.

But other than the shelves, the armory was empty.

Beth crept along the rows of shelves and double-checked them to be sure. She found a box of empty shell casings and several rifle cleaning kits. Along one side sat a large empty area where Beth guessed the cannon must've rested. She was staring at it when she heard Lieutenant Tompkins come in.

"Find something?" he called. He then coughed hard.

"The Shoshone took the cannon."

He glanced around. "And the barrels of gunpowder. There were three, sitting right there." He pointed to a spot on the floor not far from where they stood.

"What about cannon balls?" Beth asked.

"There weren't any. But maybe the dwarves could use something else. They're clever."

"Yeah," she said, "that's what I've heard."

"Maybe we can catch up to them before they get too far."

She arched an eyebrow. "Four of us against more than twenty of them?"

"You're right," he admitted. "Besides, we need to see to our dead."

It took Lieutenant Tompkins and Bannock the rest of the day to locate all the bodies and arrange them in the center of the courtyard. The fort hadn't had its full complement, but still over a hundred people had died there the night before. Bannock wrote down names when he knew them and Lieutenant Tompkins put any personal effects he found into bags to save for the next of kin. Rose demurred and said she'd take care of the horses and set up a camp outside the fort, away from the smoke and death. She'd looked pale, but never once gotten sick or avoided helping in the search.

That had left Beth free to explore all the other buildings. The kitchen hadn't been thoroughly burned and she was able to rescue some dried fruit and a large jar of flour. She found a couple of knives in the blacksmith's forge that had been overlooked by the Shoshone. But otherwise, the Indians had picked the place clean.

A few times, she tried to summon Raven, but the ghost never appeared. Bannock had been right. Beth huffed in frustration after the third time and vowed to wait until dark.

The sun had just begun to set when Lieutenant Tompkins asked them to gather near the dead. Beth's gut sank into a small leaden ball as she surveyed the rows and rows of corpses. She recognized the jailer and the cook. Too many were burnt beyond recognition, though. At least a breeze had sprung up and helped carry the smell away.

Lieutenant Tompkins held a small Bible. He flipped it open and thumbed through it until he found a passage in the middle. He skimmed it and closed the book with his finger inside to mark the page. Then he looked at the others.

"Let's bow our heads," he said.

Beth studied the scuffed dirt at her feet.

"Dear Lord," Lieutenant Tompkins began, "we pray for the souls of our brothers and sisters, who have left this world for Your realm today. We pray that You might protect them and love them and care for them as they enter Heaven. May they have Your blessings and Your mercy, even for the sinners among them. For they are Your children, just as we are."

Bannock coughed, but quickly smothered it.

"Dear Lord," Lieutenant Tompkins continued, "grant mercy on Your children here, slain by a great evil. And grant mercy on us, who must face this evil. Yea, though we will walk through the valley of the shadow of death, we will fear no evil. For Thou art with us, and Thy rod and Thy staff will comfort us. We only ask for the courage to do Thy will."

"Amen," Rose said.

"Amen," Beth belatedly added.

She looked up, but Lieutenant Tompkins and Rose still had their heads bowed. Bannock looked at her with a wry grin, but he barely caught her attention before she sucked in her breath.

Two ghosts stood among the bodies, barely visible in the last vestiges of sunset.

One was Captain Whitaker's aide.

CHAPTER SEVENTEEN

Beth squinted and stared at the ghosts. In the fading light, they seemed barely there. Almost transparent. A gust of wind brushed through her hair. She pushed the stray strands back out of her face. Her eyes were dry and she blinked.

The ghosts were still there.

She instinctively clutched her chest for Raven's pouch. But the shaman hadn't appeared during the day ...

"We have visitors," Beth said. She didn't pull her eyes from the ghosts.

"What?" Lieutenant Tompkins said. "Where?"

Beth pointed with her chin. "Ghosts."

Bannock muttered something low and almost under his breath.

Beth strolled slowly around the bodies toward the ghosts. Captain Whitaker's aide turned and watched her. The other ghost just stared down at one of the bodies.

As she got closer, the ghosts appeared more distinct. She could make out the wrinkles in their clothes and the curls in their beards. They were less transparent, too. Almost as if the rays of the setting sun couldn't quite make it through their forms.

She stopped about ten feet from the aide. The ghost stood at the feet of a badly burned body. It stared at her, but didn't move or make any other acknowledgement that she was there.

"Can you hear me?" she asked.

It nodded and then said something.

"I'm sorry," she said. "I can't hear you."

It frowned and repeated what it said. Then it pointed toward the rows of bodies.

"I'm sorry."

It shook its head strongly and stabbed its fingers toward the bodies. The more she looked blankly, the more wildly it gestured.

She reached for Raven's pouch and rubbed it.

She shuddered as a chill swept over her.

Raven's ghost formed in the shadows in front of her. It gave her only a quick glance before turning toward the other ghosts.

The aide's ghost raised his eyebrows. It said something to Raven and then gestured toward the bodies. She said something back. They repeated the exchange a few times and then Raven nodded.

Raven's ghost turned to face Beth. She held up two fingers. Then she stroked them over her shoulder. When Beth's eyes widened, she did it on the other shoulder.

"Two ..." Beth said, "two bars!" She turned to Lieutenant Tompkins, who still stood on the far side of the morbid field. "Where's the captain?" she shouted. "Captain Whitaker?"

Lieutenant Tompkins scanned the corpses. Bannock did one better and hurried down the rows and looked at each one in turn.

Beth turned back to Raven and discovered she'd moved over to the second ghost. It still stared at its body, not moving, just like the Broken One on the battlefield.

The aide's ghost was gone.

Raven said something, and this Broken One raised its head and stared at her. Its shoulders shook like it was sobbing. Raven opened her arms, and then stepped forward. The Broken One turned and flowed into her hug.

She held him close, and then a grey fog appeared behind

them. They both faded from sight. First the Broken One, and then Raven.

"He's not here!" Bannock called. "His body's not here!"

"You sure?" Lieutenant Tompkins asked. "We didn't overlook him in one of the buildings by chance?"

"We double-checked them all together, sir, remember?"

"Maybe one of the burnt ones." Lieutenant Tompkins hustled over to the nearest one. He bent and looked at it closely. He shook his head and moved onto the next one.

Rose scrunched up her nose, but bent by a third body. With Beth and Bannock also joining in, it didn't take long to confirm that Captain Whitaker was not among the dead.

"They took him," Beth said once they'd all gathered together again. Night had completely fallen, giving only the light of a lantern Rose had lit to see by. "That's what the aide was trying to tell me."

"The aide?" Bannock asked. "His ... ghost?"

Beth nodded.

Even in the low light, she could see him grimace.

"But took him alive or dead?" Rose asked She looked worn, her eyes faded without their usual cheer. "And if alive, how did he survive the dragon's attack?"

"That *is* the question," Lieutenant Tompkins said. "I can't believe he'd go voluntarily."

"Why not, sir?" Bannock asked.

"He wasn't a traitor." Lieutenant Tompkins glared at the private.

Bannock just snorted in reply.

"So ..." Rose said. "what else do we need to do?" She glanced over at the corpses.

"Nothing," Lieutenant Tompkins said. He, too, looked sadly at the field of bodies. "I wish we had time to bury them...."

"It'd take days," Beth reminded him. "And if Whitaker's alive, we need to find him."

Lieutenant Tompkins clenched his jaw. "And find out if this happened to Fort Caspar too."

They stayed in Rose's camp outside the walls that night. They lit a small fire despite it being easily seen, as they figured anyone around would've investigated the fort by now. No one talked much. Rose prepared salted pork with a couple of eggs she'd managed to find undamaged in the Fort's henhouse.

After the supper dishes were cleaned, Rose turned in. Lieutenant Tompkins didn't argue when Bannock requested second watch and the Lieutenant said he'd take the third. Both men curled up in their bedrolls. Beth sat with her gun in her lap and watched the empty prairie.

She found it hard not to stare at the fort. So many deaths. So many.

Now that they weren't busy, she felt numb. It crept through her legs and her arms and her chest. She had to concentrate to breathe. Without the busyness ...

She forced herself to turn away. She watched the prairie east of the fort instead.

The numbness didn't fade.

Lieutenant Tompkins was right, she thought. *We were too late.*

Too late for Fort Sanders, and probably too late for Fort Caspar.

She was too numb.

She resorted to counting stars until Bannock relieved her and she could sleep.

They didn't catch up to the Shoshones' wagon the next day. Or the day after that. Or even the one after that. They rode through the windy plains with nothing in sight except small mountains not too far off to the west and the occasional creek crossing their path. Rain swept through twice in the afternoons, but with no shelter there was nothing to do but keep riding. It didn't last all that long anyway.

But the third night, as dusk fell, they came upon burned out ranchers' cabins near the Medicine Bow river. The two log buildings closest to the road stood like husks about fifty yards apart, with missing roofs and heavily charred walls. The door of one had collapsed into the dirt. A torn up split rail fence marked what had once been a small corral between them. The grass in front had been trampled hard.

Lieutenant Tompkins had them pause in the road. He and Bannock searched the buildings while Beth and Rose kept watch. When the men returned they looked grim.

"They're all dead," Lieutenant Tompkins said. "It looks like they were killed in their sleep."

"Including the children," Bannock added. He clenched his fists and trembled in rage.

"They were good people," Lieutenant Tompkins said. "Good people!" He swore and glared at the northern sky. "They didn't deserve this."

"Any ghosts?" Rose asked Beth quietly.

Beth looked carefully at the buildings. She couldn't make out a single shadow. She shook her head.

"We *are* burying them," Lieutenant Tompkins said. "No *children* will be left for the scavengers."

"Amen," Bannock said. "And then we kill the dragon, if it's the last thing we do."

"Or God take our souls," Lieutenant Tompkins said.

Bannock nodded solemnly. "Or God take our souls."

Rose and Beth rubbed down the horses by the light of the campfire. They'd set up a hundred yards downstream from the cabins, where a few scattered willows gave a hint of cover. The night breeze shook the trees and also brought the sound of the men's curses from further up. Beth couldn't make out their exact words, but the tone was clear. The light of the lantern they dug by was just barely visible in the distance even though the men themselves weren't.

Rose finished with her horse and returned to the fire. She stirred a pot of stew she'd set at the edge of the coals. The men had wanted to dig before they ate, and Beth found she didn't have much appetite either. At least Lieutenant Tompkins's impromptu memorial service had been short.

Rose sagged to the ground near the stew. She didn't even sweep her dress underneath her, and instead let it trail in the dirt. She brushed some hair out of her face and stirred the stew once again. Then she rubbed her cheek and somehow smudged dirt onto it.

Beth finished with her horse. Then she gingerly walked to Rose's side and sat down.

"I shouldn't've come," Rose said.

"We're all afraid," Beth said. She watched as Rose leaned forward and stirred the stew once again. The smell of beef and sage wafted over.

"Not all," Rose said. "The lieutenant? Yes, he's afraid. He doesn't cover it well."

"Neither does Bannock."

"Maybe." Rose shot her a small amused smile. "But he's not afraid of the dragon." She brushed more hair out of her face. "Neither are you. I can tell."

"Not of the dragon, no."

"It could kill us," Rose said. She looked back toward the distant lantern. They couldn't hear or see much, but the light flickered wildly. "Kill us as easily as it did those kids and their parents."

"So could the Shoshone, or the dwarves, or those cowboys back in Golden City."

"True."

They sat in silence for a moment, with only the pop and

crackle of the fire to break the stillness. Beth let her thoughts coalesce.

"Hickok," she finally said, "used to say that a gunfighter needed to be a little afraid of death, so they'd be cautious. But not so afraid of death that they'd hesitate at the wrong time."

Rose snorted.

"We'll keep you alive, Rose."

"'Cause I can't do it myself." She shook her head again and her fist tightened around her stirring spoon. A coal popped and a spark floated out of the fire pit. When it landed on the dirt, Rose stomped on it.

"But I can *cook*," Rose said. "And I can make camp. And I can charm those men in Caspar who won't even be there. But ..."

Her lower lip trembled.

Beth put a comforting hand on her friend's shoulder.

"I'm a burden," Rose said flatly.

"No, no—"

"I *am*," Rose said. "You'd be better off without me."

Beth reached down and took Rose's hand. She gave it a squeeze. Rose returned it and they sat silently, staring at the fire.

After a bit, Rose released her grasp and reached for the spoon. "Can't let the stew burn."

"Yes," Beth said. "If you don't take care of us, who will? I mean, I might start thinking I was a *boy*."

The corner of Rose's mouth turned up and her eyes danced for a moment, but she just stirred the stew instead.

They left at dawn the next day. The trail, though more grass-covered than before, was also clear. As they rode further, more low hills appeared on the western horizon. Otherwise the flat, dull terrain stretched as far as Beth could see.

In all that flatness, they didn't see the Shoshone. They didn't push the pace too hard, but Lieutenant Tompkins still insisted they go as fast as the horses could handle without injury. Finally, it grew too dark and he called a halt for the night when they crossed a small creek. Then he rode over to Beth.

"We've got another two or three days before we get to Fort Caspar," he said, "but we should've found the Shoshone by now. Any chance Raven can find them?"

"I'll ask." She dismounted and walked a bit away from the others. Her eyes had adjusted to the low light but she still turned her back to the last vestiges of sunlight. Then she pulled the pouch out and rubbed it.

The air cooled. Raven's ghost appeared, with a curious look in her eyes.

"Excuse me," Beth said. "We can't find the Shoshone. Can you?"

Raven slowly turned. She stared out at the horizon and then turned again. After a bit, she completed a full circle and faced Beth again.

She shook her head.

"Do you know where the dragon is?" Beth asked.

Raven pointed northwest, off the trail.

Toward a small distant flickering light in the sky.

CHAPTER EIGHTEEN

The faint light almost looked like a fat star. Except it flickered. Then it went out and returned a moment later. Clouds obscured some of the stars, but not it. It danced like a spark cast up by a fire. Then it dove toward the ground and disappeared.

Beth hurried over to the others. "The dragon! The dragon's that way!"

Bannock immediately whirled the direction she pointed. His gun was already in his hand.

"What? Where?" Lieutenant Tompkins asked. He too turned to where she pointed.

"A long ways away," Beth said. "It dove toward the ground."

"Hunting," Bannock said. He holstered his Colt. "How far?"

Beth described what she'd seen and pointed again.

"Are you sure?" Lieutenant Tompkins asked.

"I'm sure," Beth replied. "Nothing else moves like that."

Lieutenant Tompkins looked northwest the way she'd pointed. Then he looked north, up the trail to Fort Caspar. Then he looked back to the northwest.

"We don't have to decide right now," Beth said. She glanced around. Raven's ghost had already faded from view.

A cold dawn broke too early for Beth's taste. She hadn't slept well. Every lump and rock had seemed to find her back. But as she ambled toward the fire, Rose smiled at her. Her friend's face was clean and her hair back in perfect place under her bonnet. She'd changed into her second-best dress, a brown one with embroidered birds on the sleeves. She poured something from the coffee pot that had been resting on the edge of the fire into a pewter mug. Then she held it toward Beth.

Beth took it, sniffed, and then her eyebrows rose.

"Real coffee?" she said. She quickly took a sip. It *was*.

"I'd been saving it," Rose said. "After yesterday with the ranchers ... I decided today was the day."

"I thought Mr. Lake took it all with him," Beth said.

Rose gave her an enigmatic smile. Then she nodded toward the approaching Lieutenant Tompkins as she reached for another mug.

He accepted it with a grateful smile and a few soft words that made Rose's cheeks dimple. Then he turned to Beth.

"I'd still like to go to Fort Caspar," he said. "We don't know for sure that the dragon destroyed it."

"But it's likely."

He nodded. "The Shoshone must've left the trail somewhere or we'd have seen them by now."

"We can guess where they're going."

"True." He glanced northwest.

"I think we should go to Fort Caspar, too," she said. "But you're the commander. Why are you asking me?"

He snorted softly. "Commander. Yeah, that's funny." He turned and smiled at Bannock as the private approached.

"We'll leave for Caspar," Lieutenant Tompkins said quietly, "as soon as everyone's finished their coffee and whatever wonders Miss Chamberlin has in store for us this morning."

"It might be a while," Beth warned.

"If those wonders match the coffee ... we'll wait."

They were back on the trail well before mid-morning. The wind died and the sun beat down hotter than before. They refilled their already empty canteens at the next stream they passed. By midday, the sweat had started to bead on Beth's forehead and neck.

They found next to no shade, though. The plains and scattered hills stretched on with only a small scattering of scruffy pines here and there. They didn't spot the dragon. Nor did they see anyone else.

Just before dusk, Rose asked if they could stop early so she could learn to shoot. Lieutenant Tompkins immediately volunteered to teach her. She looked expectantly at Beth.

"Go," Beth said with a chuckle. "I'll get supper started."

Rose smiled and let the lieutenant lead her east out of camp twenty or thirty yards.

Beth unpacked the pots and stirring spoons. She left Bannock building the fire ring and filled both pots at the nearby creek. When she returned, he stood with his hands on his hips. He was looking around with a frown.

"Problem?" she asked.

"There's no wood." He gestured toward a few thin bushes a little ways down the creek. "Those are too green to burn."

"Buffalo chips?"

"If I can find them." He looked at her pots and scowled. "How much do I need?"

"Not much. Just enough to boil these." She held the heavy pots up.

He eyed them and his lips pursed together. "So you're cooking now," he said. "You can do it all."

"You don't cook?" she challenged.

"I can," he admitted.

"Then why is it a surprise that I can?"

He shuffled his feet and then stared at the horizon. "I guess it's not," he finally said.

"It's about the ghosts," she said. "Isn't it? That I can see them?"

"And what if it is?"

"Are you afraid of them?"

"Nah." He kicked a small rock. "I just don't trust 'em. Some of them can be downright evil."

"How do you know?" she asked. "You can't even see them."

"Thank God," he said with a snort. He faced her and straightened his spine. But when he saw her glare, he continued. "I had ... a friend, a good friend ... who could talk to them."

"A witch?"

Bannock waved dismissively. "Something like that. But they scared him. He said most were angry and wanted to kill people like me."

"But they couldn't," she said. "They can't. My friend Maria, who *is* a witch, says they can't touch anyone in the physical world, just like we can't touch them. So why be scared?"

He blinked. Then he looked away. "I think I need to find something that will burn."

They rode briskly the next day. The hills to the sides grew taller, though not quite as high as the mountains around Golden City or Grand Lake. Pine trees appeared too, first at a distance, and then gradually closer and closer to the road. Aspens mixed in among them as the trail began to slowly climb.

"Fort Caspar is over this mountain," Lieutenant Tompkins said during their midday rest break. "We should be able to see it from the ridge."

Beth eyed the trees that continued to encroach on the trail. "It'd be a good place for an ambush."

"Hmm. You're right," Lieutenant Tompkins said. "Private Bannock, will you ride point?"

Bannock grumbled something under his breath, but nodded.

When they set out again, Bannock rode out alone. Lieutenant Tompkins gave him about five minutes before he motioned for the rest of them to follow.

The trail curved through the trees and the slope continued to increase. The trees grew close enough to shade them from the afternoon sun. They rode quietly for about an hour, with only the clop of the horses' hooves and the occasional jangle of the tack. The ever-present wind had actually died to just an occasional swirl of the leaves.

But no ambush came. Another hour, and then another hour, and then they came upon Bannock waiting for them. He looked grim, and pointed ahead to where the trees broke at the top of the ridge.

Beth sucked in her breath as they crested that final ridge above Fort Caspar. Even several miles off, it was clear it'd been burned and destroyed. What was left of the walls stood black against the brown prairie. Scattered greenish bushes by the river and the occasional tree made the corpse of the fort even more obvious by contrast. The hot sun cast long shadows, but there were few places for survivors to hide.

She'd expected the fort's devastation, but still felt ill at the sight. Lieutenant Tompkins muttered several curses and his face turned steely hard. He barely took his eyes off the fort as they descended the trail to the flat land.

They rode across the short plain toward the fort as the sun started to flirt with the horizon. Fort Caspar sat in a loop of the North Platte River, near the southern shore. Lieutenant Tompkins led them to a spot upstream about a half mile from the fort. A few scattered willows grew there and an old fire ring sat in the center of a large flat spot.

"Will you ladies please set up camp while Private Bannock and I scout the fort?" he asked once they'd ridden there.

Beth started to balk, but Rose quickly spoke.

"Good," she said. "Beth can keep a look out for the dragon."

Beth almost said that was silly, but after a warning look from Rose, she acquiesced with a reluctant nod. The four of them staked the horses a little ways downstream from the camp and then the men strode off toward the fort. Beth and Rose gathered firewood, started the fire, got some water heating, unpacked food and bedrolls, and then started to rub down the horses. As they worked, Beth looked over at her friend.

"You don't really expect the dragon to show, do you?" Beth asked.

"No. I ... I just didn't want to go to the fort, and I didn't want to be alone either." She scanned the skies to the northwest. "Besides, the dragon *might* be out there."

"Are you really afraid of it?"

"No," Rose said, then more emphatically, "No!" She stepped back from the horse she was working on and glared at its side, as if looking for a stain like on one of the Astor's tables. "They're going to kill it, anyway. The lieutenant promised!"

"*We're* going to kill it," Beth gently corrected. "All of us."

"I don't know what I'm going to do," Rose said. "I can barely hold the gun."

"You didn't say anything after your lesson."

"I was embarrassed. I wasn't any good."

"It took me years to get good," Beth said. "Everyone's bad after their first lesson."

"I know you want to poke around the fort," Rose said, "but ... thank you. For staying with me."

"You'd be fine," Beth said. "C'mon, let's finish up and then I can give you a shooting lesson before the men come back."

Lieutenant Tompkins and Bannock returned just as the last of the twilight faded and true dark set in. Rose had stew simmering on a low fire, along with some chicory coffee. It didn't smell at all like the real thing, to Beth's disappointment.

The breeze kept batting at the fire's flames, which caused wild shadows to dance across the ground. Beth actually started when the men stepped out of the darkness. They looked haggard and haunted.

She recovered quickly and asked, "What'd you find?"

"It's destroyed like Fort Sanders," Lieutenant Tompkins said somberly. "Everything but the stables and armory were burned first, with the men inside. We'll gather the bodies and have a memorial service tomorrow."

"What'd they take from the armory?" she asked.

"We don't know," he admitted. "Ours was wood and they burned it after the attack."

She furrowed her brow. "How do you know it was burned after instead of before?"

"The walls were still standing. We stored a lot of gunpowder there and it would've blown the walls if it'd gone off."

"Gunpowder." Beth felt the certainty of the word on her tongue. "That's it."

"That's what?"

"Why they needed the wagon," she said. Her eyes widened and her heart pounded. "That's what they were after! Sure, they wanted the other guns, but they were really after the gunpowder."

"But why?" Lieutenant Tompkins asked. "They only have half a cannon—"

"Which they probably can't use," Beth said. "Besides, they have a dragon, so they don't need cannons. They need the gunpowder for something more powerful than cannons. Or the dragon. I can't imagine what."

"Now *that*," Lieutenant Tompkins said, "is truly frightening."

CHAPTER NINETEEN

Beth stirred restlessly when dawn arrived. She'd slept poorly, with vague, alarming dreams that faded as soon as she'd finished rubbing her eyes. The day promised to be hot, with only a few clouds in the sky.

After breakfast, Rose said she wanted to do some foraging along the creek. She wanted to look for edible plants and maybe some medicinal plants. She didn't think she'd find much, but it was worth a try, she'd said. It was clear she didn't want to go to the fort.

"You really don't want to go," Bannock said grimly. "It's worse than Fort Sanders." He glanced at Lieutenant Tompkins, who just stared into the distance with haunted eyes.

"Are you all right, Lieutenant?" Rose asked.

He shook himself. "Too many friends." He looked sadly at Rose. "Some of them are ... horrible."

"How is it worse?" Beth asked Bannock quietly.

"Scavengers," he said. "Many of the bodies have been partially eaten...."

"Oh, how awful," Rose said. She placed her hand on Lieutenant Tompkins's. "It must be so hard."

He snorted and gave her a small smile.

"Take a gun," Beth said to Rose. "I'm going with the men."

Rose looked at her askance. "Are you sure?"

"You can always fire it into the air," Beth said. "We'll hear the shot and come running."

Rose slowly nodded. "I suppose...."

"We should be ready for the service at sunset," Bannock said. "We'll come get you before then."

Rose reluctantly nodded.

Beth pursed her lips. *And after sunset, I can look for ghosts.*

They held the service in what was left of the fort's courtyard. Like at Fort Sanders, Lieutenant Tompkins and Bannock had laid out the bodies in rows. This time, they'd started a small fire near the stables, where two walls still stood. It and a couple of flickering torches gave them enough light to see all but the features of the dead.

Beth considered that a blessing. The rotten smell of the bodies overwhelmed her senses. Rose was clearly struggling to keep her dinner down. Beth herself wasn't much better, but she managed.

The four of them stood side by side near the bodies and faced them. Bannock clasped his hands behind his back, while Rose did the same in front. Lieutenant Tompkins pulled out his small Bible and flipped to the middle. He rubbed the page and bent the spine back, nearly breaking it. Then he bowed his head.

The others did the same, but Beth immediately peeked up. She hadn't seen any ghosts yet, but it wasn't quite fully dark.

"Dear Lord," Lieutenant Tompkins began, "We pray for these people, your children in Christ. We pray that you take up their souls to heaven, to be with you in your Glory. They were good people, Lord. They had their flaws and sins, but they tried to do Your will. They ..."

His voice cracked.

"They ..." he continued, "they did not deserve this end ..." He broke off and stared at the page in his Bible. After a long pause, he began to read aloud, "The Lord is my shepherd, I shall not want ..."

Beth's gaze moved from body to body. Lieutenant Tompkins's voice faded as she concentrated on what she could see. No grey shapes stood near any bodies. Or knelt. Or sat. No ghosts of any sort.

She had to check.

"... yea, though I walk through the valley of death, I shall fear no evil ..."

Beth snuck a hand up to her chest and rubbed Raven's pouch through her shirt.

"... for thou art with me, thy rod and staff they comfort me ..."

Beth's skin prickled with newly cool air. She let out a relieved breath and raised her head. Raven's ghost stood a few feet away. Like always, the ghost wore a thin smile.

"... surely goodness and mercy shall follow me ..."

Beth glanced at the others. Rose still bowed her head as Lieutenant Tompkins read. Bannock, though, stared at the bodies. He must've sensed Beth's head turn, because he looked over at her.

"... Amen."

Bannock raised an eyebrow, silently questioning.

"Any ghosts?" Beth quietly asked Raven, while mostly watching Bannock.

Raven shook her head.

Beth met Bannock's eyes and did the same.

He let out a long breath and his shoulders relaxed.

"Do you know where to go from here?" Beth asked.

The ghost nodded, and then pointed west.

Beth and Rose waited in camp while Lieutenant Tompkins and Bannock did their best to set a funeral pyre. Too much of the fort had already been burnt, though. The flames barely glowed in the distance in the warm night. Beth couldn't help wondering if it was enough.

Hickok had said it'd taken a month to bury all the dead from the Battle of Golden City, even with mass graves. And they'd only buried the humans. The giants had been left for the scavengers.

He'd drunk heavily the night he'd told her that.

She could almost taste the whiskey herself. As the wind tousled her hair, she tried to look away from the fort and the flames. She couldn't. Even with the pit in her gut. Even with the tightness in her heart.

Rose came to her side. She gave Beth a forlorn smile before also staring at the fort. Then she reached over and took Beth's hand. Beth squeezed hers in return.

They kept their vigil in silence.

Lieutenant Tompkins and Bannock stumbled back through the dark. When they saw the women, Lieutenant Tompkins pulled up short. His mouth opened, as if he were about to speak, but then he closed it and shook his head. Bannock just glanced their way and headed for his bedroll.

"We have chicory coffee on the fire," Rose said quietly to Lieutenant Tompkins. "It's not much but ..."

He shook his head and gave a rueful laugh. "We should've packed more whiskey."

"Mmm hmm," Beth said.

He looked at her. "See any ghosts tonight?"

"Just Raven. She says to go west."

"Any idea how far?"

"No, but we can ask her." Beth glanced over at Bannock, but the private was already stretched out on the ground, though not quite asleep. "Let's move further away."

Lieutenant Tompkins nodded and let Beth lead him and Rose to the edge of the river, beyond where the horses shuffled and snorted. Beth rubbed Raven's pouch and let out a relieved breath when the ghost appeared.

"Hello," Beth said. "We need to know where the dragon's lair is."

Raven's ghost pointed west.

"How far?"

The ghost held up ten fingers, and then two more.

"Twelve days?" After the ghost nodded, Beth asked, "How will we recognize it?"

Raven loosely clasped her hands, like she held something round between them, like a cup, or a pole. Then she raised her arms, which lifted the imaginary cup, until it was above her head. Then she pulled her arms apart and spread her fingers as she did.

"I don't understand," Beth said.

Raven repeated the gesture.

"I still don't understand."

"What's she doing?" Lieutenant Tompkins asked.

"This." Beth moved her hands like Raven had done.

Lieutenant Tompkins's eyes widened and his mouth dropped open.

"Do you know it?" Rose asked. "Do you know what it is?"

"I think ..." he said, "I think ... that's one of the geysers in the Great Geyser Basin. The area we call Yellowstone."

Raven's ghost nodded, and then faded from view.

CHAPTER TWENTY

The night seemed warmer without the ghost. The distant whirr of the insects returned, as well as the tumbling tinkle of the river.

Beth's chest tightened as she watched Lieutenant Tompkins tense up. His shoulders went tight. His lips thinned and he sucked in his breath.

"What?" Rose asked. "What's wrong?"

"That's the Devil's land," he said. "Sulfur and hot mud bubbles out of the ground. There are ponds that will kill you if you drink from them. And then there's the geysers, shooting steam high into the sky."

"How awful," Rose said.

"It's not all bad, I'm told," Lieutenant Tompkins said. "There's supposed to be plenty of forest and meadows and places to walk without any of those things. But still ..."

"If that's where the dragon is, that's where we're going," Beth said.

"Agreed," Lieutenant Tompkins said.

Rose's eyes narrowed in thought. "It's a twelve-day trip, isn't it? Then we need food. We were going to get more at Fort Caspar...." She nodded toward the ruins.

"We can hunt," Lieutenant Tompkins said. "There should be plenty of antelope around."

"Even with the dragon eating everything?" Beth asked.

Lieutenant Tompkins grimaced, but conceded the point with a nod.

"We also need bullets," Rose said. She looked at Beth and Lieutenant Tompkins. "Unless you have enough?"

"Maybe," Beth said with a grimace. "We'll have to do less live fire practice."

"Oh!" Rose said. "I don't want—oh, of course." She looked sadly at Lieutenant Tompkins. "Can we still practice then?"

He smiled warmly at her. "I'm sure we can come up with something."

The next morning, they filled their canteens and struck out northwest across the prairie. Without any trail or track, they meandered over the next five days as they looked for streams. The hot sun parched Beth's throat and she drank greedily when they found one. Her clothes itched as they gathered dust and dirt, but at least she could wash her face from time to time.

Rose had it worse. Her coolest dress, a cotton flower print from before the War, still had a high collar and sleeves she couldn't push up far. She constantly wiped her brow with her handkerchief, but eventually used even her sleeve.

Still, as exhausted as she was, Rose insisted on shooting practice with Lieutenant Tompkins every night after they'd made camp. Beth couldn't help smile at the sparkle in Rose's eyes every time the two of them headed out of camp together. Bannock went hunting for rabbits and other small game so Beth usually headed the other way for her own practice. It'd been too long, and if she didn't keep it up, she'd suffer.

On the fifth day they reached a larger river flowing north and south, so Bannock decided to try fishing with a hook and line he'd packed. They ate well on brook trout that night, and the following morning they found a place to ford the river. They headed west up a small meandering tributary that was often so narrow Beth could've jumped across it. The land grew hillier, but the ridges to either side of their broad valley were as barren as the plains. At least the wind wasn't as fierce.

After another five days, mountains rose in front of them. The valley started to narrow and head northwest. The ridges came in closer and more cottonwoods and pines appeared along the creek. Then the slopes grew less barren with scattered lonesome pines here and there.

Beth rode nervously. They hadn't caught sight of the dragon once, nor the dwarves, nor the Shoshone. She'd begun to doubt they were headed the right way, but each night she rubbed Raven's pouch and the ghost pointed northwest.

The morning of the eleventh day, dawn broke accompanied by a stiff cool breeze blowing down the valley. They'd camped by the creek near some pines that didn't quite provide a windbreak. Beth's exposed wrists were covered in goosebumps. She sat on a small flat rock and sipped what Rose said was the last of the chicory coffee. She puckered her lips at the sour taste. It made the last of the biscuits less dry, though.

Across the fire pit, Lieutenant Tompkins and Bannock argued quietly. Bannock wanted to hunt some more before they headed further into the mountains. He hadn't bagged a rabbit or any other game in two days and their food was running low. Lieutenant Tompkins worried that the gunshots would draw attention now that they were getting close to Yellowstone.

Rose sat down next to Beth with her own cup of chicory coffee. She'd given up on more than loosely tying her hair back. Smudges of ash covered the sleeve of her dress. At least they'd both managed to wash their faces in the creek the night before.

Rose tilted her head toward the men. "You'd think they'd ask our opinion."

"Sometimes they do," Beth said with a shrug.

"Not enough," Rose said. "I truly like the lieutenant, but ..." She snorted softly. "You're rubbing off on me."

Beth chuckled. "I'd say the same, but ..." She gestured down at her pants.

"There's time," Rose said with a twinkle in her eye. "Maybe when this is over, we can go to the big city."

"San Francisco?"

"I was thinking Salt Lake," Rose said. "But San Francisco would be nice. I'd like to see the ocean."

"I hear you can see to the horizon."

"You can do that here," Rose said with a gesture to the east. "Or at least, we could. Not that I'm going to miss it."

Beth chuckled. "Yeah."

Before she could say more, Lieutenant Tompkins stood up. He and Bannock had a few last words and then he turned to the ladies.

"Excuse me," he said, "but what is the inventory of our remaining food supplies?"

"We have enough dried meat and hard tack for another day," Rose answered, "maybe two."

He grimaced, and then turned to Bannock. "Fine, hunt in the morning, after we're all packed up. That way we can run if there's trouble."

Bannock grinned. "That's fine. Let me have third watch, and I'll be ready to go by the time everyone's finished breakfast."

"I'll go with you," Beth said. "I'm pretty good hunting prairie dogs."

Bannock smirked. "Those move fast. But how are you with elk?"

"If we see an elk, I'll let you know."

Bannock woke Beth just before dawn, when the glow of the sky had started, but the sun had not yet peeked over the horizon. She jerked upright, with her hand on her Colt, but relaxed immediately. He only flinched a little, and then a slow grin crossed his face.

"You always this jumpy?" he asked. His eyes sparkled like he was teasing her.

"No," she said. "Only when there might be danger around."

"Fair enough. Get yourself ready and we'll go." He stood and walked to the edge of camp.

About fifteen minutes later, they headed to the creek and then slowly crept their way upstream. They moved carefully, with Bannock in the lead by about five feet. A light breeze fluttered the branches of the aspens and pines as they walked. Beth bowed her head a little to keep the dust out of her eyes but that made it hard to watch for prey.

As the sun crested the horizon, the morning insects hummed and danced. A fish jumped in the creek, but otherwise they saw nothing big enough to eat. Once Bannock stopped and cocked his head, listening. He glanced back at Beth. After she shook her head, he kept going.

They walked for quite a while, maybe an hour, before a squirrel rattled up one of the nearby trees, far too fast to shoot.

Maybe there's nothing to hunt, Beth silently groused. *Maybe the dragon got it all.*

But then a splash! A big one, from just around a tree-shrouded bend in the creek. Beth almost jumped in surprise, but managed to keep her feet planted. Bannock remained similarly still.

Beth slowly crept closer. When she reached Bannock, he put a hand out to stop her. She gave him a questioning look. Moving very slowly, he pointed ahead and across the creek.

Something moved and shifted behind the scattered trees. Something big like an elk, but ...

A horse. Horses. It looked like two, but the trees obscured them.

Bannock had brought his rifle and he slowly raised it high. He didn't quite put it to his shoulder, but Beth was sure he could do so in an instant. She quietly drew her Colt and rotated the barrel off the empty cylinder.

As quietly as they could, they stole forward.

After about ten yards, the trees thinned. They heard low voices, but couldn't quite make out any words. Another five yards and they could make out a small clearing ahead, just across the water. Beth smelled smoke now.

The people in the clearing hadn't noticed them yet, so Bannock and Beth continued to ease closer.

Two Shoshone warriors in buckskin shirts and pants crouched around a small fire. They were roasting a large fish impaled on a stick. They talked too quietly to make out their words, even if Beth had understood the language. Behind them, the horses shuffled and grazed.

Bannock looked at her and moved close enough to whisper, "Take 'em prisoner?"

She took a deep breath and nodded. Then she raised her gun and pointed it at the Shoshone on the left. Bannock nestled his rifle into his shoulder and aimed at the one on the right.

Then they stepped out of the trees.

The Shoshones' heads snapped up and they stared. Before they could move, Bannock barked something that Beth couldn't understand. When the Shoshone didn't respond, he said it again, louder.

The Shoshone on the right said something back. The disdain in his voice was impossible to miss. He slowly stood but didn't reach for the rifle leaning against a nearby log. The one on the left shifted in place. He held the stick with the fish, but his eyes darted toward his own rifle, which rested against a pine tree trunk just several feet to his side.

Bannock said something else. He took a step forward and barked it again.

Something moved upstream.

"Down!" Beth yelled. She dropped to one knee and whirled toward the movement.

Bannock spun and twisted. A long fishing spear flashed through the air. It grazed his side as he fell to the ground.

The other Shoshones scrambled for their guns. Beth whipped back toward them and fired. Two shots at the standing Indian. Two at the one on the ground, who'd dropped the fish. They both fell as she searched for the spear thrower.

Tree branches swayed upstream. She couldn't see the Shoshone, so she held her fire. No point in spending her last loaded bullet on a bad shot.

Bannock writhed on the ground. He cursed under his breath as he clutched his ribs.

Beth checked on the Shoshones she'd shot. The one that'd stood lay still on his face. Blood soaked his buckskin jacket on both his side and his back.

But Fish Man still lived. She'd only hit him in the leg. But he clawed the dirt near his head. He kept reaching for the rifle about five feet from his hand. It looked like it'd take him a while to reach it.

Beth looked upstream. She couldn't see the third Shoshone. Bannock cried out in pain. Fish Man pulled himself a little closer to his gun.

She knelt by Bannock's side. "How bad is it?"

"I'll live," he hissed.

She nodded and holstered her Colt. Then she picked up his loaded rifle. It felt clunky and heavy in her arms. No shots or spears came from upstream. She stood and brought it up.

Fish Man had managed to scramble another six inches.

She leveled the rifle at him. "No!"

He looked at her and froze.

"Don't do it!" she shouted.

He understood her tone, if not her words. He remained still.

With a quick sideways glance upstream, where nothing moved, she strode forward to the edge of the stream. She kept the rifle pointed at him the entire time.

Bannock called out something in Shoshone.

Fish Man slowly raised his hands by his ears in a gesture of surrender.

Beth quickly forded the stream at a spot that only soaked her to above her knees. She almost slipped on a slimy rock once, but not enough to take her eyes off Fish Man. He remained still, with one hand pressed on the wound in his thigh.

When she finally got across the creek, she scanned their little camp. Never turning her back on Fish Man, she circled to his rifle. His eyes narrowed in anger as she picked it up and quickly tossed it across the creek.

Still she kept the rifle leveled at Fish Man as she circled for the fallen Shoshone's gun. When she got there, she spotted a third rifle leaning against the same log.

The spear fisherman left his gun behind, she realized. She let out a relieved breath and switched back to her Colt. It didn't take long to reload and would be far better defense if Spear Chucker tried to jump her from the trees.

"Where's the other one?" Bannock called. He'd managed to sit up, but was clutching his side.

"Don't know," she yelled back. "But I've got his rifle!" She quickly counted the horses. "There's only three of them, too."

"Good." Bannock started to stand, but hissed in pain. He clutched his side and sank back to the ground.

Beth eyes widened in alarm. "What do you need?"

"Secure him first," Bannock replied, with a toss of his head toward Fish Man. "This," he indicated his ribs, "is pretty shallow."

"Secure him with what?"

"Dunno."

Beth glanced around. There wasn't anything near the fire that could be used as rope. Maybe they had something on their horses, or maybe she could use the bridles.

But the horses were gone.

CHAPTER TWENTY-ONE

Beth ran to where the horses had been. No sign of them. A thin trail led away through the trees. It curved around a small ridge with several thick pines which ominously shaded the path. She took a deep breath and a first stride down the trail. Then she stopped.

It'd be a perfect place for an ambush, she thought. *And you're leaving an enemy capable of action behind you.*

Her blood raced. Fish Man was down, but not out. She took another deep breath and then turned back to the camp.

Fish Man lay on his side. His hands pressed hard on the wound in his leg. Blood covered them and his trousers. He breathed fast, but didn't cry out. He glared at her, but made no efforts to move like he had before. The gun was too far away now, anyway.

Bannock had managed to sit up. He still clutched his side, but he forced a smile. Or at least a grimace that looked kind of like a smile.

"The third one must've taken their horses," Beth said.

"He's still got a knife," Bannock said with a nod of his head toward Fish Man. "On his belt." He yelled something in Shoshone.

Fish Man's eyes narrowed.

Beth pointed her Colt at him and made a show of cocking the hammer back.

Bannock called out in Shoshone again.

Fish Man slowly, carefully reached for his knife. He kept his eyes on Beth as he slowly unsheathed it and tossed it aside. Then he said something loud and sharp.

"What'd he say?" Beth asked Bannock.

"He said he wants a quick death," Bannock replied.

"What? No!" Beth said. "We're not going to kill him!"

"It's going to be hard to keep him as a prisoner."

Beth scowled. "We don't kill the helpless." She couldn't imagine doing it. Gunslingers who killed helpless men were cowards. And criminals. Hickok would never speak to her again. Heck, he might even *arrest* her.

"Didn't say we should," Bannock said. "It's just what he expects."

"Why?" She looked around the camp one more time for something that could be used to tie up Fish Man.

"It's what he'd do," Bannock said dryly. "Take the scalp. Brag about his victory. Use it as an excuse to get some firewater and get falling down drunk. Show what a big warrior he is." He said something in Shoshone, heavy in sarcasm, to Fish Man.

Fish Man narrowed his eyes but didn't respond.

"Keep him covered," Beth said. She took the bandanna from around her neck.

"What are you going to do?" Bannock asked.

"Bind his wound. And then see if he can walk. You can, can't you?"

"Yeah."

"Good. I don't want to be here if his friend comes back."

She slowly moved around behind the Indian. He twisted as best he could to look over his shoulder at her, but then winced in pain. When she knelt, he slowly pulled his hand away.

The bleeding had slowed, if not stopped. Beth quickly wrapped her makeshift bandage around the wound and pulled it tight. Fish Man sucked in his breath but didn't cry out. When she finished she stepped back. It looked good, with only a little blood seeping through.

"Can you sit up?" She asked. She gestured to show what she meant as Bannock translated her question.

Fish Man nodded and slowly pushed himself up and swung his legs around until they were in front of him. The bandage didn't show more blood, so she, with Bannock translating, had him put his hands behind his back.

Beth glanced around the camp one more time. "We still don't have anything to secure him with."

"I'd offer my shirt," Bannock said. He started to shrug but then stopped with a grimace. He glanced down at his side. "But I think it's stopping the bleeding."

"Well," Beth said, "we can't use my shirt."

"Why not? You've got something on underneath, right?"

Beth bristled, but she met Bannock's eyes. His held none of the leer she'd seen too often in the Astor's parlor. They didn't drop down her body either, like he was picturing what he couldn't see.

"No," she said firmly. "There's got to be a better way." She could use Fish Man's shirt, or—

The dead Indian. Of course.

She went to the corpse and wrinkled her nose from the smell. Already flies buzzed in a small cloud over its back, where the blood now dried a horrible brown. The seat of his pants was an equal, awful mess.

She took a deep breath. *I don't need the whole shirt. I just need enough to tie his wrists. Like a cord.*

A cord. Like he'd use to hold up his pants. She looked closer. The dead Indian's pants had one. She rolled him to his back so she could untie it. His head flopped and his lifeless eyes stared up at her.

She couldn't stop the shudder that ran up her back.

He was reaching for his rifle, she reminded herself. *And the*

Shoshone we saw outside Fort Sanders said they'd scalp us if they saw us again.

It didn't calm her stomach.

Fortunately, it didn't take long to untie the cord and remove it from the corpse. She just avoided looking at his face.

It also didn't take long to tie Fish Man's wrists. She avoided looking at his face, too, but that was mutual.

Once she was done, she reached under his armpits and pulled. He got the message and stumbled to his feet. He kept all his weight on his good leg and didn't look at her. Instead his eyes stayed fixed on Bannock.

The private managed to shuffle to his own feet. He still clutched his side, but only winced when he moved. He kept his Colt pointed at Fish Man while Beth gathered up the Indians' guns, and the fish they'd been cooking. Then they were on their way.

The midmorning sun beat down hot and only the intermittent shade of the trees kept it from being beastly. They stopped more times than Beth could count to rest. Fish Man *could* walk, but not well. After a half hour, Bannock pointed out a branch on a dead tree that could be turned into a crutch with a little work. Beth took care of it while Fish Man and Bannock drank from her canteen.

They stumbled into sight of camp another long, long while later. Small curls of smoke rose from the fire and Rose stirred the ashes with a stick. Her bonnet hung slack around her neck, but her eyes filled with shock when she saw them. She quickly called for Lieutenant Tompkins, off near the horses with their filled saddlebags, and they both rushed over.

"What's this?" Lieutenant Tompkins asked. "Who's this?"

"A prisoner," Beth said. "I call him Fish Man." She passed the fish in question to Rose, who accepted it with open arms.

Bannock said something in Shoshone, and Fish Man replied in a few short syllables.

"His name is Running Bear," Bannock said.

"We surprised them and they wanted to fight," Beth said. She described their encounter and the aftermath, to Rose's growing alarm.

Rose turned to Bannock and she looked at his side. "How bad is it?"

"Just a shallow cut," he said. "And maybe some cracked ribs."

"Let's get it cleaned up." Rose gave one last wary look at Running Bear before taking Bannock by the arm and guiding him toward the fire. "I have some water boiling for berry tea, but it might be better for your side."

"Much obliged," Bannock said. He let her lead him toward the fire.

Lieutenant Tompkins's eyes went from Beth to Running Bear then back to Beth.

"You said one escaped," he said. "He'll get reinforcements. We'll be facing more Shoshone soon."

"It depends on how long it takes him to get back to their camp," Beth said.

"True," he said. "We'll question your prisoner after Bannock's been taken care of." Then he motioned for them to follow him toward the camp.

Running Bear wasn't very forthcoming. He sat sullenly by the little fire and answered Bannock's questions in single words or short phrases. He let Rose clean and re-bandage his wound and he even accepted a little fish to eat, but neither loosened his tongue.

Lieutenant Tompkins sat next to Bannock and suggested questions to ask. His shoulders tensed and his scowl grew as Bannock relayed each non-answer. Running Bear claimed he didn't know where the tribe was camped. He didn't know anything about a dragon. He didn't know anything about dwarves or the attacks on the forts.

Beth studied Running Bear as she wolfed down her own fish. She'd been hungrier than she'd thought and she barely tasted the flaky trout that Rose had fried in a little salt and fat. But she didn't take her eyes off the Indian. From the way his shoulders slumped and the way he avoided looking at Bannock, she was sure he was lying.

"Tell him I'm sorry for shooting him," she said during a lull in Bannock's questions. "Tell him I'm sorry about his friend."

Her gut twinged. *I am sorry. Sorry I had to do it. But it was him or me.*

Bannock looked at her with a raised eyebrow, but then said something to Running Bear in Shoshone. The Indian looked up at her with surprise.

"Ask him what we can do for his friend," Beth said. "If we should bury him or what. Should we have a service?"

"Burial," Bannock replied. Then he turned to Running Bear and said something else. When Running Bear replied, Bannock's eyebrows shot toward the sky. He started talking animatedly.

Running Bear's face filled with shock, but then he started speaking quickly and gesturing wildly. Finally after several exchanges they fell silent and Bannock turned to the others.

"The dead man is—was—Grey Wolf," he said. "I knew him when we were both boys."

"You knew him?" Beth asked. "How?"

"When I lived with the Shoshone," Bannock said, "but he was older. We didn't spend much time together."

Running Bear said something and the excited conversation in Shoshone started up again. Beth, Rose, and Lieutenant Tompkins shared some questioning looks.

The conversation in Shoshone grew more animated until Bannock gasped. "No!" he said in English. "He didn't!"

Running Bear repeated what he'd said last, and when Bannock replied in Shoshone, the Indian nodded his head. Bannock's face hardened and he muttered a curse under his breath. Then he once again turned to the confused onlookers.

"If we bury Grey Wolf," Bannock said, "and take care of Running Bear's wound, he'll take us to the Shoshone camp."

"Is that a good idea?" Rose asked. She'd gotten stiffer and more pale the longer the conversation had gone on.

"I don't know," Bannock admitted. He gestured at Running Bear. "He thinks it is. But the war leader or new medicine man might not honor Running Bear's pledge of safe passage."

"Let's go back to that part where you lived with the Shoshone," Lieutenant Tompkins said.

"Ah," Bannock said. "Yes. That."

"It might've been good to know more about it before now," Lieutenant Tompkins drawled.

Bannock let out a heavy sigh. He stared off into the distance for a while.

"We don't need to know everything," Beth said. "But we need to know some."

"Fine," Bannock said. He took a deep breath. "We lived in Nebraska Territory when the Jotun came. Me and Pa and my big brother. I was seven. Ma had died." He looked at Lieutenant Tompkins. "The army came through, sir, luring the Jotun along the Platte to Golden City. Pa and my brother both joined up."

"Mmm hmm," Lieutenant Tompkins said. He gestured for Bannock to go on.

Bannock started to, but balked, and then caught himself. His chest tightened and he once again stared off into space with distant memories.

"Are they still alive?" Beth asked gently.

"No," Bannock said. He gave her a sad smile. "They both died at the Battle of Golden City. But I was too young to go with them, so ... Pa sold me to the Indians."

"Sold?" Rose said with a gasp.

"For a gun and a horse," he said. Then he chuckled darkly. "He wanted more but apparently that's all I was worth."

Beth cringed in sympathy.

"Then what?" Lieutenant Tompkins asked.

"The Arapaho," Bannock said, "took me west. I spent the summer with them, and in the fall they met up with the Shoshone for a pow wow. When it was over, I'd been traded to them for two girls." He snorted softly. "One of them married the chief's son, so apparently I was worth more than I thought."

"How long were you with them?" Beth asked.

"Three years," he said. "Then things got ... bad, and I left. I joined the army at sixteen and that's been my home since."

He left at eleven and joined the army at sixteen ... Beth decided not to ask about the missing years.

"What sort of a welcome will you get if we go to their camp?" Lieutenant Tompkins asked.

"I ... I don't know," Bannock said. He looked at Running Bear, who'd been watching the conversation in English with interest, even though he didn't seem to have understood it. "But probably not a good one. I think he hates the war leader War Eagle as much as I do."

"So we could be in for a fight," Lieutenant Tompkins said.

"But I think we have to go, sir," Bannock continued, "and soon."

"Why soon?" Rose asked.

"Because the old chief is dying," Bannock answered, "and the war leader, War Eagle, who's going to succeed him is the reason I left."

CHAPTER TWENTY-TWO

Beth stared at Bannock. He still lightly held his wounded side as he sat. Or slumped, really. The worn lines on his face made him look older than he was, she realized. She'd taken him for nearly thirty instead of the twenty he had to be. But even with the pain etched in his skin, his eyes still burned fierce. When they met hers, the corner of his mouth turned up. It wasn't a smile so much as an acknowledgement. They were alike, the two of them.

You're strong, Hickok had told her many a time. *If you were weak, you would've broken by now. Instead, it's made you fierce.*

Fierce she could be.

"Does he really not know about the dragon?" Lieutenant Tompkins asked.

Bannock asked Running Bear something, this time his tone much more casual and friendly. Running Bear answered with a couple of sentences this time.

"He says War Eagle and their shaman are the only ones who talk with the dragon. They tell the rest of the tribe what to do."

"How do you talk to a dragon?" Rose asked. "Does it speak English, or Shoshone? Or can it even talk?"

"Good questions," Lieutenant Tompkins asked. He looked at Bannock, who was already relaying them to Running Bear.

Bannock blinked at the Indian's answer. He asked something again, and Running Bear gave a one word answer and nodded his head.

"He says he doesn't know. None of them have seen War Eagle or the shaman talk to the dragon. They ride off around the lake toward the Devil's Geysers and return with orders."

"So they're taking orders from it," Lieutenant Tompkins said. "That's a surprise."

Bannock had another exchange with Running Bear.

"The dragon or the dwarves, he says," Bannock relayed. "They're on the east side of the lake. He says the dwarves can talk to the dragon." Bannock furrowed his brow and then asked Running Bear another question. Bannock's eyebrows shot up. He turned excitedly to the others.

"The dwarves have Captain Whitaker," he said. "And he's alive!"

"Why?" Rose asked. "Does he know?"

Bannock asked, but Running Bear's shake of the head was unmistakable.

"Why are they working with the dragon and the dwarves?" Beth asked.

The resulting exchange between the Indian and Bannock lasted a little while. When it was over Bannock nodded.

"He says they've been promised all the land that was once theirs and more. From the sea," Bannock pointed west, "to the distant mountains." He pointed east.

"The Black Hills?" Beth asked. "That's a long way."

"It covers their own territory," Lieutenant Tompkins said grimly. "The Arapaho's. And ours."

"We need to rescue the captain," Beth said. "So where exactly is this dwarf camp?"

Bannock asked Running Bear, who frowned. His face fell and he hesitated before speaking. When he did, Bannock's eyes grew wide and he asked him more questions before turning to the others.

"He says their camp is near the missing mountain," Bannock explained. "I asked him what that meant, and he said the mountain was there, and then one night there was a loud roar, and the next day it was gone."

Beth's breath caught. The dwarves had destroyed a mountain? In a single night?

She couldn't suppress the chill that ran down her spine.

After they'd all eaten, they went to bury Running Bear's fallen comrade, Grey Wolf. They put Running Bear on Lieutenant Tompkins's horse. The lieutenant walked ahead, holding its reins. Beth rode behind, her gun at the ready. But Running Bear made no effort to escape.

They changed roles at the Indians' camp. Bannock, with his still painful side, covered Running Bear while Beth helped Lieutenant Tompkins dig. They'd only packed two shovels, so Rose busied herself with preparing the body.

Sweat beaded on Beth's brow and along her neck as she dug. Loose dirt clumps thumped against her legs from time to time and the grime of the soil seemed to stick everywhere. Beth's stomach added a queasiness to the mix. She couldn't help glancing at the body of the man she'd killed.

It was kill or be killed, she reminded herself. *Him or me. Just like the others. Just like I had to do with the others.*

She was beginning to understand why Hickok drank.

They didn't dig deep—too many tree roots and rocks to go more than about two feet. But that was enough to keep the scavengers away. It seemed to satisfy Running Bear, anyway. They untied him long enough to allow him to say a prayer in Shoshone before they filled in the grave.

The sun had started to tilt toward the horizon by the time they finished. They debated briefly about whether to follow the thin trail the third Indian had fled down or continue cross-country on what looked to be a less forested route.

"If we follow the trail," Lieutenant Tompkins said, "it'll be faster, but we'll risk an ambush if he or his friends are waiting for us." He glanced nervously at Running Bear, who sat several feet away with his hands once again tied behind his back.

"If we stay near the stream, we can catch fish," Rose pointed out. "We haven't found much else to eat."

"But the trail by the stream's the obvious path," Bannock said, "and they know we're coming."

"Will they attack if Running Bear is with us?" Rose asked.

Bannock shrugged. "No way to know. They'll try to rescue him, but there's several ways they could do that."

Lieutenant Tompkins looked at Beth. "What do you think?"

"We need the food," she said. "We can watch for the Shoshone, and fight them if we need to. But we can't go without food much longer. I think we'll see them coming if we need to." She brought her hand to her chest, right above Raven's amulet.

Lieutenant Tompkins noticed and he nodded. "Agreed. But let's camp away from here." He glanced at the fresh grave. "Yes, as far from here as we can get."

They stopped just before dusk near a curve in the creek that had turned into a shallow side pond. The trees were still thick, but spread out enough to let the horses graze on the sparse grass. The night insects came out while Lieutenant Tompkins fished. He managed to catch one thin brook trout, which Rose cooked with some wild berries she'd found. Despite its small size, Beth savored the smoky flesh as she ate her portion. Her stomach rumbled for more, but Rose said they should save the last of their food from Golden City for the morning.

They put the fire out after they ate and the woods around them settled into deep black. Bannock claimed that his side was healed enough for him to take one of the night watches, but Lieutenant Tompkins overruled him.

"It's been less than a day," the lieutenant said. "You need rest and water."

"A little whiskey wouldn't hurt, sir," Bannock added.

"If you have some, you can drink a little," Lieutenant Tompkins said, "but just a little."

"That's all I was planning," Bannock said happily. He took a flask from his saddlebags and settled into his bedroll under a tree near the horses.

"I'll take first watch," Beth volunteered. "Will you secure Running Bear?"

"Will do," Lieutenant Tompkins said. He looked around and pointed at a beanpole of an aspen tree at the edge of their little camp. "I can tie him to that."

"Seems mighty thin to spend the night sitting against," Beth said.

"I'll leave him enough slack to lie down," Lieutenant Tompkins replied.

Beth nodded and went to find a good lookout post up the trail, the most likely direction any Shoshone would come. About twenty yards along, she spotted a small stand of willow bushes, close to the creek. She crept behind them and peered out. In the moonlight, the trail was barely visible, but clear. She herself would be invisible. Even more, the babble of the creek would drown out any small noise she might make.

She settled in, with her Colt drawn and at hand. The bugs had long since retired for the night and she only had to brush one crawling ant off her pants. Then she grasped Raven's pouch and rubbed.

The air chilled and the ghost appeared, standing right in the middle of the bushes. Beth started in surprise. Branches and leaves poked out of Raven's side and stomach and made her seem almost monstrous. Beth's own sides and gut prickled in sympathy, but Raven's expression remained serene.

"We captured a Shoshone warrior," Beth said. She quickly filled Raven in on the fight and what Running Bear had said after. "It looks like the dragon wasn't just after the buffalo, but also your Arapaho tribe."

The ghost's expression changed. Raven's eyes narrowed and her face hardened. Her lips curled into a sneer, like she was about to utter a curse. Then her eyes began to glow.

Beth gasped and rocked back. She caught herself quickly.

Raven opened her mouth, saying several things. From the ghost's contorted face, they were hot and angry, but Beth couldn't hear them. It clenched its hands into fists. It raised its right fist and shook it threateningly.

"We'll get the Shoshone to stop working with the dragon," Beth said. She had her palms out, placating. "We're going to meet their tribe now."

Raven vehemently shook her head. As she did, her whole body changed from grey to white. She stabbed a finger to the northwest, and then did it again. Then she flapped her arms.

"You want us to go find the dragon," Beth said slowly.

Raven nodded several times.

"But what about the Shoshone?"

Raven mimicked holding a rifle. Then firing it. Once. Twice. Three times. Four. Her eyes had turned white and almost burned in their brightness.

"You want us to kill them?"

Raven's ghost nodded several times. It flared bright white. Her face was filled with rage. Then the ghost faded away.

Beth sat quietly in the dark, stunned. Her mind kept racing through what she'd seen. The eyes. The anger. The rage. And the change from grey to white. She couldn't suppress a shudder. This wasn't the Raven she'd known. It was entirely unlike the Raven she'd known.

So what happens when this Raven doesn't like what we do? she thought. *We all want the dragon dead, but ... the Shoshone?* She thought of Bannock's words about the war leader who was to become the new chief. *Maybe some of them, but not all, surely.*

And what could Raven do, really? She couldn't touch anything in the physical world. She couldn't even talk to more than a few. But after that?

I don't know, Beth said. *I don't know what she can do.* This time she didn't even try to stop the shudder from running down her spine.

She forced herself to focus on the trail. She peered intently through the bushes and watched for movement. When her mind started to drift back to Raven, she took the steadying breaths that Hickok had taught her. The ones that would steady her arm during practice.

Practice. She hadn't practiced that night. That would help. She could start again in the morning.

Thinking about how to practice calmed her down further. Still nothing moved along the trail, which also helped her relax. Everything was fine. Everything was going to be fine.

And then Rose screamed.

Beth dashed blindly back into their little camp. She heard shouting—Rose's voice and Lieutenant Tompkins's. In the dark, she could see people moving, but not who was who. She pulled up against a tree and raised her gun. She held still, watching.

Two of the silhouettes converged in an embrace—both still speaking loudly. "I'm fine!" "He's gone!" Rose's voice and Lieutenant Tompkins's again.

Beth walked slowly toward them. She glanced around as she did but couldn't make out anything else other than the trees and the shadows. She didn't walk quietly, and when she was a few feet away, one of them turned.

"Miss Armstrong?" Lieutenant Tompkins said.

"It's me," she said. "What's wrong?"

"Running Bear," he said. "He's escaped."

She looked around wildly. "Where's Bannock?"

"Over here," a voice called from the base of a pine. "He punched me in the side as he ran off."

"Oh, no," Rose said. Then, "Where's your lantern?"

"With my saddlebags," Lieutenant Tompkins answered. "I'll get it."

Beth moved to Rose's side. "What happened?" she asked quietly.

Rose reached out and clutched her friend's hand. "Oh, my," she said. "I was so scared! I woke up and he was kneeling next to me. I couldn't tell it was him, but who would kneel over a sleeping woman? So I screamed. I had to scream to frighten him."

"I'm sure you did," Beth said reassuringly.

"Then he ran!" Rose said. "And there was more running, and then Lieutenant Tompkins found me and—" She took a deep breath. Then another. "Everything's fine. Everything will be fine."

Beth squeezed Rose's hand. "Yes, it will."

A minute or so later, after a few muffled curses, light sprang out from where they'd piled their bags for the night. The lantern flashed around the camp. Bannock lay on the ground, clutching his wounded right ribs. Rose and Beth rushed over immediately. Lieutenant Tompkins strode over to give them light.

"How bad does it hurt?" Beth asked.

"Bad," he said through gritted teeth.

"Let me see," Rose said. She looked up at Lieutenant Tompkins. "Move over here so the light shines on his wound."

Despite the shadows, his bandages looked bloody once again.

"The punch must've opened it up again," Rose said.

"Oh, joy," he said.

"It could've been worse," Beth said.

"Oh, I know," Bannock said. "I've *had* worse. I'm just hard to kill."

He took a deep breath and winced. "Though ... it's going to be hard to ride a horse."

"Do we have our horses?" Beth asked.

After a quick panic-stricken look, Lieutenant Tompkins shined the light toward where they'd tied up the animals. All four were still there.

"The food!" Rose exclaimed. She ran over to where she'd been sleeping. "No! That's what he took! Our food."

"So he wasn't trying to hurt her," Beth said to Lieutenant Tompkins. "That's good, at least."

"True," he said, "but how'd he escape? I tied him pretty well, or at least I thought I did."

"Let's check," she said.

They went to the aspen tree where Running Bear had been bound. Beth didn't spot any rope on the ground, even when Lieutenant Tompkins cast the light all around. But abrasions scarred the bark in several places. Beth knelt and examined them more closely.

"These were made by the rope," she said. "You tied him lying down, right?"

"Mmm hmm," Lieutenant Tompkins said. "But he must've managed to stand." He reached up and touched the bark near his head. "These go a ways up."

"To where the trunk narrows," she added She curled her hand around the tree at the highest and deepest mark. "He would've had some slack here. Do you think he could've reached the knots then?"

"He must've," Lieutenant Tompkins said. "How else would he have gotten free?"

"He moved pretty quickly," Beth said. "Probably as soon as all of you were asleep."

"Maybe we can track him in the morning," Lieutenant Tompkins said. "We can guess where he's headed." He glanced toward the trail along the creek.

"I don't know," she said as her gaze followed his. "I think that would lead us into a trap."

CHAPTER TWENTY-THREE

In the dim light, it was hard to see Lieutenant Tompkins's expression. The flickers of light from his lamp danced around their feet and occasionally cast long shadows across the nearby trees but never made it to his face.

"A trap?" he said. "How could we be walking into a trap by following Running Bear? He's on foot and we have horses. Surely we'll catch him before he gets to their camp."

"That's just it," she insisted. "We're, what, a day or two from Yellowstone? Running Bear said that the war chief and shaman could go there and back in a day, so their camp has to be pretty close."

"Which means we should easily catch Running Bear before he gets there."

"No," she said with a vehement shake of her head. "That's not the point. The point is, what were they doing out here?"

"I don't understand."

She bit back her frustration and took a deep breath. The lieutenant wasn't stupid, which meant she wasn't explaining things well.

"Running Bear and his friends were fishing when we met them," she said, "but he mentioned a lake ahead."

"There's a big one, I've heard."

"Right. So why fish out here? Not for food for the tribe. They must've been going somewhere else and we surprised them."

"Okay ..." Lieutenant Tompkins said, "but going where? There's nothing east of here except Fort Caspar, and they destroyed that. I suppose they could've been looking for the Arapaho...."

"Maybe," Beth said. "But I think they were looking for us." When she saw the surprise on his face, she continued, "They know we're out here somewhere since they saw us near Fort Sanders. If they're working with the dwarves, they know you came from Fort Caspar. They know about Raven. What they don't know is what we learned from the ghost outside of Golden City."

He nodded slowly. "They probably took a more direct route to the geysers from Fort Sanders, so while we didn't know where they were, they didn't know where we were either."

"Exactly," she said. "But they'd know to start looking near Fort Caspar. I think Running Bear and his friends just didn't think we'd be this close to them, which is why they were careless."

"So why would we be headed into a trap?"

"They know where we are now," she said, "and Running Bear's friend, the one that threw the spear, has a day's head start on us. He might even be back with the tribe by now."

"So ...?" He shifted his weight and appeared to be listening closely, though it was still hard to see his face in the dark.

"So," she continued, "the one thing they don't know is where we're going. But if we follow the trail they were using—"

Lieutenant Tompkins interrupted, "We'll walk right into them."

She scowled at his rudeness, but he didn't notice.

"So we should go cross country," he said. "We should probably move out now, just in case they're closer than we think. After all, Running Bear knows where this camp is."

"But which way?"

"Ask Raven."

Beth stood in a patch of moonlight in the clearing where an old pine had once stood. It had long since rotted. Lieutenant Tompkins or Rose had already scavenged the burnable wood, back when it wasn't so dark. Still, the scent of the rot mixed with the pine needles was nearly overwhelming.

She shifted her weight from foot to foot to release some of the tension in her legs. She forced herself to breathe normally. But she couldn't shake the image of Raven's ghost with the furious white eyes from her mind.

She pulled the pouch out from under her shirt. Then she rested her hand on her chest. After a deep breath, she rubbed the bone within the pouch.

The familiar chill hit her skin. And then Raven—the calm Raven—stood in front of her.

The ghost gave her wise smile and nodded in greeting. She had her hands lightly clasped at her waist as if she were carefully considering what wise thing to say next. She was also deep grey throughout.

"Hello," Beth said. "Are ... you okay?"

The ghost didn't move or respond.

"We need to go a different way to get to the dragon," Beth said. "We want to avoid the Shoshone." She thought she saw some white in the ghost's eyes, so quickly added, "For now. We'll deal with the Shoshone after we've taken care of the dragon. They'll be easier to deal with then."

The ghost slowly nodded. Then it pointed due north.

Beth looked northwest, the way the creek and the trail went. Due north wasn't too different, but it would have to do.

They walked and led their horses through the trees for about two hours. When Rose stumbled from weariness, Lieutenant Tompkins called a halt. He told them all to sleep and that he'd wake Beth in a few hours.

"No," Bannock said. "Let me take the second watch, sir. I'm not useless, you know."

Lieutenant Tompkins looked pointedly at Bannock's wound, but when Bannock didn't back down, he nodded. "Fine, Private. I'll wake you for second watch." He turned to Beth. "Get your rest."

Beth slept fitfully. Finally, she slowly drifted awake to the chirps of the morning birds and the first rays of sunrise. Then she jerked all the way awake and sat up, her gun already in hand.

Rose still dozed near some small spiny bushes a few feet away. The horses stood quietly several yards beyond her where they'd tied them. Beth swiveled and spotted Lieutenant Tompkins lying in the dirt near some pines. She was halfway to her feet before she realized he was just asleep.

But Bannock was gone.

She quickly stood and looked wildly around. When she didn't spot him, she counted the horses. His was still there. She let out a relieved breath.

She circled the camp, looking for where he might've gone. She briefly considered waking Rose and Lieutenant Tompkins, but dismissed the idea with a shake of her head. Danger wasn't imminent. Maybe Bannock had just gone off to relieve himself. Still, she kept her Colt drawn.

A gunshot rang out from the north.

Beth raced toward the sound. She ducked and wove through pines and leafy bushes. Then a stretch of meadow opened up—a hundred yards of musty knee-high grass. On the far side, a deer cried and bellowed as it tried to stand, and then collapsed. It tried again, and once again fell back with a horrid cry.

Bannock leaned against a tree not ten yards from where Beth had burst out of the woods. He clutched his side and grimaced in pain. When he saw her, he forced a smile through clenched teeth.

"Thought I was better," he said. He nodded toward the deer. "You'll have to finish it."

Beth's eyes widened and she swallowed. Then she marched across the field.

Blood streamed from the deer's back, where the bullet had shattered its spine. It half stood, its hind legs useless. The deer tossed its head and snuffed and snorted. Its eyes widened in terror as she approached. It tried to shuffle away, but its back legs didn't work.

Beth closed her eyes and silently prayed her shot would go true. Then she opened her eyes, cocked her Colt, and put the deer out of its misery.

She turned to see that Lieutenant Tompkins and Rose had now entered the clearing. Both looked wild-eyed. Lieutenant Tompkins's shirt was untucked and his hat missing. Rose's dress had stains and her bonnet hung over her shoulder instead of behind her neck. Rose went to Bannock while Lieutenant Tompkins strode across the field towards Beth.

"Well," he said with a touch of anger in his voice, "at least we have breakfast."

"The shots will have alerted the Shoshone," she said.

"Darn right. We'll have to work fast," he said. "Rose has some salt. We'll cook and salt what we can and be well away from here by nightfall."

If that's not too late, Beth worried.

They stayed in the camp until early afternoon. Beth kept guard on the north and west sides while Bannock watched the south and east. Rose and Lieutenant Tompkins worked on preserving the venison together. He'd had some experience in his younger days, he said. Rose, well, Rose could do anything, Beth thought with amusement.

Scattered clouds kept the day from growing too hot, but it was bright enough so the fire wouldn't be visible over any distance. The light breeze blew the tendrils of smoke mostly east, but Beth could still smell the cooking meat from time to time.

As Rose and Lieutenant Tompkins worked on slicing and salting the meat, the two of them kept smiling at each other. Lieutenant Tompkins made a few low-voiced jokes that caused Rose to laugh merrily. Beth tried not to roll her eyes in amusement. She glanced over at Bannock, but he just slumped on a small rock, his rifle lazily propped against his side. He seemed to be staring at the ground in front of him instead of the trees where enemies might appear.

Beth frowned. She checked the woods on her side of camp once more. Nothing moved. Still keeping an eye out, she went over to Bannock.

He turned his head as she approached. His worn eyes took her in before the corner of his mouth turned up.

"Get tired of your side?" he asked.

"Wasn't sure you were watching your side."

"Nothing to watch." He gestured toward the trees, which were scattered with wide spaces between them. There was as much dirt and grass as there were pines.

"So they just ride fast instead of trying to sneak up."

"Yeah, well, I couldn't shoot 'em if they did."

"I thought you weren't that hurt."

The light in his eyes dimmed. "Yeah, well, I couldn't kill that deer."

"You hit it." She tilted her head and studied his face. The worry lines around his eyes seemed etched into his skin. "That's what matters. We wouldn't be eating if you hadn't."

"But I didn't kill it. It suffered because of me." He lightly tapped his wounded side, not enough to hurt himself, but grimaced nonetheless. His eyes remained fixed ahead.

"True," she said. Her gaze followed his toward the distant grass between the nearer pines. "And that's unfortunate. But it was him or us. We'll fail if we starve."

"Him or us?" he said with a short laugh. "Is that how you think?"

"It's what Hickok taught me. A gunfighter kills when she has no choice."

Bannock couldn't hold back his chuckle. "Of course Hickok says that. He's got a lot of blood on his hands. He has to say that." Bannock glanced sideways at her. "But sometimes he *did* have a choice."

Beth's chest tightened. She'd heard half-garbled stories ... but they'd never fit the man she knew so she'd dismissed them.

"It doesn't matter," Bannock said. He struggled to rise, and reluctantly accepted Beth's hand. His grip was tight around her fingers, and his lips pursed as he wobbled before standing straight.

"Why?" she asked. "Why doesn't it matter?"

"Because Hickok's not here," he said. "If he was, things would be a whole lot simpler." He shouldered his rifle. "I gotta pee."

He walked off without looking back once.

They traveled for several hours and camped north of where they'd shot the deer. Lieutenant Tompkins took first watch this time and woke Beth when he was supposed to. Bannock had also wanted a shift, but Lieutenant Tompkins ordered him to rest instead.

Bannock bristled. "I thought we were past giving orders," he muttered.

Lieutenant Tompkins ignored him and asked Beth to consult Raven to make sure they were still on the right heading. The ghost, the calm grey version, pointed the way they were already headed.

The next day, they crossed over a low ridge and found a stream flowing north. It tumbled between small rocks and wound through trees that grew thick at first, but then thinned the further north they went. Birds chirped throughout the little valley and squirrels scampered, with a rattling of their claws on the bark. The scent of the pines mixed with the smell of wildflowers. Beth couldn't help but relax in the saddle as she rode. The pleasant spring day washed away too many wearied concerns about what might be ahead.

She still remained vigilant, as best she could. At times, when the woods ahead looked particularly thick, Bannock or Lieutenant Tompkins would scout ahead. They didn't see or hear anything other than the call of an elk off in the distance.

The creek widened and was joined by other tributaries. By late afternoon, it had turned into a full blown river. It wasn't so wide that they couldn't ford it if they needed to, but they began to stick solely to the east side. It meandered and looped and widened into mud flats more than once. Meanwhile, the steep hills to the left and right fell away and the trees grew scattered.

Finally, Lieutenant Tompkins had them stop for the night. They camped about thirty yards from the river, among a small copse of pine trees. At first he said no fire, but Rose pleaded that they needed to cook the remaining meat. The lieutenant relented and even helped gather wood.

Beth drifted down to the river's edge. She pulled Raven's pouch out and rested it gently on her chest. After a deep breath—taking in the scent of the water and the trees and the crushed plants along the shore—she looked north.

Ahead, in the sky, a flame danced.

She sucked in her breath.

The flame rose and fell, and then rose again. Then it grew bigger.

It was coming their way.

CHAPTER TWENTY-FOUR

Beth raced back to the camp. "Dragon!" she yelled. "Dragon! Coming this way!"

Bannock cursed. He'd been sitting on the ground and tried to stand. Rose dumped a pot of weak berry tea on the fire to smother it. Lieutenant Tompkins came running from the horses.

"Where?" he called.

Beth stopped running long enough to point north. She gasped for breath and jabbed her finger at the sky.

The flames were getting larger.

Lieutenant Tompkins paused long enough to look. Then he yelled, "Under cover! Everyone get under cover!"

They all raced for the base of the pines. The limbs were low and Bannock and Rose both dropped to their knees and crawled. Lieutenant Tompkins picked a different tree where he could crouch, with his rifle across his knees. Beth ran to a third with only a few low branches. She sank to one knee and drew her Colt.

It was hard to see through the branches. Eventually she crawled out enough to look up. She scanned the sky until she spotted the bursts of flames. They were larger now, when they happened, and much closer. They grew, and grew, and then—

—flew on by. Not directly overhead but past the peak of the far ridge across the river. As the occasional bursts of flame continued south, they shrunk further and further.

Beth scrambled to her feet. "Let's go! Let's go!"

"What! Why?" Lieutenant Tompkins asked even as he got to his own feet.

"Maybe we can get close enough to see where it lands when it returns!" She pointed north as she ran to the horses.

"Let's go!" Lieutenant Tompkins called to the others. A few minutes later, they were all mounted and racing north.

Beth's pulse raced faster than their horses. More than once, she had to pull up on the reins when a tree branch loomed too close. Then, after tens of minutes, the trees parted completely. The stretch of grass ahead turned flat all the way west and a great deal north. But it wasn't all grass, she realized.

They'd found a lake.

Beth couldn't see the western shore. Not at night, at least. North, the trees and the shore ran straight for a while, then curved west. To the northwest, the water extended as far as she could see.

"That way!" she shouted as she pointed north.

They rode hard along the shore. Without the constant trees, and as flat as it was, they quickly followed the curve to the promontory. Then, they paused to let the horses catch their breath. And themselves. Rose could barely hold onto her horse. Bannock's face was white as the moon in the low light and he hunched down low and twisted, as if his side ached bad.

Beth glanced back—no dragon. She urged her horse into a trot north and the others soon fell in behind.

They followed the lakeshore for another hour and a half before Beth spotted a flicker in the southern sky. They hid in the trees. Once again, the dragon flew straight past. They scrambled out of the cover to watch it go. It followed the shoreline until the flames were as small as a star.

Then it disappeared.

"Let's rest until morning," Lieutenant Tompkins said. "Can you take second watch, Miss Armstrong?" He glared at Bannock. "Someone might go hunting instead of keeping guard."

Bannock had the decency to look sheepish.

They took care of the horses and then Beth found the softest spot she could between the trees. Despite the rockiness and a tree root right next to her shoulder, she quickly fell into a deep sleep.

During her watch, Beth sat on a rock on the shore of the lake. A light breeze had blown steadily since the start of her watch and the brim of the bowler didn't keep her ears warm, but it was something. She kept hoping to see something across the water or along the shore, but blackness extended as far as she could see.

Instead, she listened to the water lap on the rocky bank below her. The trees behind her rustled. Occasionally a bird called.

I wish I knew where the far shore is, she mused. *Is the Shoshone camp a long ways away, or just over there?* She couldn't see any fires, but that didn't mean they weren't there.

Raven can see in the dark.

She hesitated as the memory arose of the ghost's change to white. *But that wasn't normal,* she told herself. She was just angry about the threat to her tribe.

Angry ghosts. That was what had worried Bannock. Perhaps she should consult Raven while he wasn't around.

She pulled the pouch out from under her shirt and rubbed it. The hair on her neck bristled with the cold.

Raven stood in front of her, waist deep in the water. Then the ghost slowly rose up until its feet were on top of the lake.

Beth blinked in surprise. "You can move through solid things?"

The ghost nodded.

"Well, we're getting closer," Beth continued, "but we don't know how close. Can you see anything?"

The ghost slowly turned in a circle. When she faced Beth again, she shook her head.

"We think the dragon is up there." Beth pointed north, along the shore. "The dwarves are probably with it. And the Shoshone are somewhere over there." She pointed across the water.

The ghost's eyes flashed. It quickly turned to face the far side of the lake. Its whole body glowed, turning from deep to pale grey.

Beth's blood froze. The hair in the ghost's braids moved. It waved, as if windblown. Not the stiff, formal way it had laid before, even when the ghost turned. Now it danced in the glow from within.

The ghost continued to stare across the water. The color of its body changed from pale grey to off white. A fiery white.

"We'll take care of the Shoshone," Beth said loudly. "We will!" Her voice carried more confidence than she felt in her gut, but she set her jaw.

The white faded to eggshell and the ghost turned back around.

"The dragon, the dwarves, *and* the Shoshone," Beth said. "We will *stop* them."

The ghost, now almost its original grey, nodded. Then it faded away.

Dawn brought a cool day with plenty of dew over everything and a constant cool breeze. In the morning light, Beth could see the far shore of the lake, but it was nothing more than a line and a haze of green. They ate a cold breakfast of venison that Rose had cooked the day before. After they finished up, they stood in a small circle.

"We have to get going," Lieutenant Tompkins said as he finished eating. "We need to find the dwarves and Captain Whitaker."

"You mean the Shoshone," Bannock said. "We've got to persuade the chief to stop this insanity, before he dies."

"What about the dragon?" Rose said. "Isn't that why we're here?"

They all turned and looked at Beth. She sucked in her breath as she took in their stares.

The dwarves were probably closer than the Shoshone. Probably. But they weren't likely to kill Whitaker, since they hadn't already. The Shoshone chief could die anytime, though. And the dragon was the real foe....

"Ah, the heck with it," Bannock said. He looked at Lieutenant Tompkins. "You're the officer, you're supposed to be in charge. Why don't you just give an order instead of asking for a vote?"

Lieutenant Tompkins's shoulders hunched and tightened. "Fine. We go north along the shore and look for the dwarves."

Bannock stood and headed for the horses. Once he was out of earshot, Rose looked at the lieutenant.

"He has a point," Rose said gently. "You keep deferring to Beth. It's ... unusual." Rose then smiled at her friend. "Not that I mind. She's got a good head on her shoulders."

Lieutenant Tompkins snorted softly. He gave Rose a winsome look, and then Beth an apologetic one. Then he let out a deep breath.

"The only reason I'm an officer is because Raven insisted," he said. "She said she needed an officer to accompany her to Golden City in case there was any trouble with the army."

His shoulders sank and he looked at the ground. "Fort Caspar doesn't have many men and my commander didn't want to send any of his officers. Since I was the one advocating we help Raven, he gave me a temporary commission. He said it was only until I returned to Fort Caspar and Mr. Weatherby would really be in charge."

He looked at Rose. "I'm sorry. I hope you don't think less of me."

"Oh, sweetie," she said with a smile, "why would I? Rank's just what they put on your uniform, not who you are."

He actually blushed in response.

She stepped forward and clasped his hands in hers. He didn't look up, but his blush deepened.

"You're still a good man," she said quietly.

He met her eyes. "I just wish I was a better leader." He nodded toward Beth. "She's better."

"That's mighty fine of you to recognize," Rose said, "that a woman can be a better leader."

He cracked a smile. "Just don't tell Bannock or any of the other men I said that."

Beth narrowed her eyes, but then she caught herself. *He'd* seen what she was capable of, even if he wouldn't admit it in front of other men.

The catcalls and insults of the men in Golden City came back to her. She closed her eyes to force herself to calm down. After a few deep breaths, she opened them.

Rose and Lieutenant Tompkins had stepped apart. They both looked at her, waiting.

She smiled back. "Let's ride."

They rode north, following the shore. Few trees grew near the water, so they could see quite a ways north. Other than a few puffy white clouds floating by and the occasional bird, nothing much moved. From time to time, a rabbit or squirrel scampered through the grass.

Beth rode point, with Lieutenant Tompkins and Rose behind, and Bannock bringing up the rear. The breeze from the night before hadn't stopped but it nicely balanced the warmth of the sun on her shoulders and arms.

After a midday stop and another in mid-afternoon, they approached a promontory where the hills spilled down to the lake's edge. It was about an hour before sunset, so Beth paused and waited for the others to catch up.

"Let's climb that butte," she said. "We should be able to see most of the lake from the top."

After a round of nods, they started up.

The slope facing the lake was steep—too steep for the horses. They rode inland along the south face until the rise became a little more gentle. Then they worked their way up sideways, as if climbing a switchback trail, walking their horses for stretches. Only a few scraggly trees dotted the butte's site. Grass grew in tufts and patches among the rocks and sandy dirt. The wind picked up the higher they went, and once Beth's hat blew off. Fortunately, it caught against a bush and Lieutenant Tompkins was easily able to hop off his horse and retrieve it.

They reached the top a little before the sun began to set. To the west, the yellow orb still hovered above the hills on the far side of the lake—which appeared more vast than Beth had expected. She couldn't make out any details on the far shore.

She turned north and let out a gasp.

A small creek flowed into the lake between their butte and the next one further north. But trees only ran halfway up the sides of that one. Everything above that was ... gone. It looked like someone had dropped a giant egg into a pile of flour, except instead of making dough, it'd made a mess. Rock debris lay everywhere, with huge boulders cast about like scattered marbles. Trees near the ridge were flattened and shoved down the slope. And judging from the slope ... the mountain should've been twice the size it was. The top was just gone.

A small figure walked among the rocks. It stopped and poked here and there with what looked like a shovel. In the distance it was hard to tell exactly what it was doing.

But not what it was. They'd found the dwarves.

CHAPTER TWENTY-FIVE

Beth glanced sideways to see if the others had seen the dwarf too. Bannock's jaw hung slack. He squinted and unconsciously wrapped the reins around his fist. Rose just sat quietly on her horse, while Lieutenant Tompkins seemed to be counting under his breath.

"Any idea what he's doing?" Beth said quietly, before she realized no one could hear them.

"Gathering something, it looks like," Lieutenant Tompkins said. "I don't know what, in that mess. Gold, I suppose."

"But why blow the mountain up?" Beth asked. "Why not just dig a mineshaft?"

"It's faster," Bannock said. "But I think they did both." He pointed to the bottom edge of the devastation where a small dark maw appeared.

"Seems like overkill to me," Bannock said. He looked at Lieutenant Tompkins. "You ever hear of any gold strikes up here?"

The lieutenant shook his head. "There were some early, fanciful stories about gold in the land of the geysers, but the scientific expedition that came through a few years later only found small amounts."

Beth's eyes went wide. "Did you say scientific expedition?"

"Yes. So?"

"Didn't Captain Whitaker say he'd been on one of the scientific expeditions?" Beth asked.

"That's right!" Rose said. "He went on and on about it over dinner. He didn't even notice we were bored beyond belief," she said to Lieutenant Tompkins.

"You noticed?" he said, surprised.

"I always pay attention," she smiled back.

Beth suppressed a smirk at their exchange, but then cleared her throat. "I think I know why they took Captain Whitaker then, and why he's still alive."

"Mmmm hmmm," Rose said with a very pleased grin. "They want him to lead them to the gold."

"But what happens when they find out there isn't any?" Lieutenant Tompkins asked. "What then?"

"And why destroy two forts just for some gold?" Beth asked. "Dwarves crave gold like we crave food, but they could've just done all this mining quietly and no one would've known."

"No one does know," Bannock said. "Except us." He grimaced. "And if we die, they'll get away with whatever they're planning."

"Let's find a place to tie up the horses," Beth said, "and then when it's darker we can sneak up closer and scout their camp."

"All ... all of us?" Rose asked.

Beth looked her friend up and down. Her dress had old mud and ash stains on it, some of which Rose had tried to wash out and others she hadn't. She looked tired and a little gaunt. Her cheeks lacked their usual happy glow. Her hair, while still combed and tucked back, hung dirty and greasy. She didn't look at all like the confident woman who'd left Golden City.

"No," Beth said. "Bannock shouldn't be crawling through the woods with his injury."

"It's getting better!" he objected. "I can do almost everything now."

She nodded in agreement. "But still. This is a scouting mission and we only need me and Lieutenant Tompkins. Rose, you can stay with Bannock. It might be a while and you can take turns resting until the lieutenant and I return."

"You could get dinner ready," Lieutenant Tompkins said in a friendly, trying-to-be-helpful tone.

"Or practice your aim," Beth said. "As long as you don't use live ammunition. I'm sure Lieutenant Tompkins can give you his spare revolver."

"She can use mine," Bannock said. "I could use a rest." He gave Rose a lazy grin, which caused her to roll her eyes.

"I'll take the gun," she said and held out her hand.

He chuckled and handed it over. Then he looked somberly at Beth and Lieutenant Tompkins. "If you need help, two shots into the air. We'll come running."

"It shouldn't come to that," Beth said. "We're just going to look around."

Beth and Lieutenant Tompkins crept down from the butte by moving from tree to tree. They made a little noise—a cracked branch here, a slide on some loose pine needles there—but each time they froze and listened for movement ahead. None came. The night breeze had largely died in this little valley so, other than the chirp of crickets and the burble of the creek, it was still.

As they approached the small creek, Beth spotted a small light flickering through the trees upstream. She tapped the lieutenant on the shoulder and pointed. He nodded, and they began to slowly sneak that way. Beth took the lead.

She stole forward slowly, with no rhythm to her steps.

Lieutenant Tompkins followed her pattern a few steps behind. He wasn't as quiet. That meant she didn't have to look back, though, to know he was with her.

She kept her eye on the light. It appeared to be a bit high to be a fire on the ground, though it flickered like one

That's strange, she thought. *Especially since dwarves can see in the dark.*

She could feel her heart starting to pound. She pulled her Colt out and spun the barrel off its empty chamber.

After another dozen steps and two dozen heartbeats, she could see something more solid through the trees. Something wide and tall, just to the left of the light.

A wall. It was the wall of a building. It had to be.

If they crossed the creek, they could come up behind the building. She took a few careful steps, but still put one foot deeper into the stream than she'd planned. The cold shocked her as it flowed over the top of her boot. She grimaced at the thought of soggy socks, but it couldn't be helped. She tried to splash as little as possible as she finished crossing. Her pants were wet below the knee, and her toes were already tingling from the cold.

Behind her, Lieutenant Tompkins made a *"kerplunk!"* in the water, followed by a muttered curse. But no one from the building responded.

Assume there's sentries, she reminded herself. *Always assume there's sentries.*

But nothing moved. No one came out or yelled or did anything. The rush of her blood almost drowned out everything she could hear, except the squish of her wet boot. Finally, she got close enough to make out the logs that made up the wall.

She could hear the clink of metal now. A regular, methodical *clink, clink, clink.* Then a pause. It came from the other side of the wall, from the direction of the light.

She stole closer, to the wall itself. Lieutenant Tompkins was right behind her. She pressed up against the wood. The pine smell assaulted her nose. She brushed against a small sticky portion—sap. The wall was made out of green logs. She stepped a little ways back and started to ease around to the left, opposite the fire and the sound.

The clink, clink, clink started up again. Beth listened and furrowed her brow until realization hit.

A blacksmith's forge. That's what this is. And the blacksmith's working.

She reached the left edge of the wall. She took a deep breath and peeked around the side. Another wall extended a good ten to fifteen feet. If she was on the side of the forge, then the new wall was the back. She couldn't see anything beyond it, so once again, she snuck forward as silently as she could. Lieutenant Tompkins followed less quietly a few steps behind.

When she reached the far end, she took another deep breath and peeked around the corner. This time she paused. While most of this side of the forge was as forested as the back, toward the front she could see a clearing and the hint of other buildings. A split rail fence corralled off an area where a pair of mountain ponies stood quietly. Behind the corral, another, larger log building sat. She couldn't make out much detail, other than the far building seemed to have a door.

The regular clink, clink, clink continued.

She looked for sentries, but didn't see any. No dwarves hid by the far building. None were on the roofs. None were tucked among the ponies, though that would've been a poor spot anyway.

They had to have known we were coming, she thought. *Running Bear had to have told them. So where are the guards?*

She checked carefully again, and listened as best she could. Then she slowly sidled along the side of the wall toward the clearing. She looked back once to see Lieutenant Tompkins still following a few feet behind.

As she approached the front of the forge, she could hear more shuffling from the blacksmith. More clanging, but also the occasional wheeze of the bellows and the scuff of boots on the ground. But that was it. She also couldn't see anything new.

Finally, she reached the front edge. She took a breath and quickly peeked around.

A solitary dwarf stood at an anvil with tongs and a hammer. He was squat and muscular and stood a bit under four feet tall. A thick beard obscured his face. The tongs held a manacle with a dangling chain. He was holding it up and examining the links closely.

Beth pulled her head back. Then she motioned to Lieutenant Tompkins for them to retreat. Once they were back at the creek, well out of earshot of the forge, she quietly described what she'd seen.

"I don't understand why it's just him," she whispered as she finished up. "They should have sentries. They know we're out here."

"Maybe they don't," Lieutenant Tompkins whispered back. "If Running Bear was headed to the Shoshone camp on the west side of the lake, we would've gotten here first."

She nodded. "But where are the rest of them? There were only two ponies in the corral."

"We should just watch for a while."

"Agreed," she said. "I'll circle around to the bigger building. You take the back of the blacksmith's shed."

He nodded and they both quietly headed their own way.

She had to cross the creek again, which she did more carefully this time, but still got the bottom of her pants wet. She circled wide away from the dwarf encampment so as to not be heard. Then she began to creep up behind the other building she'd seen.

It was built of the same green logs as the blacksmith's shed. It was much wider but only about six feet tall. She briefly considered climbing on the roof but remembered the other pony. If there was another dwarf around, he was probably inside. She reached the back and listened for several minutes, but heard nothing.

So she quietly crept around the left side, closer to the creek. She moved slowly and quietly. Once again, she could hear the regular clink from the blacksmith, but nothing else.

She peeked around the edge of the building. From this side, she could see more of the clearing. The only new feature was a post planted in the ground in the middle of the clearing. It looked like an aspen trunk stripped of branches and bark. The black-smith's shed was open on the front, and she could see tools, the fire, and the anvil. The dwarf blacksmith's back was to her. He worked steadily, and didn't look around at all.

She sank to one knee and scrunched as close to the wall as she could. She kept her Colt drawn and settled in to wait.

Nothing happened for a long time. The blacksmith was apparently adding links to the manacle chain. He finished one, and then started the next. Beth had to shift her position several times to keep her leg from going to sleep. She did her best to ignore her chilled toes. There wasn't a lot of water in her boot, but enough to distract her from time to time.

Then, uncountable minutes or an hour or two later, she heard trampling sounds. Moments later, several riders emerged from the woods near the creek. Hearing them, the blacksmith put down his tools and turned. Another dwarf emerged from the building Beth crouched beside. He slammed the door behind him.

The riders rode into the middle and milled around. Some immediately dismounted. One called something to the black-haired dwarf from the building. Others trotted toward the corral. Beth did a quick count. Five of them. Six, with the blacksmith.

The biggest—almost four and a half feet tall and as wide as a human door—rode to the post. Then he reached behind him and pushed a large bundle off the back of his pony. With a groan, it tumbled to the ground.

Beth's heart pounded. *It's not a bundle! It's a man!* She squinted and looked closer.

The man, bloodied, bruised, and mostly naked, sprawled on the ground where he'd been dumped. His head flopped to the side and he let out another painful groan.

It was Captain Whitaker.

CHAPTER TWENTY-SIX

Beth sucked in her breath. She leaned against the rough wood of the wall. Several of the dwarves were speaking now and moving about. A couple glanced around.

She jerked her head back. She tried not to breathe too fast. She had to be calm. Calm. She had to be calm. Whatever was going to happen was going to happen fast, once it started. She *knew* that.

She heard a thump and then Whitaker moan. The dwarf voices dropped to a general murmur.

She needed to know what was going on. But she couldn't risk sticking her head out and being seen.

That problem she could solve.

She fumbled under her shirt and grasped Raven's pouch. She rubbed the bone furiously through the leather.

The air cooled and Raven appeared. She stood a few feet beside her, still deep in the shadows of the wall and barely visible.

"I need to know what they're doing," Beth quietly hissed. "What are they doing to Captain Whitaker? You can go out and look and they won't see you."

Raven nodded. Then the ghost floated forward, around the corner of the wall and into the edge of the clearing.

The dwarf voices stopped.

After a half dozen heartbeats, one called out, loud and clear. Beth couldn't understand it, but from the tone it was a challenge.

Uh oh, Beth thought. *I was wrong ...*

Raven's eyes widened. She held up her hands in a surprised gesture and her lips moved as she said something.

The dwarf voice spat something again.

I have to risk it. Beth peeked around the corner.

All the dwarves stood still and stared at the ghost. The big one, the one that had dumped Captain Whitaker on the ground, said something again. When the ghost shook its head, Big One scowled. He shook his head and—

—spotted Beth.

His eyes went wide and he yelled something. Dwarves reached for axes on their belts or bows on their backs as Beth jerked back behind the wall. She stood to run. *But they'll surround me!* She quickly holstered her gun and scrambled up the logs of the low building's wall.

Two gunshots rang out. They came from across the clearing where Lieutenant Tompkins was supposed to be. The dwarves yelled—war cries, not fear. Beth pulled herself up to the roof just as a dwarf with a large battle axe raced around the corner where she'd been.

He spotted her feet and followed them up to her face. He sneered and growled at her just as she finished standing.

Her pistol was in her hand before she could blink. Her first shot took him in the eye and her second his throat.

But her wet foot slipped and she faltered.

Something hit her from behind. Agonizing pain shot through her right shoulder. She cried out as she fell forward. When she slammed into the roof's rough planks, the pain flared again.

She saw white. She gasped and gasped again. When she could take a regular breath again, she drew herself up to her knees. Blood flowed out of a deep cut about an inch below the top of her right shoulder. She clamped her left hand over it and pressed. Her knee bumped something and she glanced down to see a bloodied throwing axe. Her Colt was nowhere in sight.

She heard scrambling on the roof behind her. She tried to twist around, but the pain flared as she did. She managed to shift her knees instead and turned just as Big One climbed onto the roof.

He was indeed big and burly—almost as tall as her and twice her weight. His long black beard ended in braids at his chest and braids similarly fell near his ears. He had a scar across one cheek and a long-ago broken nose.

He also had two throwing axes in his belt. He quickly drew one and held it back.

"Move," he said in heavily accented English, "and die."

Her shoulder throbbed. She felt lightheaded—dizzy even. She could feel the blood oozing from her shoulder.

"You surrender?" Big One asked again.

"I surrender," she said. *At least for now.*

They sat Beth on the ground with her back to the aspen post in the middle of the clearing. One of them tied a dirty cloth over her cut to stanch the bleeding, but her shoulder still screamed in pain every time she moved it.

My shooting arm! she thought. Then she grimaced. *This is not the time to worry about that.*

Once she was seated, they tied her hands behind her and around the post. She briefly thought about sliding up it to where it narrowed like Running Bear had done, but that looked to be quite high. Her shoulder hurt too much anyway for those types of contortions.

They left her there for quite a while. She couldn't tell exactly how long, but long enough for her shoulder to drop from agony to purely pain. Once it was low enough for her to think clearly, she looked around.

Captain Whitaker lay in the dirt a few feet away. He moaned, but kept his eyes closed. He was shirtless and grizzled and his upper torso was covered with black bruises and burns and oozing cuts. While he still wore ragged pants, his feet were bare except for iron manacles around his ankles. Blisters covered what she could see of his skin.

Lieutenant Tompkins lay unconscious on the far side of Captain Whitaker. His face was turned away, but his chest rose slowly and rhythmically. Blood oozed from a cut on his head and the dwarves had tied a makeshift bandage around his upper right thigh. It was soaked in blood. His feet were manacled as well.

Big One moved among the other dwarves, giving orders in a language Beth couldn't understand. One rode off on his pony. The blacksmith stoked his fire and used the bellows to make it burn hotter. She spotted two bodies—the one she'd shot and another. Probably Lieutenant Tompkins's doing. That left just Big One and another.

Beth gently thunked her head against the post. Her hat was who-knows-where, but the dwarves had set her gun against the forge, along with the small utility knife she had carried at her belt. There wasn't much she could do but wait and watch and conserve her energy.

Finally Big One finished with his orders and came over to her. He paused a few feet away and crossed his arms.

"Where is ghost magic?" he demanded.

"What?" she said. She furrowed her brow in what she hoped was a convincing show of confusion.

"Ghost magic! You called ghost."

"I don't know what you're talking about."

He snorted in derision. Then he motioned to a nearby dwarf, one with brown hair and a short beard. Big One said something— guttural and deep. Then he turned back to Beth.

"I order him cut clothes. Make you naked." His eyes flicked down Beth's body. "You not have curves of our women, but Duri enjoy them still."

She shuddered. Duri's eyes gleamed as he slowly walked forward. He pulled a small knife from his belt and smiled nastily.

They'll find it anyway, she thought. "A pouch! Around my neck!"

Big One nodded, and then said something to Duri. The brown-haired dwarf's smile turned to a disappointed sneer. Still, he knelt down next to Beth.

She shuddered when he exhaled on her cheek. His breath smelled of rotten flesh and spoiled food. He pawed her breast as he felt for the amulet and she fought to not flinch under his touch. But he found the cord quickly and pulled it away from her skin. The knife flicked out and cut the cord, and then he backed up and stood.

With a satisfied grunt, he held up Raven's pouch and then passed it to Big One. Then Duri stood quietly by Big One's side, though he leered at Beth.

Big One smirked at her, loosened the cord, and poured the little bone out into his hand. He rolled it around between his fingers as he examined it.

Beth sucked in her breath.

The air cooled. Raven's ghost appeared. It faced Big One, and almost immediately its dark grey form turned blazing white. Beth closed her eyes and turned her head.

Big One chuckled and said something Beth couldn't understand. She turned back to see him drop the bone back into the pouch and then dangle the pouch from its string.

Raven's ghost faded from view.

Big One stepped directly in front of Beth. "How you control ghost?"

Beth blinked in surprise. She leaned back, and her shoulder started to hurt again when she moved.

"How you control ghost?" Big One asked again.

"I don't." Beth said.

Big One scoffed. "We saw you, on battlefield near town. On plains near there. How you control ghost?"

"I don't," Beth repeated.

Big One scowled. He stepped to her side and towered over her. She had to bend her neck to look up into his furious eyes. A vein on his forehead pulsed and his lips curled into a sneer.

"You lie," he said. "You tell us. Or else." His eyes shot sideways toward the blacksmith.

Beth's followed his gaze. The blacksmith pulled an iron poker out of the forge. The tip glowed red hot. He saw her looking and gave her an evil grin. She couldn't stop her shudder.

"It only works for me," she said quickly. "I'm the only one that can control the ghost. That's why none of the men in our group carry her."

"Of course." Big One stepped back and said something to the blacksmith, who returned the iron to the fire. "So you help us."

"Help you what?"

"Find gold. This one," he pointed at Captain Whitaker, "no help. We tired of Sterling's demands. He not trusted. So you help. You, your ghost."

Beth's spine stiffened. She stared at Big One and his arrogant smile. Her eyes narrowed.

"You will," he said again. He took the pouch and dangled it over her. Then he dropped it onto her chest. It rolled down into her lap.

Not on your life, she thought. She stuck out her chin. "No."

"No?" He laughed, loud and long. "No? You have no choice!"

The forge sizzled. She didn't have to look to know the hot iron was out of the flames again.

"You can't torture me," she said. "I can't control the ghost if you do."

He paused for a moment but then sneered. "I not need torture *you*."

He said something to Duri and the blacksmith. They strode over to Lieutenant Tompkins. Duri grabbed him roughly under the armpits and hauled him up. The lieutenant groaned and rolled his head. His bleary eyes opened, but didn't focus on anything.

The blacksmith stepped in front of Lieutenant Tompkins. He held the poker up. The shaft looked wrapped in shadow, but the very tip was white with heat. Several inches down it glowed orange to red.

"I not need torture you," Big One said. "You not help, we torture him."

The blacksmith slowly pushed the poker toward Lieutenant Tompkins's face.

CHAPTER TWENTY-SEVEN

In the dim light from the forge, shadows filled Duri's face and he looked like a demon. He even gave an evil chuckle when he saw Beth staring, but he held Tompkins tight. The blacksmith glanced at her and twisted the iron poker in his hand. In the dark, it looked oily black and evil. He turned it until the hottest side flashed toward Beth.

"You help," Big One said.

Beth's eyes went wide. *I can't! I won't! But ...!*

Big One raised a hand. He glanced back to make sure both Duri and the blacksmith were watching. Then he looked at Beth and raised an eyebrow, asking a silent question.

She couldn't breathe—couldn't think—couldn't talk—!

Gunshots! Two loud shots rang out and then a third, deeper one.

Big One threw himself to the ground and then started scrambling away. The blacksmith was already on the ground.

Duri dropped Lieutenant Tompkins in a heap and turned toward the creek.

Another shot!

Duri swayed, and then toppled on his face.

Big One disappeared into the woods.

Beth blinked in surprise as Rose raced out of the trees. She carried a Colt revolver in one hand. Bannock lumbered after her, a rifle awkwardly slung over his shoulder.

Rose ran to Lieutenant Tompkins, rolled him on his back, and sobbed in relief. Bannock went to the blacksmith and kicked the body. He glanced at Duri and then at Beth.

"Where's the third one?" he yelled.

"That way!" she said and tried to point with her head.

He frowned as he looked in the direction she'd indicated. He brought his rifle down, winced as he held it in both hands, and strode past her. After a minute or two, he cursed and came back to her.

"He got away," Bannock grumbled as he tugged at the knots that held Beth. "Are you okay?"

She shook her head. "My shoulder." She nodded toward the forge. "My knife and gun are over there."

He fetched them and used the knife to cut her bonds. "Mmmm," he said as he looked at the dirty bandage. "Looks bad. Can you walk?"

"I think so."

"Good. Let's get out of here." She scooped up Raven's pouch as he pulled her to her feet. Then he looked at the corral. "We'll use their ponies for the wounded."

Including me, Beth thought.

She stood woozily and looked around. The flickering forge made it hard to see. The two dwarf corpses from the earlier fight were laid by the building she'd climbed on. Captain Whitaker lay groaning a few feet away from Rose and Lieutenant Tompkins. Rose knelt over Lieutenant Tompkins, talking quietly to him as she undid the manacles on his feet with an iron key.

Beth walked toward them. When she swung her arm, pain lanced out from her shoulder. She grimaced and held it tight.

Rose looked up when Beth approached. Her eyes were wet with tears of relief. "He's going to live! Jefferson's going to live!"

Jefferson?

"That's good," Beth said. "But we need to get out of here. Can you get him up?"

"I ... I think so."

Beth nodded and went to Captain Whitaker. The once portly man was now almost gaunt. One eye was swollen and almost shut. He had so many bruises and burns she could barely see pink skin. One hand was missing its little finger. He labored for breath, and wheezed when he did breathe. She knelt by his side and gently touched his upper arm.

He stirred and looked up at her. At first, his gaze didn't track, but then his good eye widened. "Miss ... Miss Armstrong!"

"You're free," she soothed. "We're going to get you to safety."

He closed his eye and relief flooded his face, but then he tensed and looked at her again. "Must ... must stop them! Stop them!"

"Stop who?" she asked. "The dwarves?"

He gasped for breath and nodded. "Their new mine! I told them, no gold!" He panted a few times.

She reached down and took his hand. He weakly squeezed her fingers.

"New mine?" she asked. "Where?"

"Mud volcano," he gasped. His eye widened in terror. "But they'll set off the big volcano! Stop them! Stop them!"

He strained to sit up, but it was too much. He slumped back to the ground and passed out.

Rose and Bannock struggled to get the unconscious Captain Whitaker and Lieutenant Tompkins both onto ponies. While they were doing so, Beth tried to mount one herself. Her shoulder burned each time she moved her arm. When Rose noticed, she hurried over.

"How bad is it?" Rose asked.

"I'll live, but I can't shoot."

"Oh, dearie," Rose said, "'can't' is such a very big word. Let's use your belt as a sling until we can look at this later."

Beth nodded and let her friend undo her belt. Fortunately, her pants stayed up and only sagged a bit. She stood there, feeling helpless, as Rose looped it around her arm and pulled it tight.

"I'll be useless like this," Beth grumbled.

"As long as you're alive, you're not useless, you hear?"

"Yes, ma'am."

Somehow, they made it up the southern ridge and then down the far side into some trees near another small creek before either more dwarves or the dragon appeared. Bannock retrieved their own horses while Rose made Lieutenant Tompkins and Captain Whitaker comfortable. Both had woken up during the trip, but neither was in much of a state to talk. Lieutenant Tompkins had lost a lot of blood from the wound in his thigh, and Captain Whitaker ...

Beth shuddered when she thought about what he'd endured.

But they let Rose clean and rebandage their wounds. Rose had insisted on a little fire, despite the risk of detection, and Beth was grateful. They boiled water both for the bandages and some tea. Rose managed to cajole both the wounded officers into drinking a little while Beth tried to do something with the venison they had left. Cooking left-handed, she ended up burning the edges. Rose thanked her and somehow produced some herbs to flavor it anyway.

"We need to take care of the ponies," Beth said, but she sank to the ground next to the fire.

"Bannock will take care of the ponies when he returns," Rose said. "His side's doing much better. How do you feel?"

"Useless," Beth replied.

"Now, now," Rose teased, "that's *my* line. Let's see how bad your arm is before you steal it."

Rose put a pot of water on the fire. After it began to boil, she poured some into a mug with some leaves and passed it to Beth.

"Some medicines I've been saving," she said. "Drink up."

As Beth downed the medicinal tea, Rose boiled some bandages and wrung them out.

"This is going to hurt," Rose said. She started unwrapping the bloody bandage, pulling gently where it had stuck to the wound.

Beth hissed through her teeth. It didn't hurt as much as she'd expected. Then Rose swabbed the wound with the hot cloth. Beth gasped and tried to jerk her arm away, but Rose held it fast.

"Can't let it get infected," Rose said. "Cleaning it is supposed to help."

"Supposed to?" Beth winced and dug her fingernails into her knee.

"Mmm hmm," Rose said. "There. It doesn't look too deep. I wish we had a doctor to suture it up ... hmmm ..."

"Oh, no you don't." Beth turned her head and looked at the wound as best she could. The two-inch-long gash looked red and raw and bloody and gaped open enough to churn her stomach.

"I have my needles...." Rose experimentally moved Beth's arm, and the wound gaped a little less.

"You don't have ether," Beth said.

"No," Rose said, "and I want to save the rest of the whiskey for Jefferson. He needs it more."

Beth reluctantly nodded.

"But if I close your cut, it *might* heal enough for you to shoot again."

Beth paused. *What's a little pain? Okay, a lot of pain?*

"Do it."

Rose smiled. "I'll get my needles."

Beth lay on her bedroll. The screaming pain in her shoulder had finally eased enough that she could do more than endure. She stared at the stars above until the dryness of her mouth became too much.

"Water," she croaked.

Bannock appeared by her side with a canteen. Without a word, he helped her sit up enough to drink. Beth brought the canteen to her lips with her left hand and drank greedily. She ignored the water that slopped out and down her chin to drop onto her chest. The cool wetness was too good to care.

"The dragon flew over," Bannock said, "while you were out of it. It circled the area, but didn't see us. We'd put the fire out by then, thankfully."

Beth nodded. She vaguely remembered the light from the fire disappearing sometime in the middle of her agony.

"The lieutenant's going to live," Bannock continued, "but it's bad. He might lose the leg. He's sleeping now, and Miss Chamberlin is keeping a close eye on him."

"It was her, wasn't it?" Beth asked. "She's the one that saved us."

He snorted softly. "She was the one that killed those two dwarves. I'm the one that missed. We heard your two shots and came running...."

"Yeah," she said with a snort, "and then you waited until the most dramatic moment."

"Yeah, well ..." He couldn't hold back his blush.

"It was like something from a dime novel."

"Never read 'em."

"Fine. How's your side?"

"Good enough," he said with a dismissive shrug.

"How's Captain Whitaker?"

"Not good." Bannock glanced toward where the captain lay and grimaced. "He's got a fever, probably from some infected cuts. What they did to him ..." Bannock swore softly. "I never liked the man, but he didn't deserve this."

"No. They wanted him to lead them to gold he says doesn't exist."

"He should know," Bannock said with a snort. "He's gone on and on enough about his expedition out here."

"He also said they'd set off the volcano."

"What?" Bannock barked in alarm. "Set it off! They're crazy!"

"But what volcano?"

He grimaced. "You don't know, do you? He didn't talk about it at dinner, did he?"

She shook her head. Her shoulder throbbed when she did, but it still ached less than it had earlier, before Rose had sewn it shut.

"The expedition he was on," Bannock said. "They figured out there's a volcano under the ground here."

"What?"

"Mmm hmm. He said they found lava."

"But ... how?" Beth struggled with the idea of a *volcano* under these gentle hills.

"He didn't say," Bannock continued. "But if it blew ..."

"It'd be bad," she finished. "Really bad."

Beth could barely breathe. The thought of a volcano exploding—of an explosion that big—seized her chest. What would that look like? What would that mean?

Her friend Billy had told her about volcanoes once and offered to loan her a book on an old Roman city that had been destroyed by one. He'd told her about the ash and rock falling from the sky for miles around. How people had died because they couldn't outrun it.

How far away would it fall?

And just how big was this volcano anyway?

She swallowed hard and thought of the lake's size. If the entire lake exploded into the air ...

Golden City would be annihilated. Fort Chicago would be wiped out. Heck, even San Francisco might be buried under ash.

It probably wasn't that big. But even so, it'd be a catastrophe.

So why would the dwarves ...?

Something clicked.

"The dwarves don't believe him," she said in a rush. "They don't believe Captain Whitaker about the volcano."

"Of course not," Bannock said. "'Cause it'll kill them too, if it goes off."

"But why won't they listen?"

"Why should they?" Bannock gestured at the forested landscape around them. "What would make you think there's a volcano here?"

"Nothing," Beth admitted. "So why did Captain Whitaker say there was?"

"He never said. In all the times I've heard him tell the stories of his expeditions, he's never explained that part. He was actually pretty cagey about it."

"If there was lava on the surface, he just would've said so ..." She paused until Bannock shook his head. "So you'd have to look underground—wait a minute, Big One, the head dwarf. He said they didn't trust "Sterling" either. Didn't Captain Whitaker mention a Private Sterling who got killed on the expedition?"

"Yeah," Bannock said. "The soldier who got killed when the others were chasing him."

"So he's dead." She furrowed her brow. "No ... he's a ghost."

"Probably a really angry one, if he died because of a stupid prank." Bannock's tone wasn't light and carried a hint of condemnation. "But why would the dwarves work with a ghost?"

"Well ..." she said. "They're looking for gold but don't know exactly where it is. So they need to know where to dig." Beth froze. She felt her face drain of color. Her hand unconsciously flew to her chest, but her shoulder twinged before she touched Raven's pouch and she pulled it back. Instead, she stared at Bannock.

"Ghosts," she said. "They can move through rock. That's how

Captain Whitaker knows about the volcano. Sterling's ghost told someone in their expedition. That's also why the dwarves want this." She pointed at her chest.

He grinned playfully at her. "I presume you mean the ghost pouch and not your heart."

She couldn't help a snort. "Yes! Yes, that's what I mean." She wanted to swat him on the arm, but she hurt too much to try.

"I assume that's one of her bones in the pouch," Bannock said. He nodded toward it, but carefully did not look at her chest.

"How'd you know?" she said with a blink.

He sighed and sagged back. He kicked his legs out in front of himself. "The Shoshone medicine men have done it from time to time, especially if they're going into battle. It lets their ghosts take revenge on their killers."

"Revenge?"

"Mmm hmm. They're pretty angry."

"How do you know this?" she asked. "You can't see them like I can."

"No." He shook his head ruefully. "But ... my friend when I was in the Shoshone camp could. He was training to be the next shaman, when he got older, and then ..."

Bannock set his jaw and stared into space. Beth waited patiently. For several heartbeats all she could hear was the wind.

"Then he died," Bannock said. "A hunting accident, War Eagle said."

"War Eagle said that?" she asked.

"Exactly. When *my* friend died, *his* best friend, who's as evil and corrupt as they come, became the next shaman instead."

"Ah."

"Yeah."

They sat in companionable silence for a while. Crickets chirped to fill the quiet. But Beth's mind didn't stop working. She knew what the Shoshone wanted—the land. She knew what the dwarves wanted—gold without setting off the volcano. The dragon probably just wanted easy prey and a safe place to live. What did the ghost want? He'd died from a stupid prank and spent years alone in this wilderness, abandoned by the expedition ...

Her chest froze.

"He wants revenge," she said. "Oh, God, he wants a horrible, terrible revenge."

"Who?" Bannock asked.

"Sterling's ghost. He *wants* the dwarves to set off the volcano."

CHAPTER TWENTY-EIGHT

Bannock stared at Beth. His scruffy jaw clenched tight.

"Of course," he said. "Sterling's telling them where to dig, but he's also telling them to do things to protect himself like kill the Arapaho tribe's shaman so he can't be banished. So they know he's up to something."

"Mmm hmm," Beth said, "and so when they saw Raven become a ghost, they decided they wanted her for themselves."

"And seizing Captain Whitaker was probably their idea too." Bannock swore softly. "The torture could be Sterling's idea, though."

"But how do you set off a volcano?"

"No idea," he said.

"So what do we do?"

"Nothing," Bannock said, "at least until morning. Then we can look at that mountain they blew up."

Beth slept fitfully. Her arm hurt every time she moved. She'd wake up, shift to a new position, and try to return to sleep. Most of the time she succeeded, but not all.

Just as dawn broke, she got up. Rose had told her the night before that she could take the binding belt off and move her arm, as long as she didn't move it too much. That was fine. Beth didn't want to move it anyway. But she had to.

Rose was also already awake. She stirred the coals of the fire and tossed small sticks in. A pot of water already sat nearby, ready to heat.

Beth glanced around. The others were still asleep, so she approached her friend. Rose smiled at her, but returned to poking a thin stick at the nascent flames. She waited until Beth had settled in beside her.

"How are you feeling?" Rose asked. Her eyes flicked to the bandage on Beth's shoulder.

"Grateful," Beth said. "You were impressive last night. You shot well."

Rose blushed. "I've ... I've never done that before." She grew more somber. "I killed them, didn't I?"

"You saved Lieutenant Tompkins. And the captain. All of us, really."

Rose slowly nodded.

"You did what had to be done," Beth continued, "and everyone's going to talk about how great you were when we get back to Golden City. Hickok, Mr. Lake, even Boggs."

Rose snorted softly. "I don't care if they talk about me." She looked over to where Lieutenant Tompkins and Captain Whitaker slept. "I just want Jefferson to survive." Her eyes grew wistful.

Beth bit her lip. She didn't know what to say. What could she say?

Rose turned back to her. "I'll have breakfast ready soon."

"Then I'll go practice my left-handed aim for a while."

The cool wind tussled Beth's hair. She'd left her hat behind. The wind also pricked at her cheeks, which made her feel more alive.

That, and her Colt hanging on her left hip, where it didn't really belong. Still, she tapped it comfortingly.

The trees and grass smelled dry, and birds called in the distance. Her shoulder throbbed again, but she was beginning to know how to ignore it.

She found a spot where a distant pine tree had a branch about chest high. It forked with the smaller branches almost at right angles. She broke the upper limbs and bent them into a crude square. It wasn't much of a target, but it'd do.

She backed up about ten yards and stared at the target. She narrowed her eyes and snapped the gun up with her left hand.

She met it with her right, which hurt, and wasn't enough to actually steady it. So she tried her quick draw again with just the left. Her aim was just as bad, but the pain was less.

She holstered the gun. Then she yanked the gun out and checked her aim. She was off once again.

She let out a deep sigh and holstered her gun once again. She figured she could practice her left-handed quick draw fifty times before her arm got too tired. Seventy, if she was lucky.

So she quick-drew it for the fourth time. Four down. Forty-six or more to go.

Birds chirped and the morning insects buzzed as Bannock ambled over to Beth. Her weary left arm ached almost more than her right. Sweat beaded on her forehead, so she holstered her gun again and wiped her brow with her sleeve.

"Does that help?" Bannock asked once he'd drawn near. He gestured toward the target. "Practicing without shooting?"

"Hickok made me do it a hundred times a day," she said. "Otherwise, we would've gone through bullets too fast."

"But does it help?"

"Some," she said with a shrug. "Usually we'd finish off with a full round just to see."

"You gonna do that here?" His eyes darted warily toward the pine branch and back to her.

"No point. I already know my aim's not good enough." She gestured toward camp. "Is breakfast ready?"

"Yeah. Rose sent me to get you," he said. He looked back at her target. "What's good enough?"

She glanced at the pine herself. "At this distance? Six out of six. Hickok insisted."

"He did, did he?"

"Yeah. He said anything less would get me killed."

She gave him a firm smile and started walking to camp. He chuckled and fell in beside her.

"How long did you train with him?" Bannock asked as they walked. "Hickok, I mean."

"Every day he was in Golden City for over three years."

"So you're pretty good."

She pointed at her right shoulder. "I was."

"So was I." He lightly tapped his right side. This time he didn't wince in pain.

"Hopefully we're both good enough." She tried to picture the volcano exploding, but it was too big. Too much.

He read her mind and grimaced. "We'd better be."

After they'd eaten breakfast, Rose gave Beth and Bannock each a small pouch of salted and dried venison and a few berries.

"I know it's not much," she apologized, "but you can hunt or forage. We ..." She broke off and looked over at the still-sleeping captain and lieutenant.

"You need the food," Beth said. She thrust her bag back into Rose's hands. "Keep this. I'm sure there's more food in the dwarves' camp."

"How much do you have?" Bannock asked Rose.

She grimaced. "We didn't cure enough deer meat and the rest

is starting to go bad. We can manage for two to three days. I may try fishing ..."

"There won't be much in that little creek," Bannock said as he pointed to the creek in question. "Try the lake."

"Not until I can leave the men," Rose said.

"We'll try to be back soon," Beth said. "We can't be far from their new mine, or they would've moved their camp."

"We should also investigate their current camp," Bannock said.

"And that destroyed mountain," Beth said. "We need to find out how the dwarves did it."

Beth and Bannock approached the dwarf camp almost silently. In the early morning light, it was easier to move quickly and quietly. Bannock moved more stealthily than Lieutenant Tompkins had the night before. The morning birds and bugs were actually louder than him. The one time he did brush a tree branch, which made a soft *thwick* against his shirt, he just rolled his eyes and gave her a roguish grin.

But the dwarf camp was deserted.

The dwarf corpses lay where they'd fallen the night before. A thick cloud of flies buzzed around each of them. To Beth's disgust, the seemingly permanent wind had actually stopped, leaving the stink to hover through the camp. She did snort when she saw that the blacksmith's hot poker had actually landed on Duri's thigh and burned a hole through his pants.

Better than burning one of us, she thought.

Then she squinted and looked more closely at the poker. A thin grey fog, almost like an oil, seemed to cling to it. She moved forward and knelt next to it, and then gestured Bannock over.

"What's that?" she asked as she pointed to it.

"A poker. Used for stirring a fire."

"No," she said. "What's on it. It looks like oil or thin wool."

"I don't see anything," he said. He reached down and picked it up. "It looks normal to me." He turned it around and moved it into the sunlight.

The thin fog remained.

"You don't?" she asked. When he shook his head, she reached for it. "It looks ... well, it kind of looks like ... a ghost?"

"A ghost!" He shoved it into her hand. "How could it be a ghost?"

"I don't know." It felt cool to the touch, almost cold. Her fingertips passed straight through the tiny foggy coating. She brought it closer. It just looked like a grey fuzzy cloud.

She blinked in recognition.

"It's not like a ghost," she said. "It's like a rift."

"What?"

"When a soul ... passes on," she said, "it opens a small rift to, well, wherever it's going. Then the rift closes. At least most of the time."

"Yeah, I know," he said. "Only a witch can keep one open."

"Right. So, I can see those little rifts, too, when someone passes on. This looks like those."

"But ... it's a poker. Why would it be special?"

"I don't know." She looked slowly around and sucked in her breath. "The anvil has it, too. So does the blacksmith's hammer ... and his tongs ... and his other tools. I hadn't noticed before."

"It was dark and you were in a fight," Bannock pointed out.

The poker was starting to feel downright cold, so she set it down next to the dwarf's corpse. Then she slowly approached the forge.

"Could it be magic?" Bannock asked.

"There's no such thing as magic."

"In our world. What if these didn't come from our world?"

"Of course," she said with a wry chuckle. "Dwarves are master smiths, right? The stories say they forged magical weapons. Wouldn't they need magical tools to do that? I bet these were magic in their world."

"But here?"

"I don't think so." She touched the anvil and felt the same cold as the poker. "If magic worked after coming through the rift, we would've seen it by now. You know the trolls would've used it."

He snorted in agreement.

Beth furrowed her brow as she thought. "So ... if the tools were magic in their world and not in ours, then they changed when they went through the rift."

"And that's what you're seeing," Bannock said. "What the magic changed into."

Beth nodded. It was as good an explanation as any.

"So does anything else have that fog?"

She looked around and then turned to survey the rest of the dwarves' camp. "I don't see anything, but let's take a closer look."

They didn't spot any magic, but they did see another body. The corpse lay at the start of a well-worn trail through the woods that Beth hadn't seen the night before. The dwarf sprawled on its side, with a large wound in its chest where he'd been shot by someone. Beth wasn't sure who. The flies covered both the wound and his lifeless face.

Beth stared down the trail. It ran pretty straight over the sloping ground toward the lake. The trees obscured her view before she could tell if it curved. She turned back to the clearing.

The building opposite the forge turned out to be a combination barracks and warehouse. Twelve small wooden beds stood in two rows toward the back. Some had blankets pulled up tight and neat where others were messily unmade. At one end, a small fireplace sat against the wall. Beth noted the chimney she hadn't spotted when she'd been on the roof.

Of course, I was a bit busy, she mused. Her shoulder twinged in sympathetic black humor.

They found a lot of dried fish in a barrel near the doorway, along with buffalo jerky on a shelf. Beth also found some dried berries in a metal pan. She ate several of them greedily. They had only a hint of tartness and were almost too hard to chew. She sucked on them as she continued to search.

In addition to the food, the building contained various mining tools and personal effects. There weren't very many, though, and the clothes were worn and the tools often dull. She pointed that out to Bannock.

"I think this was their first camp," he said. "They've taken the good stuff to where they are now."

"But they brought Captain Whitaker back here. Why?" She thought for a moment. "Oh. The manacles."

"Yeah. They didn't move the blacksmith's forge."

"But why move at all?"

Bannock gestured up the mountain. "I'll bet the reason's up there."

"True."

They loaded their saddlebags with food and checked for weapons. All they found were axes of various types and bows and arrows. Bannock didn't know how to use them, and since Beth didn't either, they settled for breaking them into pieces. After piling the splinters near the forge, they mounted their horses and rode toward the hill.

At first, it looked like it would be rough going, but Bannock spotted a path. It ran straight up for the most part but dodged scattered boulders and downed trees in places. When they cleared the last of the standing trees, they could see the path ran to a dark opening in the rock about a hundred feet below the shattered rim.

"Is that the mine shaft?" Bannock asked.

"Looks like it," Beth said. "Let's check the rim, too."

They rode to the mine entrance, where the trail ended. The slope up was too steep for the horses, so they dismounted. They took the opportunity to look down the shaft. It ran straight as far as they could see. There might've been some faint light far down, but Beth's eyes could've been playing tricks on her too.

"Look at this," Bannock said. He pointed to wide scrapes through the dirt and dust at the entrance floor. "Something's been dragged here. Several things."

Beth stared at them. They reminded her of something ... of the marks in the dirt behind the Astor after Mr. Lake received new deliveries.

"Barrels," she said. "They dragged barrels down into the mine."

"Gunpowder?" Bannock mused.

She nodded in agreement. Then she pointed down the shaft. "That's pretty dark. Let's check it out later."

They scrambled up the fractured slope to the rim. A crater formed the top of what had been a mountain, and rocks and dirt filled the slopes. Halfway down almost directly below them, they saw a black hole.

"The other end of the mineshaft," Beth murmured.

Carefully, they picked their way down the debris field toward the mine. Here and there, Beth saw scrapes and other signs that rocks had been pushed aside or broken up. She pointed one out to Bannock.

"Looks like marks from a pickaxe," he said.

"There's not many of them," she said. "There must not have been much gold."

He shrugged in agreement.

As they made their way down to the mineshaft, the rock took on stranger shapes. More and more, it looked like ash from a fireplace, now squished solid. Not all of it, though. A fine grit soon covered their boots. At the bottom, some of it looked like dark glass.

Bannock pointed at it, and then the surrounding bowl. "There was an explosion here that created all this. Like some sort of dynamite."

"That's a pretty big explosive. It melted the rock." She glanced inside the mineshaft and it looked as dark as the other end. The rocks here were more jagged. She looked closely at the ground and didn't see any scrapes. Just a lot of dust. She knelt for a closer look. "Do you think the gunpowder they took could've done it?"

"No," Bannock said emphatically. "Not a blast this big."

Beth ran her hands through the dust. It felt cool, almost cold. She scooped a little onto one finger and brought it close to her eye.

It had the same grey sheen as the forge. It was faint, but it was there.

"Why?" she asked aloud. When she saw Bannock's confused expression, she added, "Some of this dust has the same shadow as the forge."

"Maybe the dust is what blew this up," he said with a gesture to the crater. "Maybe the dwarves brought something from their world that could do this."

"Like gunpowder. Only more powerful."

"Mmm hmm," he said. "But that begs the question ... why'd they steal the gunpowder?"

"Maybe they needed the gunpowder to set off their bigger explosive."

"That's so crazy," Bannock said with a laugh. Then he grew somber. "But ... it might be right."

"It might?" Beth had just said the first thing that came to mind.

"Yeah," Bannock said. "Maybe it's something like nitroglycerin. That stuff's real unstable as a liquid, so they used to ship it frozen, before dynamite was invented. So maybe the dwarves needed the gunpowder to, uh, 'warm up' whatever their dust was."

She nodded.

"C'mon," he said, "let's get out of here."

They worked their way back to the rim. There, they paused to catch their breath.

Bannock looked down at the crater. "They went to an awful lot of work for that gold."

"Seems like a waste of time," Beth said.

"Compared to what?"

She shrugged. "I don't know." *Practicing your quick draw* came to mind, but Bannock would scoff if she said it. "I just don't understand their lust for gold."

He chuckled. "And that's what makes you a good person." When she raised a questioning eyebrow, he continued, "You're not interested in the usual vices."

"No," she said. "I want other things."

"Like what?"

She met his eyes. They were wide and he didn't blink or look away. The corners of his mouth were soft. His shoulders and jaw carried no tension.

He was honestly curious.

"To do this," she said. She gestured across the small valley, but mostly at the dwarvish camp. This time it was his turn to raise a questioning eyebrow, so she continued. "Out here, no one's telling me what to wear, or what to do, or what I can't do. I can be ... me."

"And who is that, exactly?"

She blinked in surprise at the question. *Wasn't it obvious?*

Movement in the corner of her eye caught Beth's attention. She whipped her head sideways. There was nothing on the mountain other than the bare rock. But farther to the west, toward the lake, something flew through the air.

Something big and round, with wide bat-like wings, a long serpentine tail, and legs as thick as tree trunks. Its head, on a snake of a neck the length of its body, turned their direction. Its cat eyes widened and its teeth-filled maw opened.

A stream of flames a few feet long shot out of its mouth. Even a thousand yards away, Beth could hear the pop and crackle of the fire.

The dragon had found them.

CHAPTER TWENTY-NINE

Beth sucked in her breath. Her heart pounded. Her first good look at the dragon!

She looked closer. It didn't look like the sleek lizard she'd imagined. It was fatter and rounder, like a grey-green pillow with wings and limbs. Or a big blob of dough, drawn thin at the head and tail. It also floated, rather than swooped like a bird.

It's like a balloon, she thought. *A big hot air balloon.*

Except balloons didn't have claws. Or fangs. Or long, broad wings.

Which it began to beat. With a roar, it shot forward fast.

"Into the mine!" Bannock shouted.

"No!" Beth yelled back. "We'll be trapped there!"

She raced pell-mell down the steep hill toward the dwarf camp. The horses whinnied behind her, but there was no time to turn back. All too soon, it was all she could do to not fall—gravity was carrying her body downhill just a little faster than her legs could keep up.

Bannock too. He was to her right and huffed and gasped as he tried to keep from tumbling as well. He swore once but didn't fall.

About when they reached the trees, one of the horses screamed. Beth glanced back just in time to see the dragon's claws slice through the unfortunate animal's neck and back. She couldn't see the other horse. Hopefully it'd escaped.

Bannock didn't stop running, and neither did she. They finally slowed up and skidded to a stop just at the edge of the camp's clearing. The scattered trees obscured the view of the slope behind them. Beth drew her Colt, clumsily, with her left hand. Bannock frantically scanned the skies.

"There!" he said. He pointed to a flash of scales between the branches, high but uncomfortably close.

The dragon roared to the north of them. Flame whooshed and, even in the bright morning light, Beth could see it in the sky. Then the dragon flew to their east. It roared once again.

"It's marking us!" Beth realized. "Our location!"

Bannock nodded hard in agreement.

"Go down the trail," she urged. "Ambush whoever's coming!"

"What about you?"

"I'll keep the dragon distracted."

He shot her a look that could only mean "you're insane" before running for the trailhead.

Beth took a deep breath. Then another. The dragon had already flown to the south of the dwarf camp where its roar echoed off the hills.

What's the best way to distract a dragon?

She couldn't avoid chuckling at the silliness of the question. The smart thing to do would be to *hide* until it was safe.

There weren't a lot of places to hide, though. The building was the obvious spot. The door was even half ajar. But it was as much of a trap as the mine.

Beth sprinted for the blacksmith's lean-to and crouched behind the forge. She grimaced as her right shoulder twinged, but tightened the grip on her revolver in her left hand.

The dragon had finished its circuit and flew back to the sky above the clearing, where it ... floated. There was no better word for how it hung in the air. It flapped its wings from time to time to rotate its body this way and that as it looked around. Thankfully, it spotted the open door before it spotted her. It swerved around to face the door and coiled its neck, like a rattlesnake about to strike.

She forced herself to breathe quietly. *How good is its hearing? Or its sense of smell?*

But its back was to her. Maybe she could get the jump on it.

She studied its hide carefully. Overlapping grey-green scales like a snake's covered its tail and back. On the underside, its stretched hide looked more like a lizard's, but also tough like a buffalo's. It was probably as thick as a giant's skin. Tough and nearly impenetrable.

Hickok had told many a tale of shooting a giant in the arm or chest only to annoy it. He'd likened regular bullets to mosquitos or bee stings for them. Only the difficult shots to the eyes regularly brought them down. That and swords to their vulnerable spots like knees and ankles.

She didn't have a sword. She couldn't see the dragon's eyes to shoot. And if she could, that'd mean facing the dragon's flame.

The wings looked more vulnerable. They were membranes stretched tight between ribs that ran straight out from the dragon's back. A bullet would probably pierce them. But then what? They were so long and wide that a few small holes wouldn't knock the dragon out of the sky.

If the best she could do was bee stings, she needed to find where it was allergic.

Unfortunately, she couldn't see anything good from the back. There wasn't a missing scale to be seen, or an obvious soft spot, or much more than the joints in its legs and wings. Could she hit a knee hard enough to damage it? She didn't even know what part of the knee to aim for.

She'd have to go for the eyes when it turned.

She quietly brought her Colt up. Her left hand shook a little, so she braced it with her right. She aimed down the barrel and waited. She took a steady breath and waited some more.

Gunshots rang out from down the trail. She blinked in surprise —that'd been faster than she'd expected.

The dragon whipped around. Its head snaked out toward the trail. She could see its eyes.

She fired twice.

The dragon twisted its neck and then roared. One shot had missed completely, but a red splotch appeared on one ear.

Its gaze quickly found her and the cat eyes widened. It reared back its head and—

—Beth dove forward—

—flames exploded behind her and the blacksmith's shed burst into fire.

Beth ended up in a somersault. Somehow she lost her gun. She twisted sideways just as claws raked the ground where she'd dropped. She rolled sideways again as another set of claws scraped her right arm.

Pain shot through her shoulder again, but she kept rolling until she hit something. A cloud of bugs flew into her face and eyes and she had to cough to keep them out of her mouth.

More gunshots rang out.

Beth reached sideways and shuddered. She'd just put her hand on a dwarven corpse. She fumbled around with her hand as the bugs scattered and her vision cleared.

The dragon hovered right above her. Its back legs were only two feet above her head and off to the side. Its big fat belly obscured everything else. But it seemed to be distracted, at least for the moment.

Her gun! Where was her gun?

She clawed left and right. No gun! But her hand found the blacksmith's poker. She quickly slid her hand down to grip it by the handle. Once she had it, she moved into a crouch.

The dragon began to float up and turn.

She jumped and stabbed up with all her strength. The poker hit the dragon's skin and—

—went in!

Just a little, but the poker lanced through the tough hide. No more than a bee sting if there ever was one. Black liquid flowed out of the wound and bubbled down the poker.

The dragon screamed.

The liquid hit Beth's right hand and burned. Then the dragon's tail whipped around and smashed into her legs below the knees. She fell as more of the black liquid dripped onto her shoulder and back. It sizzled on the cloth.

With a huge blast of fire toward the shed, the dragon rocketed straight up.

Beth wiped her hand on her shirt and rolled to her stomach. She struggled for breath as her back and stomach screamed in pain where the liquid burned through her clothes. She rolled and tried to rub it out in the dirt. As she did, she looked for the dragon. She couldn't see it.

The dirt helped, but not enough. She sat up and fumbled for her shirt buttons. Her breath came in shallow gasps as the pain coursed through her from almost everywhere.

She groaned as the buttons didn't give. Finally, she grabbed and tore the cloth. The stubborn buttons flew as she tugged her shirt up. She finally, finally got it off and yanked her chemise over her head as well. Agony shot from her shoulder. A quick glance showed the stitches hadn't opened, though. Thankfully.

"Beth?" Bannock's voice called.

She swiveled toward the sound. He strode into the clearing from the trailhead. His eyes widened when he saw her and he immediately stopped and turned away.

Without thinking, she dropped her arms in front of her bare breasts.

"Where's the dragon?" she asked.

"Flew off," Bannock said. He studied the trees intently. He started to turn his head, but balked and looked back the other way.

Beth staggered to her feet. She kept her arms in front of her. She drew back as the heat from the burning shed washed over her.

"The dwarves had spare clothes in their quarters," she said.

They weren't much smaller. Maybe she could find something that fit.

"Good thinking," Bannock replied. "I'll make sure the fire doesn't spread."

Beth sagged onto one of the dwarf beds. She sat on the edge and drank some water from a tin cup she'd found. It was warm and tasted metallic, but it helped. She also found a shirt which she could fit over her slim frame. It was too short in the arms and didn't tuck into her pants well, but she was decent.

And she hurt. Her shoulder hurt. Her back hurt. Her stomach hurt. Her hands hurt. Her legs hurt. It was all she could do to not lay back and collapse into tears. Except crying probably would hurt, too.

So she sat. And tried to drink her water. And focused on her breathing to calm herself and keep back the sobs. And let the weariness flow through her.

A knock came from the door.

"Miss Armstrong ...?" Bannock called from outside. "Are you decent?"

"Come in," she croaked.

The door opened slowly. Bannock stepped in, quickly looked her way and then at the ground. Then he looked up again. His face was red with embarrassment.

"Miss Armstrong, I ... uh, apologize for earlier ..."

"Apologize for what?" she said wearily. "You had no way of knowing. I had to get my shirt off. The dragon's blood burned." Her shoulders sank.

"I figured it was something like that." He still didn't look her in the eye. "I, uh, have your shirt. And your gun." He held it up. "The shirt's a mess."

But the gun wasn't. She let out a sigh of relief. "Oh, thank God."

He looked up. "Huh?"

"The gun," she said. "Hickok would kill me if I lost it."

"You talk about him a lot."

She shrugged. "He's my mentor. My friend."

"Oh." The guilt snuck back onto Bannock's face. "I always thought it was because you and he were ..."

"I'm half his age," she said with a glare. "We started my training when I was thirteen."

He blushed. "Uh, yeah. I hadn't thought that through."

"You're not the only one." She sagged even lower in her seat, but then held up her hand. "Can I have my gun?"

Instead of replying with words, he strode across the room and handed it to her. He pointedly looked at the spot on the bed next to her. She slid over and he sat down. He waited while she sat quietly and wrestled with the crowd of old memories.

"I'm sorry," Bannock finally and firmly said. "I see a pretty girl who talks about a man all the time. I just assumed ..."

She snorted softly. "A lot of people do. Even my mother, at one time. Now ... now she just thinks I can't make it on my own."

It was Bannock's turn to snort. "Please, Miss Armstrong. I've seen you shoot. I've seen you in a fight. You're better than most of the men I know." He thought for a moment. "All, maybe."

"Thank you," she said. She couldn't hold back the water pooling in her eyes anymore. "And please call me Beth."

"I can do that, Beth. And you can call me Winthrop if you like, but I prefer Bannock."

She started in surprise. "Winthrop? Winthrop!"

He grinned, the first he'd done since he'd come in. "Named after a rich great-uncle, who did *not* include us in his will. I think 'Bannock' is a much better fit."

"I'll say!" She smiled again and straightened up a bit. As she did, her arm brushed his, but he didn't flinch or move away. Instead, he just sat still and attentive. She straightened a bit more, and winced from the burns on her back. At least her hands and stomach only stung a little from the burns. Her back felt much worse.

He noticed. "Do you need something?"

"Bandages, I think," she said. "I wiped the dragon's blood off, but I think my back's blistered."

"I can find some bandages, but, uh …"

"*This* is the problem," she snapped. "If I was Lieutenant Tompkins, you'd be helping without a second thought. But I'm a girl and you—"

"I'll get the bandages." He stood and strode off toward the dwarves' supplies.

She stared at his back. *What is it about men?*

Bannock rummaged through a couple of bins on the shelf. With an "Aha!" he pulled out several strips of soft cloth and a small bottle. Then with a smile he walked back toward her.

"Iodine," he said, holding up the bottle. He nodded toward the shelves. "There's a salve that looks like it'll be good for your burns, too." He stopped in front of her. "Turn sideways and pull your shirt up as best you can."

She nodded, and as she did so, he sat down behind her.

"You're right," he said as he began dabbing her wounds. She winced with the sting. "The problem is you're a girl. It's not *your* problem, but mine. Dressed as you do, it's easy to think of you as just a boy with funny pronouns."

"So I'm a boy."

"No." He unrolled one of the bandages and passed her the end. "Take this and run it across your chest and back under your arm." He held the center over her back wounds as he did. "You're not. I … saw. And every bone in my body says I shouldn't've. So …"

"You feel guilty," she said.

"I do," he said, "or at least, I did. And I know I shouldn't, because you didn't have a choice—"

"But that's it," she said. "How can I be a gunfighter if the sight of my breasts is going to reduce men to gibbering idiots?" She sucked in her breath, but the insult was already out.

Bannock didn't seem to mind. He chuckled instead. "Maybe you should show them to your enemies. Turn *them* into gibbering idiots."

She laughed at the absurdity of the idea. Neither the dwarves nor the dragon would care at all about her breasts.

"But your partners?" Bannock continued. "No. Gibbering idiots would be bad."

"So we're partners now?" she asked.

He finished tying the bandages. She felt his posture shift as he straightened. His voice fell too. "I can't think of anyone else I'd want watching my back."

"Thank you."

He tugged at her shirt. "You can pull this down." She did so and turned back to face him.

His eyes were wide and deep. The half-mocking smile still held traces of embarrassment, that he couldn't quite hide. But he didn't look away. And his eyes didn't drift lower, but stayed with hers.

"So," he asked, "what now, partner?"

"Hickok would say we needed to chase after the dragon."

"So?" He smiled and shook his head softly in amusement. "Hickok—who cares? What does *Beth* say we need to do?"

She blinked in surprise, but he just nodded.

Then she realized she knew what to do.

"Captain Whitaker said they were digging near 'the mud volcano,' whatever that is. Let's follow the trail and find out."

CHAPTER THIRTY

The dwarf camp outside the building wasn't as hellacious as Beth had feared. The green wood that made up the blacksmith's shed burned, but not well. Bannock had pulled anything dry away from it and so it didn't look like the flames would jump to the grass or nearby trees. Instead, the shed crackled and smoked. Fortunately, most of the smoke went straight up.

Bannock's ambush had been nearly perfect. He took her to the spot down the trail where several small pines had given him a shooting blind. He'd been able to prop his rifle on a tree limb, which gave him the steadiness he'd lacked since the injury to his side.

And he'd gotten both of the dwarves that had charged down the trail on ponies.

"Well, not right away with the second one," he admitted with a red face. "I hit his pony instead. It turned into a game of hide and seek, but I won."

His face beamed, like he was proud of himself. But his eyes held a hauntedness his mouth did not.

Unfortunately, neither of the dead dwarves was Big One. The first one Bannock had shot even looked more like a youth than a warrior. His pudgy cheeks and wispy beard hinted he was barely into manhood.

But he was still trying to kill us, Beth reminded herself. *They all are. Them, or us.*

They couldn't find the remaining pony, nor Bannock's horse. Beth's horse—she couldn't look at it. She had to struggle to keep her stomach under control when she even glanced that way. The horse's guts were splattered all across the bare rock. Blood puddled and dripped down the slope like runoff from melting snow.

"We need the food and ammunition in my saddlebags," Beth said to Bannock.

"I'll get it," Bannock said. His grimace made it clear he wasn't looking forward to it. "You see if you can find some haversacks or packs. We're gonna have to walk from here."

"Yeah," she said with an exasperated sigh. "And thanks." She nodded toward the horse's remains without actually looking its way.

Beth found a few small pouches in the dwarves' barracks, but nothing large enough to carry more than a double handful of dried and somewhat mealy apples. She packed them anyway. They'd put all the good food on their horses and she didn't think she could eat anything that Bannock managed to retrieve.

So we'll go hungry if we have to. We have to be close to their new camp. Maybe we can find something there.

She snorted. *If they won.* The dwarves wouldn't give them food. And if they didn't win ... well, hunger wouldn't matter.

Beth did one more check of the barracks and then went outside to check the blacksmith's shed. Maybe something hadn't burned. The flies on the dwarven corpses had thinned with the smoke. The burning wood also masked the scent of decay.

She spotted the poker she'd used a few feet from one of the bodies. It looked badly corroded, so she picked it up. The sharp point was gone and pockmarks covered the top. It was also thin in several spots—almost brittle. The dragon's blood had eaten it away.

Still ... it had worked. It had gotten through the dragon's hide.

She scanned the blacksmith's shed. Most of it was charred or ash, but on one far side, she spotted another poker. The flames hadn't gotten to it, so she darted in and retrieved it. It was warm, but not hot enough to burn her hand. Away from the fire, she held it up. It was just a long rod of iron, about three feet in length and a quarter inch in diameter. One end had been sharpened to a wicked point and the other had a makeshift handle. But it held the grey sheen of the other tools.

It worked once. Why not? But how to carry it?

She doubled back into the barracks and found some twine. With it, she converted her empty right side holster into a sheath. With her Colt riding on her left hip, the weight felt balanced and right.

Bannock had returned when she strode back out of the barracks. He took one look at her and grinned.

"Sir Beth the Knight?" he teased.

"No," she said with a roll of her eyes. She put her hand on the "hilt" of the poker. "I'm not sure I can even use this thing. I'm still a gunslinger."

"Good," he said, "because you're gonna need to make every shot count. We don't have a lot of bullets left."

"How many?"

"Maybe twenty, thirty rounds for the revolvers. Less for the rifles."

"How many dwarves are left?" She looked at the corpses nearby.

"At least six," Bannock said, "plus the Shoshone, the dragon, and Sterling's ghost." He grinned. "And the possible volcano. Can't shoot that, though."

She grinned back. "No. We don't have a big enough gun."

The trail wound down to the lake and then followed the shore north. Here, the trees were even sparser and grass covered the land. The incessant breeze was back, blowing across the lake. The sun beat down on Beth's head and sweat beaded on her brow and around her ears. She momentarily wished she hadn't lost her hat.

After about an hour of walking, they reached the north end of the lake. A half hour after that, they reached a large river that flowed out of the lake. This one was hundreds of feet across and looked too deep to ford. Fortunately, the trail turned and headed north along the river's eastern shore.

Along the river, the trees grew thicker in stretches as they moved north. Squirrels scampered through the underbrush and at times the shady stretches of the trail were downright cool. When they were in the open areas, the midday sun made it hotter.

As they walked, Beth kept eyeing the underbrush. If horses thundered down the trail, where could she and Bannock jump? Where could they hide?

She saw plenty of spots, but none they needed to use. They walked until midday and nothing came down the trail toward them. Nothing flew overhead. It was almost idyllic, if not for the aches all through her body.

Bannock moved a bit better. He said his side felt much better. He'd certainly stopped clutching it. But he also still didn't trust his aim.

Not that she trusted hers, either. She tried not to think about her shoulder. For a few short stretches, she even succeeded.

The forest gave way to a large stretch of grassy plains that nestled between the river and the mountains to the east. The trail took the easiest, flattest route, which was also the most exposed. The river remained wide and swift and uncrossable.

Speed or safety? Beth wondered. They'd driven off the dragon and killed the dwarves who'd come to find them. How long until more came looking?

They stuck to the trail. When they took short breaks, they headed into the trees.

Then after another two hours or so, the river wound into a wide bend, about a hundred yards from shore to shore. It slowed and grew shallow. Beth could see the round rocks underneath for quite a ways out.

And the trail led right to the edge.

"Looks like we found a ford," Bannock said.

Beth shaded her eyes and scanned the surrounding area. The river looped east here, with few trees close on either side. They'd be exposed as they crossed and for some time after. On the other hand, there wasn't anywhere for ambushers to hide.

Then something caught her eye to the northwest, across the river. She looked closer and then pointed.

"Is that smoke?" she asked.

Bannock stared at it for a good long while. "I believe it is."

The river was cold. Freezing cold. It might've been fine to ford on horseback, but wading across took forever. The water got up to Beth's waist and the current was strong. Her legs were numb before she was even a third of the way across. But she didn't dare stop. One frozen step at a time.

Finally, finally, finally, she made it across. Bannock was only a few steps behind her. They flopped on the grassy shore and gasped for breath. Beth shivered heavily. She twisted her legs to keep them in as much sunlight as possible.

If we get attacked now, she thought, *we're in trouble. I don't think I can move.*

But eventually Bannock found the strength to climb to his feet. He extended a hand and pulled her up as well. They staggered to the trees a bit away from the trail. Bannock found a spot where they could sit in the sun but still be hidden from the trail. Beth tried wringing out water from the ends of her pants.

Bannock stretched out on the grass and propped himself up on his elbows. Then he noticed what she was doing. "Do you want me to leave so you can take 'em off and do that?"

She glared at him and twisted the fabric a little further up her shin.

"Yeah, sorry. I shouldn't say that to a lady."

She sat back in surprise. "Now I'm a lady and not a boy?"

He scoffed at the sky in exasperation. "I don't know! You're not a lady. You're not a boy. What are you?"

"Me. Beth. What does it matter after that?"

He snorted and thought about it a moment before nodding.

"What matters," she said, "is do we have each other's backs?"

"That we do."

"Good."

He didn't reply but just lay back and rested in the late afternoon sun. When the chill had finally left her legs, she sat up. By the time she stood, Bannock was also on his feet.

"Let's go," he said with a gesture toward the trail.

The trail led across a wide meadow—easily more than a quarter of a mile across. They'd be completely exposed for some time if they followed it. After a brief discussion, they decided to take the long way around and stay in the trees at the meadow's edge. The lodgepole pines weren't very dense, nor did they offer many places to hide, but it still felt safer.

It took nearly an hour and they saw no one.

The smoke was closer now. Thin and white and, it was harder to pick out against the sky than it had been before. It curled and drifted with the wind.

"Shoshone," Bannock said quietly from behind her.

A half dozen Shoshone warriors on horseback were splashing through the river at the ford. Beth peered closely, and one in the middle looked like Running Bear. A chill went up her spine.

She gestured to the west, away from the trail. The pines here were still quite thin, and the ground cover sparse. Beth and Bannock ran from tree to tree and kept looking back. When they couldn't see the Shoshone any more, they paused, but Beth pointed west again. When Bannock nodded, they ran further.

Finally, both gasping for air, they flopped down on the grass behind a small stand of short pines. The trees were dense enough for cover and probably far enough from the trail to let them evade any casual eyes.

"Did you see Running Bear?" Bannock asked once they'd both caught their breath.

"I think so. But I thought only the shaman and war leader rode this way to talk to the dragon."

"They must be bringing him in to answer questions."

"About what?" Beth asked. "The dragon knows all about us." Her back twinged at the memory of its blood hitting her. "What can Running Bear tell it?"

Bannock shrugged. "Maybe they're bringing him to the dwarves instead of the dragon. But I think we follow them."

"Agreed. If they stick to the trail, it shouldn't be hard."

Dusk was just beginning when Beth and Bannock reached the end of the trail. The cool wind had picked up again and they'd lost sight of the smoke, but it didn't matter. The trail emerged from the thin trees which opened up into another large field. A log building stood on the far side of the field with horses staked in front of it. Shoshone and dwarves milled about, but were too far away for Beth make out exactly what they were doing.

Fortunately, a small spiny hill rose nearby to the west. Beth and Bannock left the trail and headed just south of it. Once they'd gone a few hundred yards, it cut off the view of the camp. The ridge, just a few hundred feet up, was covered with short trees and spiny bushes. They carefully climbed it. Beth stopped every few feet to look for sentries, but never found one.

As they neared the top, Beth had to crinkle her nose. The smell of sulfur and decay seeped through the air. Finally they crested the small hill, still hidden in the trees. A thin shallow valley lay before them with another small ridge running opposite them. Beth realized the building had to be at the mouth of the valley to the east. They moved along the northern slope until they could see the building again.

Beth sucked in her breath. About five hundred yards in front of them, they could see the entire second dwarf camp. The building she'd seen earlier wasn't finished on all sides and appeared to be filled with barrels. Some small tents were pitched nearby. She also spotted a wagon pulled up against one side.

Off to the west of the building, a dark hole opened in the far hillside. Timbers braced the side and roof. A tall pile of what looked like mining equipment clustered to the side.

Further west beyond the mine entrance, the ground turned swampy with large patches of black and brown and grey swirled together. While grass did grow here and there, it looked more like a cauldron of bean soup than true land.

Beth narrowed her eyes. Was some of the mud ... bubbling? In the low light it was hard to tell.

She turned to Bannock. "I think we've found the mud volcano."

"That's not all." He gestured toward the building. "Those barrels are the gunpowder they stole."

"But where's the dragon?"

"I don't see it." He pointed toward the mining equipment. "Is that the cannon?"

Beth squinted and looked closer. A long metal barrel the size of a cannon sat on wooden wheels. Except the barrel pointed toward the ground instead of up, like cannons she'd seen before.

"I think so," she said. "But why is it pointing at the ground?"

"For mining?" he speculated. "Maybe shoot holes in the rock?"

"Could be," she said. "Some miners near Golden City use big hoses of water. It probably works the same."

"It'd have to be on hinges or a wheel, so they could point it where they needed."

"It probably is. Dwarves are clever like that."

Bannock gestured toward the Shoshone and dwarves, who were still mostly just standing around. "What do you think they're waiting for?"

Beth just shook her head.

Beth and Bannock settled onto the ground behind some low leafy bushes. As they watched, the dwarves and Shoshone didn't do much. Instead, they appeared to be just waiting. Beth's shoulder ached, as did her hand and back, but she did her best to ignore them. Instead, she kept her eyes forward as the dusk finally turned to darkness.

One of the Shoshone lit a torch and held it aloft. The dwarves and Indians moved to the edge of the mud volcano. They appeared to be waiting for something.

And then a blazing white figure appeared over the ooze. It looked like a man, but it shone so bright Beth had to turn her head.

"What are they staring at?" Bannock murmured.

Beth blinked and looked back at the figure Bannock couldn't see.

It had to be a ghost.

CHAPTER THIRTY-ONE

Beth studied the ghost. Its light dimmed or her eyes adjusted. From where she was, she couldn't make out much. It was taller than the dwarves and so probably human-sized. She couldn't make out its face or the details of its clothes, other than it seemed to be wearing a hat of some sort with a broad brim.

While the dwarves pulled back to the building, the Shoshone party approached. They shoved two of their own to the front, toward the edge of the mud. Those two looked wildly around and clearly didn't or couldn't see the ghost. But one behind them did. He seemed to be saying something.

The ghost flared brighter, like Raven had done when she'd grown angry. The Shoshone who could see the ghost, whom Beth figured was the shaman, shook a fist at it. The ghost flared brighter still. The shaman said something to the other Shoshone. They seized one of the two Indians in front and shoved him to his knees. Then they grabbed the other and yanked him back.

"Oh, God," Bannock muttered. He pointed up, above the ridge on the far side of the little valley.

A burst of flame seared across the sky. The dragon hovered above the ridge.

"How does it do that?" Bannock whispered. "Just float there? Magic?"

Beth frowned until she realized he hadn't seen the dragon do it before. "There's no magic on this side of the rift. I think the dragon's full of hot air, like a balloon. That's how it flies."

"Oh." He didn't ask any further questions.

Enough of the last rays of sunset remained to bask the dragon in a reddish glow. It stared down at the ghost. It seemed to be listening as the ghost spoke. Then with a roar, it floated down.

The kneeling Shoshone looked up in terror and began to rise.

The dragon dropped! Fast and sudden, its back claws tore into the Indian. The poor man had barely a chance to flinch before he was nearly ripped in half.

Beth's stomach lurched and she fought to keep the vomit down.

The dragon rose up carrying the body. It floated to the height of the ridge, and then its wings began to beat. After a few powerful thrusts, it shot over the far hill and dropped out of sight.

"I think that was Running Bear," Bannock murmured.

"I think so, too," Beth replied. "And his people let it happen!"

"If that's War Eagle," he pointed at the tallest of the warriors, "I'm not surprised."

They watched as the remaining Shoshone strode to their horses, unstaked them, and started to mount. The ghost said something to the shaman and he raised his hand. The other Indians stopped and waited.

"Let's go!" Beth said. She started scrambling back the way they'd come.

"Go where?" Bannock asked as he quickly followed.

"They're leaving. I don't know why, but if we hurry, we can catch them at the ford."

The Shoshone weren't in a rush, thankfully. Beth and Bannock made it back to the trail before the Indians. However, after all the running, Bannock had started to limp. One hand held his injured side. Beth's shoulder ached as well. She felt lightheaded, too, as her stomach reminded her of the dinner she'd skipped.

"I think we should ambush 'em here," Bannock said. "More cover."

She looked around and nodded. While the trees were scattered here, the big field between them and the ford offered nowhere to hide.

"Anywhere you can brace your rifle?" she asked.

He glanced around. "Nothing good. Maybe against that tree trunk." He pointed at a scraggly pine that was missing most of its branches on the far side of the trail. "Are we just going to shoot them?"

"Maybe not the other prisoner," Beth said. "But the shaman and the war leader? They just killed one of their own, not to mention what they did to the forts."

"Yeah," Bannock said with an unsavory chuckle. "Shooting's too good for them, but it's the best we can do. I'll wait for your signal."

He headed across the trail toward the tree. Beth found a bushier short pine she could kneel behind. Its long needles formed a near-perfect screen as long as she didn't stand. She found a comfortable position, hoisted her Colt in her left hand, and waited.

And waited. And waited some more.

And waited long enough for kneeling on the ground to become down right uncomfortable. The Shoshone had been heading for their horses. Where were they?

Finally, the dark shapes of horses appeared in the distance. They cantered down the trail with two in front and the others bunched up behind. Beth shifted her seat and raised her Colt. It felt heavy and wrong in her left hand. She held it as steady as she could.

As the Shoshone approached, Beth aimed at the one on the left, who looked like the shaman. She sighted down her barrel, and—they stopped! About fifty yards away. The one she'd been aiming at held up his hand. The two on the far side raised their rifles and aimed them toward Bannock's hiding place.

They'd spotted him!

Beth fired. Then fired again. Other gunshots rang out. One looked her way so she deliberately froze.

The one she'd targeted was still on his horse, but it bucked and screamed in pain. She'd hit the animal instead of him, she realized. It bounced into the horse behind it hard enough to dislodge the rider. The other Shoshone had slid from their horses. She got a glimpse of some of them stealing into the trees on the far side of the trail.

Gunfire sounded to her right—Bannock's—and the bucking horse collapsed. As the Shoshone she'd targeted jumped free, his back turned, big and broad. Beth fired twice again and he fell to the ground without a word.

But that meant three, maybe four, were in the trees somewhere. Her blood raced. In the dark, she couldn't make them out at all, and they probably knew where she was.

She quickly scanned the woods while she reloaded. She couldn't see anything moving her way. To her right, just one thin lodgepole pine stood between her and the trail. She scrambled to her feet and ran for it.

No shots came. No bullets whizzed by her head. She reached the tree and dropped to a crouch behind its trunk and its low, thin branches.

Across the trail, she could just make out a dark lump behind the tree where Bannock was hiding. He seemed to be holding still, as still as possible.

Something moved in the corner of her eye. Further up the trail, a dark shape—had to be a Shoshone—dashed from one tree to another. He, Dasher she quickly named him, paused at his new location and blended into the deep shadows too far for Beth to target.

She grumbled in frustration. She needed to see in the dark!

Raven. Raven can see in the dark.

But can the Shoshone see her? Beth's shoulder throbbed at the memory of the dwarves.

Only the shaman, she realized. *He's the only one that saw Sterling's ghost.*

She fumbled for Raven's pouch while keeping an eye on the spot where she'd seen the Shoshone. She rubbed the pouch between her forefingers and waited for the chill.

Raven appeared, in calm dark grey. She looked at Beth and her eyebrows went up in a question.

"Shoshone," Beth hissed. "In the trees. Where?"

Raven frowned and her dark grey lightened to mottled cream. She spun slowly in place. Then she pointed four places—two spots across the trail, one down by where the horses milled about, and the fourth, Dasher, on her side of the trail. Raven shook her finger at him.

So, he's close, Beth realized. She swiveled around to face the way Raven pointed, but kept near to the ground.

Raven floated past her and then to her left side. She went about ten feet and then pointed again. This time at an angle.

Beth followed the sight line from Raven's outstretched arm. Two trees in that general area were full and bushy enough to hide someone.

Raven again floated past her, to her right, and right through the tree. She again pointed forward. Beth sucked in her breath and nodded. Dasher was hiding behind the front tree.

Beth aimed her Colt into the darkest shadow of the tree. She braced her left hand with her right. Then she took a deep breath and fired twice.

The branches of the tree whipped back and forth as a body crashed through them. It fell still on the ground.

Bannock's rifle went off to her right. She turned just in time to see a black figure dashing between trees. She fired and he, Dodger she thought, threw himself to the ground.

"Did I hit him?" Beth whispered to Raven.

The ghost shook its head.

Beth stood and shifted to get a better look at where the figure had fallen.

A Shoshone war cry ripped the air further to her right. She didn't let it distract her. A metal clang rang through the air and then another howl of fury.

Dodger scrambled to his hands and knees. Beth fired before he could get to his feet. The first shot went wide, and she winced, but the second was on target. He collapsed.

She glanced sideways at Raven, who nodded this time.

More clangs. Two figures fought in a clearing. One swung what looked like an axe and the other kept blocking with something long. In the dark it was hard to be sure exactly what. The defender —Beth was sure it was Bannock—kept retreating under the onslaught of fast and furious blows.

Beth ran closer. She still couldn't get a clean shot, so she hesitated and looked at Raven. "The other one?"

Raven pointed back toward the Shoshone horses. That warrior, whom she hadn't nicknamed yet, hadn't moved. She turned back to the fight.

Maybe if she circled to the side she could get a good shot ...

Bannock tripped on something. As he fell back, the Shoshone warrior yelled in triumph and swung his axe straight down.

But then Bannock rolled sideways and kicked out! His feet caught the Shoshone's and the Indian tumbled to the ground. The axe went flying and then Bannock was on top of him.

The two wrestled and rolled on the ground. Beth raced over. She holstered her revolver and drew her knife. She paused on the balls of her feet—she still couldn't make out exactly who was who.

The one on top gasped, and the gasp turned into a groan. He flopped a few times and then went limp. The man underneath started shoving him aside.

"Gimme a hand?" Bannock said.

Beth let out a huge sigh of relief. She helped roll the corpse off Bannock. He sat up and panted to catch his breath. Then he looked over at the body.

"That knife didn't help you, now did it?" he taunted.

"What?" Beth said.

"War Eagle," Bannock said. He gestured toward the Shoshone. "He liked to keep a hidden knife strapped to the small of his back. Other boys would think he was unarmed...." Bannock let out another sigh, this one of satisfaction. "Well, a secret knife's only good if it's a *secret*, you know?"

He extended his hand and Beth pulled him to his feet. "The others?"

"Three dead," she said. "The fourth's back there," she nodded toward the spot. "He's not moving though."

"So you got two more, huh?"

With some help, she thought. She looked around for Raven, but the ghost was gone.

"Are you hurt?" she asked Bannock.

"Bruises," Bannock said. He gingerly touched his ribs and his elbow. "Yeah. Nothing serious."

Beth's chest relaxed in relief. "Good. Let's go see why this last one didn't join the battle."

They walked down the trail, side by side. No point in being subtle, they'd agreed. This Shoshone had already decided to skip the battle and was likely injured. Even if he wasn't, he'd had plenty of time to hide in the trees and hadn't.

Still, they'd reloaded and had their guns out. Bannock's rifle was too banged up to use, so he'd switched to his revolver. He scuffed the ground with his right foot as he walked and winced when he tried to step higher.

"Just bruises?" she murmured.

"Just bruises," he said back through gritted teeth. "Knee, thigh, foot, side, arm, gut. Just bruises."

She grinned but then looked ahead.

The Shoshone horses had scattered. Beth spotted one through the trees off to the right, but her eyes quickly settled on the man sitting in the middle of the trail. He had one leg bent under him and the other outstretched. He clutched the ankle of his bent leg and just looked at them as they approached.

Bannock barked something in Shoshone and got a two-word reply.

"He's surrendered," he said.

"That was quick."

Bannock said some more, and the Indian pointed to his ankle. They exchanged a few more words before Bannock murmured, "Ah, good."

He turned to Beth. "His ankle's broken, but he's not going to fight us anyway. He saw what you did a few days ago. He's the one that threw the spear. He says you're too good with the gun to fight."

Beth's eyebrows rose and she blinked.

"He was also happy to hear War Eagle was dead."

"Really?"

"Mmm hmm. War Eagle had offered to let the dragon eat him, too."

Beth's chest tightened. Her stomach churned at the memory of what the dragon had done to Running Bear.

"Will he help us?" she asked after she'd regained control of her innards.

Bannock talked to the injured warrior some more. Then he turned back to Beth.

"He'll tell us what he knows," Bannock said, "and then if we put him on a horse, he'll ride back to their camp and tell the chief what War Eagle did. He thinks they'll stop helping the dragon then."

"So what does he know?"

Bannock turned back to the Indian. It looked like it might be a long conversation, so Beth carefully walked over to the horse she'd seen in the trees. It skittered away, but she still managed to snag its bridle and lead it back. When she returned, Bannock looked grim.

"He says," Bannock said, "they helped the dwarves move the gunpowder into the mine before they left. On the orders of the ghost, apparently. The dwarves were preparing some delayed charges for the cannon. And yeah, they rigged it so it shoots up or down."

"Oh, God," Beth said. "They're going to set off the volcano!"

"Mmm hmm. Tonight." Bannock kicked a rock in frustration.

Beth tightened her grip on her Colt. She stared up the trail toward the mine.

"No they won't," she said, "because we're not going to let them."

CHAPTER THIRTY-TWO

They strode side by side through the night. The breeze slid coldly across Beth's face. She set her jaw and marched on. Bannock matched her pace. He too had his gun out, held low as they walked. What she'd thought would be a long trek flashed by. The trees fell away and the dwarves' storage building came in sight.

Beth and Bannock didn't slow. The clouds had fallen away, and the moon, just a sliver short of full, shone bright. Even so, deep shadows filled the nooks of the valley. They passed the last of the trees. Sterling's ghost glowed at the mud volcano, but his light didn't reflect. Something moved near the mineshaft, but it was too dark to see.

Beth reached for Raven's pouch, but paused. The dwarves would see the ghost and that would give her position away. Then movement atop the building caught the corner of her eye.

"Down!" she cried. She tugged on Bannock's arm and they both dropped to the dirt.

An arrow whistled overhead. Then a second. She nestled deeper into the long grass.

She peeked up. The archer stood atop the building. He'd stopped shooting, but still held his bow at the ready. She judged the range. It'd be a tough shot.

"Can you hit him?" she whispered to Bannock.

He shook his head. "But we've got more company."

Two short figures jogged toward them from the mine entrance. "Where are the rest?" Beth asked.

"Dunno. In the mine, hopefully." He shifted to his elbows and brought his gun up. "Think we can get these two?"

Beth raised her Colt but pain shot through her right arm. She winced. She'd shifted her weight and her shoulder *hurt*. She adjusted her position, which helped, but made it harder to aim left-handed.

"Oh, no," Bannock said.

Beth looked ahead. The two approaching dwarves had slowed to a walk. One circled left while the other went right. She couldn't make out their features, but the one moving left held a throwing axe cocked back by his shoulder. She couldn't be sure, but the other could've had an axe too.

"They don't know where we are," Bannock hissed.

Beth shook her head. "Dwarves can see in the dark."

Bannock swore.

The dwarves slowly crept forward. The bowman was looking their way too.

"Attack on three?" Beth murmured. When Bannock nodded, she started counting. "One ... two ... three!"

She jumped up to her knees and fired twice at the dwarf on the left. Bannock's gun barked as well. Then she dodged sideways and rolled through the grass. An arrow stabbed the grass where she'd been. The poker she wore at her belt smacked across her leg and pain shot through her shoulder when it hit the ground.

She popped up from her roll to see Bannock's dwarf was down. She'd missed hers completely and he reached for something in his belt. Bannock ran toward him, weaving, as arrows flew by. But then a thrown axe clipped his arm and he dropped to the ground.

Beth steadied her Colt and aimed down the barrel. The dwarf with the axe took a step closer to where Bannock had fallen.

She fired twice.

The dwarf collapsed and fell to the ground. She didn't wait but fired twice again toward the archer. Then she sank to one knee to reload.

The archer ran to the side of the roof and started climbing down.

"You hurt?" Beth called to Bannock.

He clambered to his hands and knees. "Not bad. The handle hit me instead of the blade."

Beth let out a sigh of relief. She looked for the archer and saw him running toward the mine shaft.

"What about you?" he asked.

"Nothing new," she said, "but ..." she double-checked her ammunition pouch. "I'm down to my last eight bullets."

"I'm about the same."

She walked to his side as he finished getting to his feet. As she did, she watched Sterling's ghost. It stared back at her with its fists clenched.

"The mine next?" Bannock asked.

"You guard the entrance," she said, "while I check the building. We don't want any other surprises."

They warily approached the two structures. As they got closer, shadows resolved themselves. The wagon sat near the building, with a team of two horses hitched. They shuffled nervously and snorted, but didn't pull away. Beth guessed they had blinders on.

She glanced over at Sterling's ghost. It raised a fist and shook it at her.

The building was easy to check. It was empty of anything big. The barrels of gunpowder were gone. There wasn't anywhere anyone could hide within it, and a quick look around the back showed no one there as well.

She joined Bannock at the mine's entrance, or more precisely at the cannon. It rested a dozen feet from the mine's threshold. The dwarves had fashioned two large iron wheels to hold it, along with a third wheel in back for balance. Huge notches in the side wheels allowed it to be pointed up or down at large angles. At the moment, it was aimed toward the dark opening.

"Let's move that," Beth said as she pointed toward the cannon.

"Yeah," Bannock said with a dark chuckle. "Can't have it going off accidentally."

"Assuming they loaded it," Beth said.

But as they moved closer, it became clear that's exactly what the dwarves had been doing. Several small iron spheres about the size of apples were stacked in short piles near the cannon's mouth. Each had a long fuse cord running out of a hole in the sphere's side. Several of these had been twined together. Nearby, a small, shuttered charcoal lamp sat on the ground. Its dim glow lit up a small patch of ground around it.

"Those are delayed charge cannon balls," Bannock said. "You light the long fuse with that," he pointed at the lamp, "and then fire the cannon. They explode in flight."

Beth checked the barrel. A bundle of cords hung out the end. "It's already loaded."

"Let's move it." Bannock didn't wait. He pushed on the barrel until the cannon began to roll backward. Beth joined him and found it surprisingly easy to move. While it was heavy, the dwarves had been smart in building the wheels and they turned easily.

They pushed it about ten feet down the gentle slope from the mine entrance, and then gravity took over. It rolled another thirty or forty feet and turned slightly, until it was pointed more at the building than the mine.

"Think that's far enough?" Beth asked.

"Let's take those explosive charges out to be sure," Bannock said. "We probably should've done that first."

"Wait. We can't let them set off the ones back there." She gestured toward the piles on the ground. "Let's at least take the lamp."

He nodded in agreement and waited while she raced back to

get it. Then they headed down the slope and had just gotten to the cannon when a voice rang out behind them.

"Die, humans!"

Shoot first, taunt second. Beth snorted at the memory of Hickok's words and dropped to the ground. A thrown axe whistled through the air where her head had been. She twisted around and fired toward the mine.

She missed, but two of the dwarves that had emerged scrambled to the sides of the mine entrance. The third was Big One. He snarled. His arm flicked almost too fast to see and another axe clanged off the cannon near where Bannock had been.

Beth scrambled behind the cannon barrel. She crouched and peered beneath the barrel. Big One had moved out of the center of the mine entrance. There wasn't enough moonlight for her to make out exactly where the dwarves were, but they weren't running forward.

"Bannock ... you okay?" Beth called.

"Yeah," he called back. His voice put him a few feet away on the far side of the cannon's wheels. "His throw was really wide."

"I think we're at the edge of their range," Beth said, "and they can't come closer or we'll shoot them."

"I can barely see them," Bannock replied.

"But they can see us fine, so we can't charge either."

"So we've got a stand-off. Three to two."

Four to two. There was another dwarf somewhere. But maybe she could make it four to three. Keeping her gun level with her left hand, Beth started to reach under her shirt for Raven's pouch with her right. But then she stopped as a thought struck her.

Wait. What about Sterling's ghost?

That ghost still hovered over the mud volcano. It still glowed angry white and had its hands cupped around its mouth, like it was shouting.

Or calling something.

Oh, God, it's summoning the dragon! Beth's heart hammered so hard she thought her chest would explode. She had to take several deep breaths before she could speak.

"Hey, Bannock," she called.

"Yeah?"

"We're about to have company," she said. "The dragon."

He cursed sharply.

"I think we can use it," she said, "as a distraction. When it comes over the ridge, it may distract the dwarves and we can attack."

"Yeah, but the dragon'll burn us to a crisp the minute it sees us. We'd be better off distracting it. Or getting it to attack the dwarves."

Get it to attack the dwarves ... she had an idea!

She furiously rubbed Raven's pouch. When the ghost appeared, she pointed back to where the cannon had originally stood. "Go!" Beth said. "Stand there and draw the dragon's attention!"

Raven's ghost nodded, but then took a moment to stare sharply at Sterling's ghost. She yelled something out while she floated to where Beth had pointed. Sterling's ghost stopped its calling and raged at Raven for a moment, before returning to its summons.

"Bannock," Beth called, "I need you to help me with the cannon."

"What? The dwarves will see us!"

"But they can't hit us. We need to aim the cannon at the top of the mine."

"Seal them in! Good thinking!"

She hadn't been thinking that, but this wasn't the time to tell him.

A roar ripped through the sky, followed by a burst of flame in the air above the ridge. The dragon floated over the top and its head whipped this way and that. It gave another angry snarl. With one quick stroke of its wings, it zoomed down toward them all.

Beth crouched under the cannon barrel and made herself as small as possible. She had to shift her "poker sword" to do so, and then kept her hand on it. She shivered and couldn't stop stroking her gun handle with her left thumb. She forced herself to breathe as she watched.

Raven turned from grey to blazing white. She faced the dragon and shook her arms at it. Her mouth opened in a yell that Beth couldn't hear.

But the dragon did. It pulled back its head like a snake about to strike. Then it opened its mouth and flames shot down toward Raven's ghost.

"Now!" Beth yelled to Bannock. She stood and started shoving the barrel into place. He adjusted the levers at the wheels and it tilted up.

The dragon's flames went right through the ghost. They hit the stack of gunpowder charges that she was standing over. Raven winked out as it did.

The charges exploded. Flaming debris flew all around and smoke obscured their view of the mine and the dragon.

"Now!" Beth yelled again, but Bannock was already pushing the wheel around.

Beth pulled the poker from her belt. She took it off and dropped it down the barrel, pointy side out. Then she grabbed the charcoal lamp from where it had fallen. It hadn't broken or gone out, thankfully. She lit the fuses hanging out the end of the barrel and raced back to Bannock.

He'd already pointed the cannon up. He took the lamp and lit the cannon's firing fuse.

The smoke cleared. The dragon hovered in the sky above. Right where it'd been before.

The cannon fired and kicked back. Bannock jumped out of the way, but Beth wasn't so lucky. It slammed into her and knocked her sprawling. She landed on her back.

Which meant she watched as the poker flew through the sky and lanced the dragon in the belly. It howled, but then the fused bombs hit. The first one exploded and then—

—the sky went white. The boom deafened Beth and she

threw her arm over her face. The sound echoed off the hills, followed by other explosions. Then she heard the clatter of falling debris.

"My God!" Bannock mumbled from somewhere nearby. "Did we ...?"

The debris stopped. Beth's vision slowly returned as she sat up. The dragon was nowhere to be seen.

No. *Pieces* of the dragon were everywhere. Lumps and limbs and scales scattered across the valley.

"I don't think it was filled with hot air," Bannock said. "Maybe it ate too many beans that gave it gas. Explosive gas at that."

Beth laughed, and then she couldn't stop laughing. Her laughter turned to sobs of relief. She just sat on the ground as they wracked her body.

Bannock knelt by her side and put a comforting hand on her shoulder. She shook her head.

"I'm fine," she said. "I'm fine." She wiped the moisture from her eyes. "What about the dwarves?"

"I'll check."

She nodded and took several deep breaths. Once she'd managed to calm herself, she stood.

Bannock stood near the mine entrance. He looked around and then back to her.

"Three dead dwarves," he said. "It looks like they tried to attack and then got caught in the explosion."

"Three? Not four?"

He shook his head. "Only three bodies." Then he pointed to the timbers holding up the entrance. "These look pretty weak. We can probably pull them down and collapse the entrance."

"We'll do that," she said. "But first ..." She turned toward the mud volcano.

The fiery white ghost still floated over the mud. It raged and shook its fist at her. Its face was almost a snarl. For once, she was glad she couldn't hear ghosts.

"We have to get rid of Sterling's ghost," she said. "Otherwise he'll trick someone else into fulfilling his plan to set off the volcano."

"But how?" Bannock said. "We can't get rid of a ghost. Only a witch or a shaman can do that."

A shaman. Beth pulled Raven's pouch from under her shirt and furiously rubbed it.

The familiar chill arrived, even with the heat from the fire. Raven appeared in front of her, her normal grey. Her normal serene expression. Which lasted only for a moment as she cocked her head like she was listening. Her brow tightened in confusion.

When Raven gazed back, Beth hurriedly said, "The dragon's dead. But it took its orders from him." She pointed at the other ghost.

Raven's ghost turned blinding white.

"He ordered it to kill the Arapaho," Beth said. "Can you send him away?"

Raven only gave a quick nod before she shot forward toward Sterling. And then stopped suddenly about thirty feet short. She strained, as if pulling on a leash.

Beth's eyes went wide. She looked at Raven's ghost, then at the pouch with the bone in it. Then at the ghost again.

A ghost was tied to its body. Raven couldn't get any farther away from her toe bone.

Beth took a deep breath. Then she hurled the pouch at Sterling's ghost.

It arced through the air and fell just short. The hot mud popped and sizzled when it hit.

Raven's ghost zoomed into Sterling's. Both ghosts flashed brighter as they struggled, so bright Beth had to look away. When it dimmed a little, she looked back.

Raven had one arm around Sterling's neck in a chokehold. Her other hand held something against his back. Her eyes met Beth's. She gave a small nod of acknowledgement.

A grey disk shimmered above them. Then both ghosts disappeared.

Beth sagged to the ground with a sigh.

"What happened?" Bannock asked. "You destroyed Raven's pouch—"

She cut him off with a shake of her head. "She took him," she said. "She took Sterling."

"Where?"

"I don't know. But I suspect he's not going to like it."

CHAPTER THIRTY-THREE

Bannock let Beth rest while he went to the weakened mine timbers. He pushed and pulled and then jumped back when they gave way and collapsed. Then went to the wagon near the storage building and got the horses calmed and unstaked. Then he got the wagon turned toward the trail. He gestured for Beth to climb up.

She glanced around one last time. Was there anything they needed? Anything left undone?

The ghosts were gone. Not even a flicker of light came from the mud volcano. She hoped Raven's soul had gone to a better place.

Proof. She searched the ground until she found enough pieces of the dragon to make it unmistakable. Rose could probably preserve them, or they could strip them down to the bones. But people would know.

Wearily, she stretched out in the back of the wagon. She closed her eyes and tried not to think about her wounds. The wagon bumped along down the trail. Somehow she fell asleep soon after they crossed the ford.

She awoke, still in the wagon, to someone lightly shaking her. She cracked her eyes open. Streaks of red creased the dawn sky behind Rose's head. Her friend's eyes were filled with concern.

"Where do you hurt?" Rose asked.

"Everywhere," Beth replied. Her dry lips cracked when she tried to smile. "Nowhere bad, though."

"Water," Rose said. "You need water. I'll be right back."

Beth slowly sat up. She *did* hurt, everywhere. Bruises she couldn't remember getting now sang their hellos. She sagged in exhaustion. At least she was alive. The bruises and other wounds made that clear.

The wagon was parked in a wide grassy expanse near the lake. Waves rippled across the water and carried the fresh smell of morning. The horses had been unhitched and now grazed in the tallest grass about ten feet away.

Rose knelt at the shore of a small stream feeding into the lake. Her dress was torn around the bottom and her sleeve was a splash of mud. Every hair on her head seemed to want to fly a different direction, but when she glanced back at Beth, her face glowed with triumph. She stood and held up a canteen like it was a trophy. Then she marched back to the wagon.

Beth took several deep pulls from the canteen. She wiped her mouth of a few dribbles when she finished. "Where is everyone?"

"Bannock's asleep in camp," Rose answered. "He didn't think the wagon could handle the terrain. He'll bring Jefferson and Captain Whitaker down on the horses later."

"How are they?"

Rose bit her lip. "Alive," she finally said. "But for a little while there ..."

"They'd've died without you."

Rose's smile barely creased her lips. "The captain's fever broke a little while ago. He's sleeping now. It wasn't from my doing, though. At least, I didn't do anything special."

"Anything Rose Chamberlin does is special."

Rose rolled her eyes. Then she playfully swatted Beth's arm.

"Come on. If you're not badly hurt, you can help me fetch the supplies and load the wagon."

Beth groaned. "The work never ends, does it?"

"You can rest in Golden City," Rose shot back. "Until then, we've got work to do."

Lieutenant Tompkins was sitting up near the remnants of a small fire when they got to camp. His face almost glowed when he saw the two women, though his eyes were more on Rose than Beth. He looked worn and pale, but alert. He clutched one of Rose's small tin cups in his hands as if it was full of gold.

A few feet away, Captain Whitaker snored lightly. He lay on his side facing away. His entire back was bandaged, and blood and pus had still soaked through in spots and mixed with dirt. But he breathed normally.

Bannock was harder to spot. He'd found a shady spot near a copse of thin trees and was on his back with his hat over his face.

Lieutenant Tompkins gestured for Beth to join him.

"You're alive!" she said as she knelt next to him.

"Thanks to Rose," he said. He tapped a thin tree branch that had been splinted to his leg. "I bled a lot, she says."

"But you'll be all right."

He grimaced and shook his head. "But it's better than being blown up by a volcano." He looked longingly at Rose. "Maybe I can get a discharge from the army now."

Beth suppressed the desire to roll her eyes.

"But," he continued, "at least now everyone will believe me about the dragon."

"They will indeed." *But what will they think about it? About all of this?*

Beth's mind drifted to her ma. Would Ma be upset, or proud? She'd risked her life, but ... she'd won.

She mused on it while she helped Rose pack.

It only took one trip to get all their gear to the wagon. When they returned to camp, Bannock was awake. They managed to gently load both Lieutenant Tompkins and Captain Whitaker onto horses. The captain awoke, but his eyes never quite focused. His mind and his seat drifted as he rode, and only Bannock's frequent steadying hand kept him from falling.

When they reached the lake, they found a surprise. A small band of Shoshone, four of them, waited on their horses a respectful distance from the wagon. One of them was the Indian they'd spared after the ambush the night before.

"Go talk to them," Beth told Bannock. "We'll get the lieutenant and captain into the wagon."

He nodded and rode over to them.

It took a little bit of shuffling to get the men off their horses and comfortably seated in the wagon. Rose checked their wounds and gave them each some water. Beth helped her tuck blankets over each of them after that.

Bannock rode back with a huge grin. "How would you ladies care for an escort back to Golden City? Or at least as far as Fort Collins?"

"What?" Beth said in surprise. "The Shoshone?"

"Mmmm hmmm." Bannock turned somber. "The old chief died. With War Eagle dead too ... well, they're gonna have a tribal council. But they did agree on one thing. They don't want a war with us, on account of Fort Sanders and Fort Caspar." He gestured toward the Indian warriors. "So they're going with us as kind of a peace mission."

"I don't know if we can forgive that," Lieutenant Tompkins said. His voice was strained with exhaustion, but his eyes lit with fury.

"Forgive?" Beth said. "No. But the responsible ones are dead. Why should the rest suffer for following orders?"

Lieutenant Tompkins's face soured. "Well ... we forgave the rebels from the War Between the States, but that's because we had a bigger enemy to fight ..."

"Which we still do," Beth said. "We have no idea how the army's doing against the trolls."

Lieutenant Tompkins grimaced.

"Yeah, well," Bannock said, "the Shoshone will also share their food. They'll help with the hunting, too."

"Well, why didn't you say so!" Rose said. "They're coming with us, aren't they, Jefferson?"

Lieutenant Tompkins snorted softly but couldn't keep the small smile off his face.

"Rose does know best," Beth added.

Lieutenant Tompkins nodded. "Far be it from me to disagree."

They followed a shorter route south to Fort Sanders, the one the Shoshone had taken on the way up. It still took weeks. The summer heat was in full sway, but they found plenty of water and game along the way.

Captain Whitaker started to truly recover after a few days. He started drinking broth and began to regain his wits. When Bannock asked him what he remembered, the captain said he didn't want to remember. He barely talked at all. Instead, he mostly just stared at the scenery or slept. Rose said he was doing better, but his eyes remained haunted without respite.

Lieutenant Tompkins did better. He grew restless after only a week and tried walking in camp, but his injured leg just wasn't strong enough. He managed short rides on horseback, but had trouble holding on with his bad leg. So, as he rode on the wagon, he started carving himself a crutch from a long branch Bannock brought him. When he wasn't doing that, he'd ask Beth or Bannock questions about the battles they'd fought after his rescue. To Beth's surprise, he seemed to find new questions each day and didn't tire of her repeating, "I don't remember."

"We'll want the report for the army to be complete," he said when she asked about his continued curiosity. "The army loves its reports."

"But you're not writing it down," she said.

"No paper." He gestured toward the wagon in emphasis. Their supplies were mostly blankets and cooking gear. The remnants of their months on the trail. "Don't worry. I've got a good memory."

She just rolled her eyes.

Beth herself felt better physically as the days went by. The bruises faded and the scrapes and scratches slowly healed. Her right arm grew stronger, strong enough to start exercising it. Her quickdraw was still horrible, though. Her right arm started shaking after only a few practice draws, though "a few" grew larger with time.

Bannock too seemed to heal. The second night out, he and the Shoshone got rip-roaring drunk on some whiskey the Indians had. He had the decency to be chagrinned the next morning. He didn't shirk from his turn at the wagon's reins either. He just gave Beth a pained smile and let her sit quietly on the buckboard beside him.

Rose thrived. When they dropped out of the mountains, she slipped off to bathe in one of the streams. At nights when she could, she washed her clothes. She produced a comb magically from somewhere and once her hair was perfect, offered to help untangle Beth's.

They sat by the fire early one evening of the fourth week. Rose was behind Beth with her comb and a bowl of warm water. Captain Whitaker and Lieutenant Tompkins were asleep, while once again Bannock and the Indians carried on their own conversation just out of earshot of the ladies.

Rose gently tugged at one of the knots in Beth's hair. When Beth hissed, her friend just clucked and kept working on it. "You really should take better care of this."

"I have more pressing things to do," Beth shot back.

"Mmm hmm. But you don't need to practice with your gun all your free time. I don't."

Beth snorted softly. "You barely practice at all."

"But I *do* practice. At least when Jefferson's able." Rose finished tugging one rat's nest apart and moved onto the next.

Beth bit her lip to avoid saying anything. *Just how hard had her friend fallen for the officer?*

Rose apparently read her mind. "Oh, sweetie. Give me some due. I know it may not lead to anything. The army will reassign him when he's healthy, and then what?"

"They could always assign him to Golden City."

"True," Rose said, "but Jefferson thinks that's unlikely. Besides, I may not be there."

"Where would you be?"

"Why, on the road with you, of course." She teased another tangle apart. "Who's going to take care of you otherwise?"

Beth smiled at the thought of Rose making her dresses and combing her hair as they rode through the wild.

When they arrived at the ruins of Fort Sanders a few days later, they camped near the river where they'd once hidden to watch the Shoshone attack. Lieutenant Tompkins insisted on riding over to the fort. Bannock and the Shoshone went with him. Beth considered it, but then decided she didn't need to see the destruction and the bodies. She was actually sleeping without nightmares, which was a small blessing.

The men came back at dusk in surprisingly good moods. Rose and Beth stood to meet them at the edge of camp.

"The army's been here," Bannock said. "They buried the bodies and left a note. Fort Collins, at least, is still intact."

Beth nodded. "The dragon never made it that far."

"I suspect they'll reclaim Fort Sanders once the trolls are driven back," Lieutenant Tompkins said. "Though I doubt Captain Whitaker will want his command back."

The captain just continued to stare at the fire without looking up.

"The poor man," Rose murmured.

"Yeah," Bannock said. "There but for the grace of God...."

"We were lucky," Beth said.

"No," Lieutenant Tompkins said. "I was lucky." He patted his bum leg. "*You* were good. You're the reason we're all alive."

The others nodded and Beth blushed, uncertain of what to say.

When they were about a day out from Fort Collins, Bannock grew noticeably impatient. Despite the beautiful summer morning, he seemed in a cloudy mood. After breakfast, he spoke with the others and rode ahead, carrying one of the dragon's claws they'd kept from the battle. He left the Shoshone behind, but by now they seemed like just part of the group. Lieutenant Tompkins had even started teaching one of the warriors English.

About mid-afternoon, Bannock returned, but with a squad of soldiers. They rode hard and their dark blue uniforms almost sparkled in the sun. Rose had been driving the team, and she pulled up on the reins and brought the wagon to a halt. Beth stood up on the buckboard and watched.

Bannock and the soldiers halted right in front of them. His grin spread from ear to ear.

"The trolls ran away!" he said. "The army's back!"

CHAPTER THIRTY-FOUR

Beth's jaw dropped. She shaded her eyes and looked at the soldiers. They nodded in confirmation. The one with thick black curly hair and sergeant's stripes spoke up.

"It turned out it was more of a raid in force than an invasion," he said. "Once our army showed up en masse, the trolls turned and ran for the Mississippi."

"Not all of them made it," one of the privates added with a grin.

"And you're back already?" Beth asked. *Have we really been gone that long?*

"Most of the reserves weren't needed," the sergeant said. "Once it was clear the trolls were on the run, they sent us back."

Rose let out a deep sigh. "They're safe. Mr. Lake and all the others are safe."

"In part thanks to us," Bannock said. His grin hadn't faded a bit, and Beth wondered if his cheeks were sore.

"Private Bannock told us a little and showed us the dragon's claw," the sergeant said, "but my captain wants a full report as soon as you all are able." He nodded toward the Shoshone, who'd been nervously hanging back. "From them too."

Bannock said something in Shoshone, and the Indians nodded.

One of the privates dismounted and handed the reins to a soldier. He walked toward the wagon.

"Private Hanson will drive the wagon," said the sergeant. He smiled at Beth. "So, Miss Armstrong, can you ride?"

After the debriefings and the report writing and a very late dinner, Captain Jameson, the Fort Collins commander, ordered three kegs of Adolph Coors's beer to be tapped and shared with the troops. He held a fourth keg back for the soldiers on watch with the statement that everyone deserved a chance to celebrate.

From somewhere, a soldier produced a fiddle. Then another found a fife while a third brought out a drum. Soon a merry party with music and dancing filled the Fort's courtyard. Rose consented to dance a few songs with some of the soldiers, though never with the same one twice. Between partners, she smiled and waved at Lieutenant Tompkins, who sat on the side and tapped his crutch in time to the music. During one break, she sat with him. When she was asked to dance again, she gave Lieutenant Tompkins a kiss on the cheek before she stood.

Beth just sat on a stool in the shadows and watched. She sipped water since she hadn't cared for the beer. After the first few songs, a private hesitantly approached, like he was going to ask her to dance. She raised an eyebrow and he skittered away.

She never saw Bannock. After a dozen songs, she decided to go to bed.

She awoke at dawn the next morning. Her body didn't seem to know how to sleep longer. It still ached, though. All the familiar wounds. All the familiar stiffness. She couldn't help wondering, *would she ever feel right?*

Eventually she shook off her maudlin thoughts. She climbed

out of bed, found her pants and shirt, and then her gun. There had to be a shooting range, or somewhere else good to practice, somewhere.

She ended up just outside the fort's main gate. With the sentry's permission, she scratched an X on the wall with her knife. She backed up twenty feet and let her left hand hover over her Colt. She took a steadying breath, and then drew.

Her aim was off by a good six inches. She grumbled under her breath. *I'm surprised I managed to hit any of the dwarves!*

"Getting better?"

Bannock stood near the open gate. He grinned and adjusted his hat against the morning sun.

"Some," she replied as she holstered her gun.

He sauntered toward her and nodded toward the target on the wall. "I'm gonna miss seeing this."

She blinked in surprise. "You're not coming to Golden City?"

He shook his head. He stopped when he reached her side and squinted at her makeshift target.

"Why not?" she asked.

"Orders."

"Ah."

"Captain Jameson wants to have a peace conference with the Shoshone and Arapaho."

"And he wants you to lead it."

Bannock shook his head again. "I'm just the translator."

"Ah. Think it'll work?"

"Dunno. He wants to offer them land in exchange for promises of help against the trolls and Jotun."

"Think Congress will go for it?"

"Maybe," he kicked a small clod of dirt. "With the forts gone, we couldn't stop 'em from taking it anyway."

"So then what?"

"We'll see," he said with a shrug. "I've got another year before my enlistment term's up ... but I think the army's not for me."

She raised an eyebrow.

"That insubordination thing," he said. The corner of his mouth turned up in a grin. "I do better with a partner than a boss."

She couldn't resist smiling back. "Even if she's a girl?"

"Best partner I ever had was a girl." His eyes twinkled. "She had my back when we fought a dragon. How many people can say that?"

"Not many," she said with a laugh. "Not many at all."

"Mmm hmmm." They shared a long grin before he gestured toward her target. "Let's see what you can do with a live round."

"With pleasure."

Days later, a much smaller group arrived at the northern edge of Golden City at dusk. Bannock and Lieutenant Tompkins had remained behind. Rose and Beth were instead accompanied by two seasoned veterans who weren't interested in casual talk. Not that there needed to be. The story of their fight with the dragon had spread like wildfire and a messenger with Lieutenant Tompkins's full report had preceded them by a full two days.

But as the buildings of the town appeared in the distance, Rose pulled up on her horse. She turned to Beth.

"You should see your ma," she said.

Beth's throat caught, but then her heart started hammering. A good hammering.

"Yes," she said, "I should. The turn-off's just ahead."

"Why don't you spend the night?" Rose suggested. "You can get some rest and clean up before you face the town. Remember that dress I made you way back when? I put it in your saddlebags. You can wear it tomorrow."

Beth laughed in surprise, but her friend just gave her a knowing grin.

"Fine," Beth said at last, "I'll see you in the morning."

A lamp shone through the cabin's window as Beth approached. She tied her horse up to the hitching post. A light breeze tickled her hair and brought with it the smell of the barn. At least the animals were quiet.

Nearer to the cabin, the garden bloomed with vegetables and the raspberry bushes hung thick with dark red fruit. Beth thought of the strawberries she'd missed and her shoulders sagged. Had she really been away so long?

She steeled herself and knocked on the door.

After a moment, it opened. Ma's face went from surprised to stunned and then she threw her arms around Beth.

"My girl!" Ma said. "My darling girl's back!"

Beth stiffened at the words, but then the emotions overwhelmed her. She hugged Ma back as the older woman shed tears of relief.

Finally they pulled back enough for Ma to put her hands on Beth's upper arms and look her square in the face.

"You haven't been eating well," Ma pronounced. "Better come in." She stepped back and held the door.

Beth entered. The cabin was as clean and tidy as ever. In fact, a little tidier than she'd seen it last.

"No Wayne?" she asked.

"No," Ma said. Her face fell. "He didn't come back."

"He was killed?" Beth asked in alarm.

Ma shook her head. "He ... found another interest."

"Oh, Ma," Beth said, "I'm so sorry."

Ma shrugged. "It can't be helped." She forced a smile. "I've got a raspberry pie in the pantry. Join me?"

"You baked a pie for yourself?" Beth blurted. Ma never did anything just for herself.

Ma's smile turned sly. "I might've been hoping someone would stop by for dinner." When she saw Beth's surprise she explained,

"An army messenger stopped by yesterday with a message from Miss Chamberlin."

Beth rolled her eyes and smiled. Then she looked at Ma and grew earnest. "I'm here for the night if you'll have me."

"Your old bed's made up. But first I want to hear all about your adventure." Ma gestured toward the table and headed for the pie.

They talked long into the night. To Beth's surprise, she found herself telling Ma everything—the wounds, the fears, the risks she'd taken. Ma took it all in without a single admonishment. She perked up when Beth mentioned Bannock, but didn't ask more than what he looked like. Beth grinned when she realized how much Ma was restraining herself.

When she'd finally wound through her tale, Beth stifled a yawn. Instead, she asked, "But what about you? How are you doing with Wayne not coming back?"

Ma actually chuckled and shook her head. Then she reached across the table and took Beth's hand.

"I've lost a husband," she said, "and I've lost a beau. But my daughter has returned safe and sound. What more could I want?"

Beth blushed. Her chest caught and she didn't know what to say. Instead, she squeezed Ma's hand and accepted her squeeze in return.

"I love you, Beth," Ma said.

"I love you, too, Ma. I didn't think you understood ..."

"I don't," Ma said. "But does it matter? You're alive. You're healthy. And you're happy. Maybe you'll be happier when Private Bannock comes to visit."

Beth rolled her eyes and shook her head. She let go of Ma's hand and leaned back with a smile.

"You should get some sleep," Ma said. "After all, tomorrow you might have to save the world again."

Beth laughed, but the laugh turned into a yawn that made Ma smile.

The sun had been up a few hours as Beth rode into Golden City. She basked in the warmth and brushed a strand of hair out of her face. The sleeves of her dress dropped as she did. Rose hadn't made the cuffs too tight. Beth adjusted them with barely a thought. She rode slow, her mind on her conversation with her mother. The horse didn't seem to care. It clopped along at a steady pace.

She reached Boggs's place and the bridge over the creek. With a start, she looked up. The road was lined with people. Soldiers, shopkeepers, women and children. She even saw Boggs himself off to one side, holding a broad brimmed hat in his hand.

She didn't know what to say, so she just kept riding on. Her gut and shoulders tightened, and she couldn't help wondering if she had something on her face. But then she caught a little girl's look of awe.

They weren't disgusted with her at all. In her man's hat that Bannock had given her. With a gun on each hip. They seemed ... respectful.

Mr. Lake stepped out of the crowd. He also held his hat in his hand, but he smiled.

"Welcome home, Miss Armstrong. On behalf of the town of Golden City, and the rest of the United States of the West, we thank you."

She blinked, unsure what to say. But then the words came.

"I just did what had to be done," she said.

"We know," he said, "and we're grateful." Then his face resumed its usual business expression. "I've moved you to Room One in the Astor House. The cook has left sandwiches in the ice box if you're hungry. While everyone is eager to hear your story, I've spread the word that you are not to be disturbed. But once you've rested up ...?"

She nodded. "It might be a few days."

"Take as long as you need. I'll make sure everyone leaves you in peace."

She nodded again and rode forward. The crowd dispersed as she passed, and by the time she reached the Astor, she was alone. She took her horse to the stables, where a young boy of about ten promised to take good care of it. Then she slipped in through the kitchen and found the promised sandwiches. She pushed open the door to the parlor and froze in surprise.

At the far table, Wild Bill Hickok sat with his chair pushed back and his feet up. His long hair was brushed back and his clothes impeccably clean and pressed. A sly grin appeared when he saw her.

"Bill!" Beth shouted. She set the sandwich on the sideboard and rushed across the room with her arms wide. He lowered his feet and stood, but put out a hand just before she hugged him.

"Now, now, Beth, people will start to talk."

"They already do. Besides, there's no one here."

He chuckled and let her give him the hug. He then patted her back and gestured toward the table and a spare chair. "Have a seat."

She did. A small glass rested on the table in front of her filled with a clear liquid. "What's this?"

"Your first whiskey. You've earned it." When she blinked, he continued, "It's Jane's favorite brand. We used to celebrate our survival with a shot from time to time." He gestured at it. "Drink up. Though you should probably go slow."

She lifted it and took a sip. It danced like fire in her mouth, but it was smooth, like liquid gold. When she swallowed, it burned down her throat. She coughed once, and then caught herself before she coughed again.

Hickok just smiled at her. "I heard about your exploits. Good work there, especially with the dragon. Though most gunfighters prefer a smaller caliber."

"It's what I had," she said with a grin. "Besides ..." she nodded toward her right shoulder. The bandage there was now just a lump under her dress.

"Ah yes, we did not practice left-handed shooting enough. We will rectify that."

She shrugged in acknowledgement and took another sip of whiskey.

"So tell me all about it."

She did, sipping slowly as she went. He asked a few questions but mostly sat rapt at attention, when he wasn't drinking his own booze. His eyes were wide and he seemed to be taking in every detail.

Like I used to do when he told stories, she mused.

She finished her tale and raised her glass to find it empty. She stared at it until Hickok chuckled.

"Just the one today, I'm afraid," he said. "One brings out the stories. Two brings out the tears."

She nodded, suddenly sober for a moment. "Too many good people died."

"That they did. But more would've died without you. Many more."

"Maybe," she said. She looked piercingly at him, and he met her gaze. "I wish you'd been there, Bill. There were times ..."

"No," he said. "I would've just messed it up." He set his glass down and stood. "You didn't need me at all, and if you really think you did, we have some training to do."

"In what?"

"Swagger. If you're gonna be a gunfighter, you gotta have swagger."

"You're joking!"

He grinned and tipped his hat. Then he sauntered toward the door. At the last minute, he paused and looked back.

"Enjoy your day off," he said. "Tomorrow after breakfast, we start training."

"In what? Swagger?"

He shook his head. "Nah. In shooting left-handed. You might need it again next time."

"Next time?"

"Mmm hmm. You're a gunslinger. You've got a reputation now. That means there's always a next time."

Beth sucked in her breath. She set down her glass and stood. He was right, which meant she had a lot to do. At least a hundred left-handed quick draws. But in the morning, after her well-deserved day off.

ACKNOWLEDGMENTS

It takes a tribe to write a novel. First, my wife Sarah has kept me sane and been my best cheerleader and first reader. I also want to thank Griffin and Gwyneth for their patience when Daddy is off writing. I'd also like to thank Marcia Knight, Elizabeth Knight, and Steve Hartmeyer for brainstorming and proofreading, and Terry Mixon and Sam Sheddan for their on-going support. Finally, Peter Sartucci, Anne Larsen, and others from the Superstars Writing Seminars tribe encouraged me, for which I'm extremely grateful. Thank you.

AUTHOR'S NOTE

Beth first appeared as a secondary character in my novel *Sidekick*, but it quickly became apparent she deserved her own starring role. I wanted her to be someone my daughter would admire, so, like her, Beth's determined and driven. She's smart and intuitive and always figuring things out. Most important, she's not willing to let her society dictate what girls can and cannot do.

In my alternate histories, I strive to keep the magical elements to a minimum. We have monsters (dwarves, trolls, giants, dragons) that came through a rift from another world and we have ghosts. Giants are roughly based on dinosaurs for size, skin thickness, and so on. Dwarves and trolls have human equivalents. But that left the dragon—what would a realistic dragon be based on?

To answer that, I drew on Pete Dickinson's wonderful book *The Flight of Dragons*. He posits that dragons could have actually existed if they flew by being lighter than air. The chemical reaction to create hydrogen gas could be accomplished in a biological organism, and would, of course, require the dragon to get rid of excess hydrogen from time to time by burning it. The big concern for the dragon would be if those hydrogen storage cavities in its abdomen were somehow pierced and the gas ignited. It would be the fantasy equivalent of the Hindenburg, even though Beth and her 1881 cohorts would have no idea what had happened.

Beyond the monsters, the historical and geographic elements are generally as accurate as I could make them. There is indeed a super volcano under Yellowstone, and the dwarves' mine is in the vicinity of the Black Dragon Cauldron, which erupted in 1948 and created a new geological feature. I relocated the mine shaft closer to the mud volcano for the sake of the story. The current city of Golden, Colorado, was named Golden City in the 1880s and the Astor House was its first stone building. The names of the forts that founded Laramie, Wyoming, and Casper, Wyoming, are correct. The hardest part of historical extrapolation was reducing the number of American settlers. I decided that, after a major war with trolls and giants, there wouldn't be as many in the American Great Plains as was historically the case.

That said, current (2021) science knows of no way to set off a volcano at a specified time. The characters in the 1880s would not have known this, though, so I had to bridge their ignorance with the modern reader's knowledge. Since anything magical that entered our world would be transformed, it made sense that any explosives from the dwarves' world would become something different. In this case, they became the equivalent of an anti-matter bomb. It still might not set off a volcano, but the blast would be rather impressive. Since anti-matter would be unstable in our world, I extrapolated that it would have to be neutralized somehow until triggered. My model was not nitroglycerin as Bannock suspected so much as an atomic fission bomb where conventional explosives push the radioactive elements together to create a critical mass.

Finally, I've long had a love of "smart" adventure stories where the heroes puzzle things out instead of just getting lucky. I enjoy competent villains and realistic, worldly concerns. Is it fun when the heroes never get hurt, never get hungry, and never have to look for supplies? Perhaps, but I think it's a lot more fun when they have to deal with the real world just like us.

ABOUT THE AUTHOR

A fourth generation Coloradoan, Edward J. Knight only left the Denver area long enough to learn how to put a satellite into orbit. Four satellites (and counting) later, he's returned to both the mountains and writing fantastical fiction. Along the way, he met the love of his life and became the father of two amazingly curious kids. He's a huge fan of tightly constructed universes and smart plots. He  hopes his own Mythic West stories hold up to those standards. More of his work can be found at edwardjknight.com.

.

IF YOU LIKED ...
GUNSLINGER, YOU MIGHT ALSO ENJOY:

The Best of Penny Dread Tales
Edited by Kevin J. Anderson
& Quincy J. Allen

City of the Saints
by D.J. Butler

OTHER WORDFIRE PRESS TITLES BY EDWARD J. KNIGHT

Unmasked
Stories of Risk and Revelation

Our list of other WordFire Press authors and titles is always growing. To find out more and to see our selection of titles, visit us at:

wordfirepress.com

facebook.com/WordfireIncWordfirePress

twitter.com/WordFirePress

instagram.com/WordFirePress

bookbub.com/profile/4109784512